**"You've got to help me, Abbott.
Do an exor
whatev
Get this w
I'm**

 "Do you swear you didn't kill her?"

Lucas laughed out loud. "And if I did, would I say *no*? Come on, Lila, I swear it wasn't me, and I have a really bad feeling one of us is going to take the fall for her murder."

"I sat there and squirted that cheese onto those crackers with my own hands. There is no way someone could have tampered with that food. Even if I delivered the poison, I didn't mean to kill her." Lila put her hand over her mouth. Her eyes teared up a bit.

"You didn't. I know that, but the sheriff is going to question you. He asked me specifically if we had a relationship." Lucas took in her curvaceous body thinly veiled in the cotton robe. He was toying with the idea of running his hand over Lila's smooth leg and pulling her over to his end of the bed. She looked like she needed comfort.

God knows he needed . . . *something*.

**"Macpherson is . . . the freshest
and most delightful new voice
to hit the romance genre in years . . .
Love and laughter at its very best!"**
Jill Barnett

SUZANNE MACPHERSON

The Forever Summer

A V O N

An Imprint of HarperCollins*Publishers*

This is a work of fiction. Names, characters, places, and incidents are products of the author's imagination or are used fictitiously and are not to be construed as real. Any resemblance to actual events, locales, organizations, or persons, living or dead, is entirely coincidental.

AVON BOOKS
An Imprint of HarperCollins*Publishers*
10 East 53rd Street
New York, New York 10022–5299

Copyright © 2007 by Suzanne Macpherson
ISBN: 978-0-06-116126-1
ISBN-10: 0-06-116126-8
www.avonromance.com

First Avon Books paperback printing: August 2007

Avon Trademark Reg. U.S. Pat. Off. and in Other Countries, Marca Registrada, Hecho en U.S.A.
HarperCollins® is a registered trademark of HarperCollins Publishers.

Printed in the U.S.A.

10 9 8 7 6 5 4 3 2 1

To my cousin Mary Elizabeth Izzo
with great love and admiration.
And her little dog, too.

Acknowledgments

To all the checker chicks and guys at Safeway and the great information you've shared with me over the last year. Party on aisle nine when this comes out!

One

Lila Abbott dropped her aluminum demo tray of Ritz Crackers, Cheez Whiz, and green olives on the unforgiving floor of Market Foods with an earsplitting clatter. The sound echoed throughout the store, but no one turned around to look. Not even one person.

A pure panic swept through Lila, and it wasn't because of her lost Cheez Whiz demo. The panic was for Emily Ruth Griffin who lay face down on the floor of the produce department surrounded by lemons.

Lila ran past the spilled tray and fought her way through several other customers circled

1

around Emily Ruth. *What in God's name did I do that would make Emily Ruth keel over?*

Larry Pierson had gotten to her first. He checked her breathing, which wasn't happening, and frantically began administering CPR to Emily Ruth. Lila prayed he could bring her around. *Please, God, don't let the beautiful Emily Ruth die in our store.* She might be perfectly rich and perfectly dressed, and perfectly bitchy, but she didn't have to be perfectly dead, did she?

Mr. Trent, the pharmacist, came running over. He kept checking Emily Ruth's wrists for something—maybe a pulse, and tried to talk to Larry.

Pilar, from the deli, called 911 from the upstairs office phone. She must have been looking out the observation window and seen the whole thing. Even with Pilar's very cool but complicated Argentinian accent the 911 crew must have gotten the general idea. Within twenty seconds Lila heard sirens.

Tom Boscov, the store manager, was running up and down the aisles trying to calm his regular customers. Tom would do that. The townies were the meat and potatoes of his year-in-and-year-out business. His short-sleeved white shirt had big wet spots under the arms and on his back. He was sweating it, for sure. Lila saw him round the back end of aisle two and heard his quick footsteps down the next row toward Emily Ruth.

Everything went all cold and slow during the next few minutes as the paramedics arrived at a run. Boy, those guys were fast.

Lila helped them back people away. A goodlooking gray-haired man with a nautical outfit soothed a crying Mrs. Gordon. The summer people and the townie people coming together over a tragedy, Lila thought. How touching.

Lila tried not to look at Emily Ruth's body, which wasn't pretty anymore, as the medics worked on her valiantly.

Larry Pierson was having a complete meltdown. He wept over Emily Ruth like his heart was splitting in two. Poor Larry, and what a good effort he'd made. The medics had to move him out of the way several times.

Lila kept thinking about the last thing Emily Ruth had put in her mouth.

It wasn't like Emily Ruth to eat a non-natural thing—that's what she'd said when they'd chatted just moments earlier. Lila remembered Emily Ruth carefully reading the ingredients on both

the Cheez Whiz and the crackers, compliment-
ing Lila on her olive and pimento artwork, then
ever so casually, popping one in her mouth.

She had commented how starved she was
from South Beaching herself to bikini weight
and that maybe just this one cracker wouldn't
kill her. *Just one little carb moment.*

Had it killed her? What in God's name could
be in a blob of Cheez Whiz that would *kill* someone? Was it a tainted olive? Was the cracker
moldy? Lila trembled all over. It was like the
shadow of death had formed a dark misty cloud
over the entire store.

Emily Ruth was dead.

Dave McInnis, chief paramedic, declared time
of death, then he and an orderly gently lifted
Emily Ruth onto a gurney. Larry clutched the
side rails. He was a high-strung kind of guy, and
trying to revive someone like that had probably
been too much for him.

Dead. Dead as a doornail. Lila shuddered
again. Then she thought how good-looking
those McInnis boys were. Then she thought that
was a terrible thing to think—*but, hey, she wasn't
dead—just coming out of hibernation from seventeen
years of being a single mother.*

4

Just suffering empty-nest syndrome from her only daughter Mallory leaving for college at the oh-so-young age of seventeen. Just freaking out for not being able to reach for and hug her only child right this minute. Her mom instincts went into high gear and all her fears about letting Mallory go early to that math-geek-club-sorority-rushing-welcome-to-your-new-life-away-from-the-parents thing came surfacing up. *Anything could happen to her!*

It must be the heat making her think like this. The summer heat always got to her. Plus, one tends to take stock when death comes lurking around. Lila's life flashed before her in a strange series of disconnected thoughts, including a certain summer night many years ago when she'd gotten herself knocked up.

Nothing she could think right now would make any sense or feel correct so she gave up torturing herself about her thoughts. Apparently her mind was trying to grapple with the whole situation and doing a rather random job of it. It must be shock.

The local chief of the Port Gamble Police Department came in the store. He took a look at Emily, talked to the paramedics and Mr. Trent, all very matter of fact. Tom Boscov joined the other men in their short-sleeved-shirt pow-wow. Many forms were passed between the officials and signatures given. Why did life come down to paperwork in the end?

Lila skirted around the death area sweeping up fallen crackers and cheese and doing recon on the side. They extended the gurney and rolled Emily Ruth out of the store, no sheet to cover her once-beautiful face. *Talk about your cleanup on aisle one,* Lila muttered.

She picked up Emily Ruth's expensive lime green leather clutch. It was the size of a doll's purse. Or a little girl's. Lila clutched the clutch. Police Chief Bob Boniford came toward her. He looked a little flirty but still maintained his professional air, if such a thing was possible.

"Lila." He tipped his hat.

"Chief," Lila nodded.

"Looks like Ms. Griffin had some sort of severe allergic reaction."

"Oh God, Bob, I let her eat a Ritz with Cheez Whiz off the demo table. And it had a green olive and pimento garnish. I did it. I killed her." Lila felt a little woozy. She leaned on her broom and tucked Emily's purse under her arm.

"Now, Lila, the woman was a grown adult. She would have known if she were allergic to any of that. It's not your fault. It was probably a fluke." Bob got way close and put his arm around her. Bob was nice, but . . . married. She took the comfort anyway. And the support. Support was always good.

"The paramedics gave her a shot of epinephrine, but it was too late. Is there anything else you noticed? Did she have anything else to eat in the store?"

"Not that I know of, I'm the only demo today," Lila answered. "Her cart is right over there." Lila pointed to the abandoned cart next to the lemon bin. She sort of disengaged herself from Bob at the same time.

"I'll take a look at the cart. Just let me have all those food bits, and the containers—we'll have the lab in Seattle run a few tests on the stuff."

"The food is all in this trash bag. I can get you the containers. I've got them under the demo table," Lila answered. It occurred to her that the store might have some liability issues if indeed some part of the sample food was tainted. That would be terrible. "Just take it." Lila picked up the bag and handed it to the chief. She felt too guilty to sort out liability issues at the moment.

"I'll get the containers," Bob said.

Pilar came up behind them and tried to tell Chief Bob something that looked important. Bob spoke pretty good Spanish and they managed well despite the difference between her Argentine Spanish and his local yokel. Lila had only taken one high school quarter's worth of Spanish. Getting pregnant had sort of cut her academic education short. But she'd picked up quite a bit since.

"Lila, Ms. Griffin's dog is locked up in her car barking its fool head off. Let's get the keys and take the poor thing out of there. It's damned hot today." Bob indicated the purse.

Guess the expensive little green purse didn't much blend with her white poly pants and blue checker's vest. Not that she'd entertained stealing Emily Ruth's purse. Lila snapped open the bag. Inside was a sleek black tube of Chanel lipstick, a round gold compact, a set of car keys, and a miniature wallet, folded and snapped, with quite a bit of money in it from the bulge factor.

Just the Emily Ruth essentials nestled in the lime green silk lining. Lila pulled out the car keys. Bob looked at her with a smirk and took the purse away from her, leaving her with only the keys.

"Chief Boniford?"

Everyone turned at the sound of one booming male voice.

"Lucas, over here. Lila, get that dog, will you?"

Lila wasn't moving. Lucas Griffin was too amazing for her to leave the scene of *this* crime.

He walked like he owned himself and everything else. He looked like tennis in the afternoon, expensive cars, and country clubs. His dark brown hair behaved just the way it should.

He had on Ray Bans or some other sunglasses that only the rich could afford. When he removed them his blue, flashing eyes made Lila's throat catch with surprise. A small sound squeaked out of her. Those eyes did not behave at all.

Then there were his perfect rich-boy jeans and his black polo shirt. The real Polo: Ralph Lauren. Great shirt. Great body.

"What happened to Emily Ruth?" he asked.

"I'm sorry son, she's dead. It was very quick. She didn't suffer."

"Too bad." He stopped in front of both of them and looked straight at Lila.

Bob ignored Lucas's horrid comment. "Are her parents in town?"

"No, they moved to Seattle permanently last year. Her lawyer can get in touch with them."

"Did she have a severe allergy you know of?"

"Peanuts. She was a walking time bomb. Is that what got her?"

"Looks like it. How did you know to come here?"

Lucas took a small pause. "I went looking for her. She missed an appointment we had. I saw her car in the parking lot."

"Oh, the dog. Her dog is in the car. And where would you like her vehicle taken?"

"Geez, Bob." Lila gave them both a stern look.

"I'll take her car. Hell, I paid for it." Lucas held his hand out in Lila's direction, indicating the keys.

Lila just about dropped the keys on the floor, gaping at Lucas for all the comments that had just come out of his mouth. *Darn, buddy, that was just cold.*

Didn't Mr. Griffin know it wasn't proper to speak ill of the dead? Lila's mother's etiquette-phraseology voice popped into Lila's head. Rose Abbott would no doubt be giving Lucas Griffin the evil eye for his crass, cruel comment. Lila did it for her.

"What is that *look* for? Emily Ruth made everyone's life she touched a living hell." Lucas glared back.

"I thought your legal issues with her were settled," Chief Bob interjected.

"Hardly, she'll probably find a way to screw me from the grave."

Lila shut her mouth tight. Nothing good could be coming out of it anyway. Her best friend Bonnie told her she'd heard Lucas Griffin was a no-good cheating son-of-a-rich man that messed around with a string of townie girls here in Port Gamble while his wife, the former townie, formerly alive Emily Ruth, was skiing in Switzerland—or something like that. That was enough to put him on her permanent *s*-word list. Lila didn't want *anything* to do with Lucas Griffin.

On second thought, the dog deserved better. "Your dead ex-wife's dog is in the car. I am going to get it out of there." Lila gave him the iciest glare she could possibly muster and walked past him, car keys in hand.

* * *

Lucas shrugged and followed the nasty, but appealing woman with Emily Ruth's car keys dangling from her pink manicured fingertips.

He knew he should feel really, really bad about his ex-wife's untimely demise, but the relief it was going to bring to his life was so immense it prevented him from any initial grief. Later, perhaps, he'd reflect on the woman he thought he'd married years ago. Or at least the woman she'd pretended to be. The fantasy she'd fed him before he'd caught her in bed with his own brother.

Oh hell, there was nothing to reflect on except that a woman as smart and beautiful as Emily Ruth had wasted her talents in the wickedly evil pursuit of wealth. His family's wealth, to be exact. He regretted she'd misspent her God-given gifts on manipulation and lies, and that his family had been destroyed because if it.

If he had anything to reflect on it was the swift and deadly karmic retribution of her death. *Damn, that was fast.*

Here they were last week in court over his brother's will, the stupid local judge gives her a life estate in the beach house and she drops dead four days later. That was one short life estate. Of

course, she'd been living there with Jason since
. . . since it all went down with them, so she'd
had a few years of fun.

Poor Jason, he never knew what hit him when
it came to Emily Ruth. But he should have been
stronger. He should have put his family first.

There wasn't anything that could be done
about it now, no chance for reunion, reconcilia-
tion, or communication. Jason's motorcycle accident last winter took that chance away. And so
did Emily Ruth.

He might as well take her car. Maybe he could
sell it. He needed the money. He'd come back
for his Jeep later.

As the automatic doors of the grocery store
swooshed open and Lucas stepped outside,
the heat of August midday rolled over him like
a wave of lust. Something he hadn't felt for a
while. This was somewhat connected to the very
nice behind of the woman walking in front of
him. He liked a girl with some curves. He could
see her pink lace bikini underwear through her
white pants.

He had a twinge of guilt for thinking like that
in the oh-so recent aftermath of his ex-wife's
death.

But hell, *she* died, not him. He'd just been so pissed off at spending the summer in lawyers' offices trying to wrestle his family's estate out of the clutches of Emily Ruth instead of regaining some much-needed tranquility, he hadn't had time to think about much of anything else.

Even now his younger brother's stupidity in marrying her after Lucas divorced her, and not making her sign a prenup, grated on him—like gravel under the wheel of a motorcycle going too fast around a corner. If he didn't know better he'd think Emily Ruth killed Jason herself. She'd sure vanished for a while after the funeral, only to turn up like a bad penny this summer.

The pale yellow Jag sedan looked fairly undamaged from Cruella De Emily Ruth being at the wheel. The dog wasn't just yapping, it was howling. Its tiny red furry nose with its black button tip stuck through the crack in the window Emily had left for her. He could see a bowl of water on the floor. At least she was kind to animals, just not people.

The pissy but curvaceous girl that had commandeered the keys was cooing at the dog, but nothing was working. Howls were punctuated by growls and snaps.

"I'm going in for dog treats. Stay here. Don't you dare hurt that dog." She ran back in. That left him with Schatzie, Emily Ruth's crazy dog.

"Schatzie, shhhhhh." Lucas kept his voice low. He reached over and tried to pet Schatzie's little nose. He got snapped at instead. Emily probably trained the damned thing to bite him. He kept at it until Schatzie reduced herself to a whine-howl. He got a little closer and managed to stroke her under the chin. That seemed to calm her a tiny bit. He kept it up. Poor thing, we don't get to pick our owners.

He thought about the store girl. She was familiar. Thirty-some summers in Port Gamble gives a guy plenty of time to get to know the locals.

He remembered who she was in an interesting flash of long-ago gossip and foolish attractions from his teenage years here. Lila Abbott.

Foolish attractions. Too bad he hadn't had the sense to let his attraction to Emily Ruth slide on by. These local girls were nothing but trouble.

"Move."

"Aren't you Lila Abbott?" Lucas asked.

Lila was slightly impressed with the fact Lucas had calmed the dog down just by his touch.

She'd come through the door and seen him bent over, stroking it under the chin. Of course, if he stroked her under the chin like that she'd probably calm down, too. Or get excited. One of the two.

"Yes, I'm Lila Abbott. What's the dog's name?"

"Schatzie. She's a girl. Emily Ruth named her after a character in a movie. You know, Lauren Bacall in *How to Marry a Millionaire*?"

Wow, interesting. Emily Ruth must have had a broader understanding of her own life than it seemed. She'd lived out that—how to marry a millionaire—part. It wasn't often a townie girl nabbed one of the summer boys. Emily had done a pretty good job of it. Lucas was a hottie.

Lila thought about her own situation and gritted her teeth. She hadn't nabbed a summer boy; the summer boy had nabbed her, used her and thrown her away. Oh well, she was a big girl now. She was long over it. Really. And she'd gotten a terrific daughter out of it. A daughter she missed terribly today. She'd have to call Mallory later just to hear her voice all the way from that college she couldn't have afforded if Mallory hadn't gotten all those scholarships—Stanford University in California.

Well that, and the bribe money she'd been getting all these years from a rich family in Texas that didn't want their name sullied with an illegitimate child. Hey, it worked for her. It'd kept rubber boots and books and bread on the table.

"Here you go, yummy yum, here Schatzie." Lila held her hand out flat so Schatzie couldn't nip off a finger. The dog licked the treat off her palm. Oh, if only men were that easy.

She unlocked the car door and made sure she was armed with more treats. The smell of hot white leather baked by the summer sun and long-haired dog mingled with the clean, outdoor scent of Lucas Griffin, who had wedged himself close in—apparently to prevent Schatzie from bolting into the parking lot.

He made her nervous. "Could you give me a little space here, Mr. Griffin? The dog doesn't seem to like you." Lila had Schatzie by her little jeweled collar and held her tight against her store vest, but the little thing was squirming like a weasel. Long red hair flew up in Lila's nose. She flipped it away with her other hand. "What kind of a dog is this, anyhow?"

"Pomeranian." Lucas put his hand behind his neck and smiled at Lila.

Oh, he had quite the smile. As if that would do him any good, the snake. "Oh, that's right, Pomeranian. I should have known that," she stumbled through the reply.

"You two have the same color hair," Lucas said.

Oddly, that was true.

"And what do you intend to do with her?" Lila asked, ignoring the hair comment, holding a growling Schatzie so they could both look at Lucas. She was a little sensitive about the whole red-haired thing anyway.

"I don't know, I was thinking of putting her in the dog shelter, or a kennel or something."

"Why can't you just take her to your place?"

"I'm staying with friends. I don't think they'd appreciate my ex-wife's dog."

"Don't you people have any sense of charity? The poor thing just lost its owner."

"You people?" Lucas stared at her.

"Oh, you know perfectly well what I mean. Like it would kill you to have a little dog in whatever fifty-room, fifty-acre estate your friends own."

Lucas took in a quick hissing breath through his teeth. "My, my, we are quick to judge."

"Oh, *please*." Lila wasn't going to let him get away with that bull. I mean *really*. "Fine, *I'll* take her while *you* find poor Schatzie a good home. And no, we won't be putting her in the pound to be gassed. I think the dog deserves better, don't you?"

"I didn't mean I'd let her be gassed. I just thought they might find her a new owner, but I can do that just as well, as you've pointed out. Thank you very much for your generous offer." Lucas looked into her eyes with a deep, edgy, too-bright stare that made her stomach flip over for some reason.

He reached into the open car and popped the glove box open. "She always keeps the dog's leash in here." He handed the red leather leash to Lila.

Then he shut the passenger door, moved around the back of the car, and slipped himself into that Jag. He started the engine before she had time to thank him for the leash. Jags always purred. Lila remembered that from . . . another time. He was out of there in a sleek streak of expensive car.

"Heartless snob!" Lila yelled after him. Schatzie yapped in agreement. Lila looked down at her and the dog's little black eyes gleamed as if she knew something. Schatzie was shaking like a leaf. Well, if Lila was going to be a dog-sitter . . . oh, good grief, she'd just gotten herself in the middle of a commitment with Lucas Griffin.

Lucas. What an arrogant ass. He probably would have killed Emily Ruth himself if he could have, and her little dog, too. What the heck was his problem anyway? These summer boys, they had everything in the world and yet their discontent ate them up. Good looks, money—old money, even, girls at their beck and call. What else did they want?

Poor Emily Ruth had been a beautiful, intelligent woman. The short interaction between her and Emily had been fairly civil. They'd gone to the same high school; just hardly known each other. Emily Ruth, the elusive, disappearing and reappearing in town several times over the last few years.

Sure, Emily did have—or had, in her past tenseness—that slight condescending edge all the wealthy people had toward the "help," but not overly so. The woman did *speak* to Lila, and even moaned about her diet woes and confessed a weakness for cheese and crackers.

So why did a man like Lucas not find her enough of a wife to stay faithful to? Why did they end up divorced? These guys were never satisfied. No woman was ever good enough for them.

And she should know.

She hugged Schatzie, who growled. They marched back into the store and headed straight for a cart. She was going to need doggy supplies. She plopped Schatzie in the child seat and held on to her. Schatzie scrunched down and started whining. Poor thing. A dog can mourn, too.

It was hard to believe they had to finish up a work day after the death of a customer. Only two people had come into the store since it happened, and they'd acted very nervous. This was not going to be good for business.

Lila couldn't get Emily Ruth off her mind.

Or Lucas Griffin for that matter.

Two

Lucas sat in the tiny cubicle they'd put together for him in the *Port Gamble Gazette* and stared at the blank blue screen of his laptop. He had to admit it was hard to write about who looked promising on the Port Gamble High swim team after seeing the dead body of his ex-wife just a short while ago.

These days he'd developed a strange jaded shell where his heart used to be. Probably being in a war zone for a year or so didn't help his outlook.

Being in Port Gamble used to be so restoring. He'd hoped for that on this trip, despite the ugly legal battles. But not having access to the family house had really put a damper on his spirits.

The only thing cheering him up now seemed to be the kooky redhead who commandeered Emily Ruth's dog. She sure had an attitude. And a great behind.

```
Chelsea Dodge, a two-year veteran of
the swim team held her record in timed
trials for the breaststroke. Chelsea
was last year's district champion in
this event. It looks like freshman Tory
Harrison will be giving her a challenge
this season, or perhaps the extra com-
petition will push Chelsea to the state
finals.
```

Lucas speed-typed his notes into article format and hit save.

He leaned back in the wooden swivel chair with his hands behind his head and almost flipped backward. Antique office chairs sucked. Once he established a good balance he gazed out the window onto the main section of town from his second-story window.

Even though Emily Ruth did have that extremely fatal allergy, she was completely driven to protect herself. After all, self-preservation and self-gratification were all that really mattered to the woman.

Where was her EpiPen? It just wasn't like Emily Ruth to be unprepared. Could it have caught her so fast she didn't have time to use it? She always had that allergy kit on her. He hadn't seen one in the car either.

Lucas leaned forward on the desk and brought up his search engine page. He typed in *fatal peanut allergy* and spent some time educating himself about the finer details of his ex-wife's condition. When he was with her he'd been fastidious about keeping anything peanut related away from her. And as he read, he remembered the bracelet she always wore.

What could have happened? Lucas rubbed his chin and carefully leaned back in the chair. Maybe they didn't see her bracelet. Of course if she didn't give herself a shot in the first thirty seconds—or if someone else didn't—she'd be a gonner.

He ran through possible scenes in his head. Was it just that simple? Her allergy got her? But where did the peanut substance come from?

Would the autopsy explain her death in more detail?

Most of all, would he be considered a suspect?

His reporter brain went in ten different directions. Lucas printed out the information and got back to the stats on the swim team. That woman, she'd always found a way to distract him from anything resembling productivity or peace.

Although, he had to admit his mind was also on the other woman he'd met today: Lila Abbott and her charmingly difficult personality. Why was he always attracted to difficult women?

The produce aisle was still buzzing with officials. It hadn't been taped off or any of that, but it was the point of much discussion by Bob's crew and the medics and whomever else happened to be in the store. Death, Lila had learned, fascinates some people.

By all accounts she should be over there, but she needed a break. No doubt they'd be bugging her soon enough since she had a talent for resolving the problems of the deceased, but not fully or dearly departed.

Lila avoided that scene and headed to aisle

seven: Dog, Cat, Pet. If she were going to dog-sit she'd have to get some supplies.

After a few quiet minutes to herself, Chief Bob came strolling down from the other end of the aisle.

"Lila, I'm going to need a statement from you. Is that Ms. Griffin's dog?"

"Yes, apparently I'm stuck with her." Lila put a protective hand on the little dog. "Why do you need a statement from me?"

"Just routine. Young woman dies suddenly, you know. We probably should have done a regular crime scene on it, but Tom Boscov doesn't need his store closed down and, heck, it's just too damn hot. This isn't CSI, it's Port Gamble. Besides, Ms. Griffin had a deadly peanut allergy. That's a no-brainer."

And Bob should know all about no-brainers, Lila thought. "But there weren't any peanuts in that stuff she ate, were there?"

"Probably some trace peanut oil from the factory or something like that. Kind of like a boulder dropping off a hillside and squishing someone flat. It's just their time, you know? They'll test the food and do an autopsy. Then we'll know."

Lila felt queasy thinking about it. "Oh, whatever, I'll give you a statement. What about that nasty ex-husband of hers?"

"You can hardly blame him, can you?"

"What?" Lila felt her gossip meter tick higher.

"She cheated on him with his own brother. Then after they divorced, the brother married her. Jason Griffin had an untimely death and that left Emily Ruth with the family estate here in Port Gamble. Lucas contested the will, but just last week the judge sided with Emily Ruth and gave her a life estate in the property."

"Maybe Lucas's bad behavior drove her into the brother's arms."

"Word around the Blue Goose is that Emily duped the whole lot of them, that she had a lover or two on the side since the day she married Lucas. That she cleaned Lucas out then moved on to his brother, who had a rather nasty drinking habit. I know that for a fact; I've drunk-tanked him at least three times myself.

"Anyhow, Annie, the old caretaker, says she's been living in the big house out on Hidden Cove since the brother died last winter. Lucas has been staying with the Beckers out by the Sea Crest Country Club for the past few months battling her in court."

"Ah, tough life. The country-club set," Lila said snarkily.

"Hardly, the Beckers are the caretakers out there. Lucas came back this summer and took a job at the newspaper. He had been in Iraq reporting for some big national press and caught a shard from a car bomb in his leg. There's more to it, but I didn't hear every little detail."

Sounded like Bob had gotten plenty of details. "Boo-hoo, poor little rich boys," Lila snapped. Schatzie yapped one short yap. "And playing newspaper reporter, too."

"I hear ya, Lila, but there is more to Lucas than that."

"If Emily hadn't dropped dead in public I'd have pegged him for doing her in myself."

"You read too many mystery books," Bob grinned.

"So do you, Bob, and maybe too many romance novels. And it sounds like you and Annie have been hoisting a few too many brewskies together, *Bob*. Wouldn't want the wife to get the wrong idea, now would we." Lila gave Bob a knowing look.

"Oh, shut up Lila," he said. "Now come on, after you're done here meet me at the station. I've got a foot of paperwork because of this. I'll be in my hot office till after supper and will miss my wife's grilled salmon. You don't want to make me later, do you? She's making blackberry pie for dessert."

"Fine." Lila gave him a little half-smile and rolled her cart past him, squeaky wheel and all.

So, Lucas lost his brother and their old estate over Emily Ruth. Damn, that had to hurt, really hurt.

She stood still for a moment and noticed how dumb her sympathy for Lucas Griffin was. Chief Bob must have it screwed up. Of *course* Lucas cheated on Emily Ruth, not the other way around. He probably treated her so badly she turned to his brother for sympathy and things just got out of hand, and really, after Lucas divorced her, she did *marry* Jason, so it must have been one of those tragic, true love kind of triangles. Sure, that was it.

Chief Bob was full of it. Men always sided with men. Emily Ruth was one of those high-strung, hair-in-place, painted fingernails kind of girls. She didn't seem like any wanton sex kitten.

More likely Lucas was one of those husbands you can't ever tame. He had that look about him.

The look of a man who knew his way around a bedroom.

And she should know. She'd seen that look in a man's eye before. And fallen for it.

Lila got mad and started throwing doggie toys in the cart. The little blue plastic *doggie news* newspaper squeaked. Schatzie got all wound up and yipped seventeen times, with a few attempted leaps. Lila held her down and offered up another one of the doggie treats she'd stuffed in her vest pocket.

God, she felt weird. Lila took a deep breath and the sharp, off-kilter energy of the morning shifted like the downside of a sugar rush.

She steered the cart around the end of the store to grab a steak. She'd treat the poor dog to a good dinner. Pretty soon Lila found herself moving down the back aisle toward produce. She couldn't help herself.

Larry was sitting on the floor with a pile of paper lace. She wheeled over to him. It was the edging off the lemon, lime, plum orchard bin.

"Larry, honey, you need to let me take care of that." She helped him off the floor. He didn't really speak. His pale hands fluttered. "I'm going to let Tom know you need to go home now.

Go home and take a rest. It's been a terrible morning."

"Yes, I'll go home," Larry said. He handed her the lace paper edging. Poor Larry. His eyes were red from crying.

"Fine now, that's good." Lila patted his back.

"Throw everything in her cart away." He clutched her arm and looked wild-eyed.

"I'll do that, Larry. You go on now."

Larry wandered off. Lila parked her own cart next to the former cart of Emily Ruth.

Emily Ruth's cart had been arranged according to type of item and weight: canned goods, corner back right, jars center back, dog biscuits and other dry boxed items like brown sugar, corner back left. Breads, top front right, two steaks bagged and perched on the canned goods, a bottle of nice red wine, and Larry's beautiful produce, with its own spot, front, left.

Fresh green beans, yellow fin potatoes, romaine lettuce, and baby gourmet carrots. She could see a menu forming here—a steak, fresh beans, glazed carrots, and grilled potato dinner. Also Emily Ruth had obviously been assembling a Caesar salad since she'd headed for romaine and a lemon in her last moments of life.

It dawned on her that Emily Ruth had been expecting company for dinner. This was not the cart of a single woman. This was the cart of a single woman on the prowl. Lila found that *very* interesting.

She poked through the cart contents. Low and behold, there were the two white taper candles wrapped in tissue and the bottle of Cabernet Sauvignon to prove it. Emily Ruth had *plans* before she died.

Lila also found a hunk of very expensive imported Parmesan cheese, the good kind—not that stuff Lila used out of the green can. And three other kinds of cheese: a pepper jack, a blue cheese, an Alouette herbed cheese spread, and a can of the fateful Cheez Whiz. My-my, the woman did like her cheese. Lila shuddered thinking of the deadly Cheez Whiz she'd handed Emily Ruth. Could that be true? Could it have had a trace of peanut oil in it?

She couldn't just throw all this stuff out. Lila wondered why the chief didn't take these items in for evidence. Lazy Bob. Maybe ol' Bob thought it was a slam-dunk accidental death deal, but Lila wasn't so sure. She had a feeling. Bob was being a dope not doing a full police investigation on this.

Lila decided to leave all of Emily Ruth's groceries for a while . . . just in case Bob got a clue. She also wanted to be sure to remember the cart, so she took her black Sharpie pen out of her store vest and made a little star on the plastic flip-down seat.

She should shop like this—healthy and wealthy. Instead of frozen entrée's she could stand a nice dinner for a change.

As she was scribbling her little star, Lila found Emily Ruth's shopping list stuck underneath the flip-down child seat. More like her entire day's itinerary done on some computer program complete with the shopping list. She read the schedule, which listed *6:30 P.M. Dinner*. As she suspected. Lila slipped the list in her pocket. She put Schatzie under her arm.

Dates. Well that was something she hadn't been on in a while. She was just getting used to being alone, with Mallory off to her new college campus. Lila felt a twinge of mother emotion. She missed her daughter. She needed to talk to her. Seeing someone keel over made you want to talk to the people you loved.

This was a whole new phase in both their lives. She was going to have to get used to being a long-distance mom. And if she was going to start a new phase, she could stand to lose a few pounds. Maybe shake a better figure on the dance floor of the Blue Goose. Better something like the carrots Emily Ruth picked out than the Cheetos she really wanted to eat an entire bag of to shake off this terrible day.

What was she doing, standing here, thinking about dancing, thinking about dieting, when someone had died right on this very spot less than an hour ago?

Schatzie stared at her. Lila stared at Emily Ruth's cart contents. Schatzie yipped. Lila gave the dog another treat for sympathy and left Emily Ruth's death cart where it was, except for a box of dog biscuits. Emily no doubt knew her dog's preferences. And the bottle of wine. She'd need that herself.

A cold step-on-your-grave shiver ran down her spine as she passed close by the lemon display again. She pictured Emily Ruth Griffin's well-dressed body arranged on the black-and-white linoleum squares like a fallen chess queen.

One-handed with the dog tucked under her arm, she parked in check stand three and stacked her own things on the conveyer. Then she set Schatzie down in the child seat. Schatzie kept her eyes on the dog biscuits from Emily's selections. Nice of Emily Ruth to think of her dog in her last moments.

"Jeez, Lila, kind of fancy wine, isn't it? Are you expecting a gentleman caller?" Becky teased her as she scanned each of the items.

"This isn't my wine. This is from Mrs. Griffin's cart," Lila answered. She pushed the emptied cart to the bagging area, with the dog looking very warily at her, then picked out some paper bags and doubled them, helping Becky finish the job.

"Wow, Lila. This whole thing gives me the willies."

"I know what you mean. Ring this onto my account, okay?"

"Sure. God, the place is empty as a tomb. Oh, that's so creepy to say, isn't it?"

"But true." Lila picked up Schatzie and came around the checkout counter.

The hairs on the back of Lila's neck prickled as if someone had whispered in her ear. Schatzie growled, which freaked Lila out more. Her whole body did a horrible tingling shiver. For a minute she thought she was going to pass out.

"Becky, leave everything here. I'll come back in a minute." Lila grabbed Schatzie and quickened her pace as if something was after her, which might have been true. She shot up the stairs, dog and all, to the break room.

The room was empty, which was both good and bad. She scrunched herself down in the corner of the ugly beige vinyl break room sofa, thinking that would hide her. Schatzie seemed exhausted, too, and found the granny square afghan throw Cindy Fisher had brought in for catnaps. The dog made six little circles and settled on the blanket for a dognap.

Lila loosened her shoes and tried to calm herself, leaning back on the sofa. Her cell phone was a lump in her Market Foods blue vest pocket, begging her to call her daughter and her best friend, Bonnie. Mallory might not be out of bed yet, night owl that she was, so she autodialed Bonnie Forbes instead.

When Bonnie answered she didn't say Port Gamble Antiques or even hello. She launched right in. "I can't believe it took you this long to call me. I would have called you at work, but your boss grounded me from doing that, remember? I heard the entire story from Dave

McInnis already." Bonnie thumped on the desk with her fist. Lila could hear it over the phone.

"Why does he talk to you and not me?" Lila pouted.

"We've got history, babe. So spill your guts. Tell me as much as you can."

"It was an allergy. A peanut allergy. I probably killed her with peanut oil–tainted Cheez Whiz. I just went past where she died and got completely spooked."

"This is the best story I've heard in years. The newspaper will finally have something to write about. I suppose Lucas Griffin can't report on his own ex-wife's death. I think there's some kind of law against that. He's the sports dude anyway."

"Emily Ruth was so *young*," Lila said. "Poor thing. Why, she was only four years older than me!"

"Two years older. Two," Bonnie rudely reminded her.

"You complete *b-word*! Like I like being reminded I turned thirty-three years old last week." Lila always tried to use letters to indicate swear words whereas Bonnie went straight for the actual curse. "The whole thing has really made me think, you know?"

"Obviously, we need to live life to the fullest. We could drop over dead at any moment." Bonnie sounded very philosophical but in a beer commercial kind of way. "Sorry about that age thing. We're both still young and wild."

"Okay, I forgive you. I hope they do an autopsy. I need to know I didn't cause her death. I can't believe there was peanut anything in that Cheez Whiz, but I can't figure out where else she would have gotten it. Who knew an allergy could kill you that fast? I mean, Larry administered CPR, but it was already too late. She must have died instantly."

"I'm surprised Larry actually put his mouth on a woman's lips." Bonnie cracked her witty whip. She snickered over the phone.

"Tell his wife that." Lila took a stalk of celery out of her lunch bag and crunched in Bonnie's ear. "He almost fainted when it was over. He wept like a baby and flung himself on her body. I was just surprised he remembered all that CPR stuff from our training."

Lila had a pang. She would have done it herself. She would have. It surely would have come back to her in an emergency. Lila winced. Owing to her lack of attention span she'd been way too busy flirting with Dave McInnis, her favorite paramedic, when he'd been doing the demonstration last year.

Lila was feeling guilt for being a CPR flunkie. Then again, it hadn't helped anyway.

She picked up her end of the conversation. "Poor Larry had pleated, like, a hundred and twenty yards of white lace paper edging material for the summer fruit displays. You should have seen him tucking it under the rows of plums and grapes in the center orchard bins. When she went down, Emily Ruth made a lunge for the citrus and dislodged the entire frilly thing on the lemon bin."

"Oh my gawd, what did you do?" Bonnie laughed. Although they both knew it wasn't a laughing matter.

"I just now found him trying to re-pleat the edging. I sent him home. Geez, he tried to revive a person and she died. That would freak anyone out; but Larry, well that's just too much for him, as you know."

Bonnie knew. She knew every detail of everyone's life at Market Foods, via Lila, and Lila smiled thinking of that.

Like the time they'd both said a silent prayer

for Larry's wife the week he completely rearranged the entire produce department according to color of item. He'd waved his hand like a game show hostess and babbled about monochromatic unity. He'd put yellow bell peppers next to the lemons, and worked his way through the color spectrum, ending with eggplants next to turnips. ROY Gee BIV he'd said, as in Red Orange Yellow Green Blue Indigo and Violet, the rainbow spectrum. As she remembered the story it made a weird kind of sense.

Everyone knew better than to mess with Larry's produce, even the customers. They gingerly picked their items off the top and knew that Larry would be right behind them, restacking. But a sort of mutual appreciation had grown out of that, because Market Foods produce was the best in the county.

People drove thirty miles from Silverburg to buy Larry's beautiful Jonagold apples in the fall, plums and raspberries in the summer, squash and persimmons in the winter. It was almost a cult thing. The local jam makers claimed his berries were the only ones worth investing in.

And woe to the supplier who tried to pawn sub-par produce off on Larry. At least once a year they'd hear a sound like a high-pitched air-raid siren coming from the backroom regions of the store. They all called that a Larry Alert. It was a distinctly different kind of sound than oh, say, a *screamer* in the candy aisle. That's code for a toddler having a "gimme" meltdown.

Bonnie knew all this, of course, so Lila didn't thought-dump the entire contents of her mind. She was on a short freak-out break; she had to be selective.

Only best friends listen to you repeat stuff about your life ad nauseam for twelve years straight without hitting you over the head with a cast-iron skillet.

"So did *it* happen?" Bonnie asked expectantly.

Of course, all Bonnie wanted to know was if Lila had gotten the *feeling* today. She hated that feeling. The last time she'd had that feeling she'd run into the whispy, smoke-scented spirit of Old Man Turner, four years ago. Seth Turner.

There'd been a fire at the old Grange hall that week, and old man Turner had died of smoke inhalation in the basement. Seth had bugged her for days until she'd gone to the chief and told him to look into the whole event more carefully.

It took a ghost to get Chief Bob to agree to

have an arson team investigate the fire. Bob was always the lazy type and didn't want to create more paperwork than necessary. He sure hadn't changed.

But for some reason he listened about Lila's ghostly encounters. This was no doubt due to the Strawberry Queen incident of 1995. Everyone in town took Lila's gift seriously after that.

The whole thing with Seth Turner had turned out to be true as well. Two really horrid local boys had been kicked out of a dance at the Grange that Saturday night and had decided to torch the place in the wee hours of the night. They hadn't known about Mr. Turner in the basement. It was tragic. They were minors, but were duly punished.

Bonnie thought her feeling was a great gift and always asked if Lila's "spidey sense" was tingling before or after any tragic town event.

She and Bonnie had tried to apply it to potential boyfriends—sort of an early-warning system of trouble to come, but it only worked for spirits who had departed their earthly bodies. Not living, breathing people. So they were stuck with trying to figure out the boyfriend thing on their own.

All this thinking led to a long silence on the phone, which Bonnie was used to. Lila had a tendency to drift off.

"Lila, I've got a customer. Come to the store after work."

"I will." Lila looked up to see the store manager. Her never-ending break was definitely over. Tom Boscov gave her the stink eye, so she told Bonnie she had to run. She stashed her cell phone in her blue checker's apron and tied her lovely white sturdy running shoes back up tight. It'd been a good breather for her poor feet.

Schatzie was snoring. The little thing would probably be fine up here. She'd tell everyone to keep an eye out for the dog.

She clunked down the stairs onto the selling floor.

It was hard to believe they had to finish up a workday after the death of a customer. Only two people had come into the store and they'd acted very nervous. This was not going to be good for business. All the more reason Bob should have shut the place down and done his job properly.

Until today Emily Ruth was always a distant blur to Lila. She didn't know her well, and they didn't travel in the same circles.

Lila did remember the announcement in the paper a few years back that she'd married Lucas Griffin, now that she thought of it.

Wow, Lucas was a catch, no doubt about it—those piercing eyes and classic good looks. Had Emily Ruth strayed from that? It was hard to understand. Lucas gave a woman this feeling that sort of . . . *haunted* her after he left.

At least he haunted *her* ever since she'd seen him this morning. She'd found herself thinking about him most of all.

But apparently he hadn't haunted Emily Ruth. Lila had only seen Emily Ruth a few times this year, mostly just this week in the produce department. Emily was definitely the kind of woman who had a keen appreciation for the obsessive-compulsive produce tendencies of Larry.

Which reminded her of the groceries she'd bolted from. There they were, waiting for her, neatly packed by Becky. She'd have to store everything in the dairy cooler for the rest of the day. Lila gave Becky the *"thanks and be right back"* wave and wheeled the cart with her groceries back toward dairy. She'd sneak in her call to Mallory from the stock room.

She'd forgotten to tell Bonnie about the schedule she'd found. And the dinner-date thing. Now, who the heck was Emily Ruth having a candlelit dinner for two with tonight? Whomever he was, his dinner was cancelled.

Three

 All week long the energy at work had been off-kilter. Things were too quiet. The early freestone peaches had come in and Larry hadn't even screamed at the supplier about the bruise ratio. Plans were in the works to change the patio furniture area into the Back-to-School area. But nothing was back to normal. Lila felt herself on guard most of the time.

Bright and early this Monday morning Lila knew why she'd felt that way all week.

It was even worse than the commotion Emily Ruth's fall from life had created. It was one horrendous blood-curdling scream by a full-grown adult.

Usually that indicated a big ol' Edgar Allan Poe–sized raven in the rafters, dive-bombing customers, or a truly not-nice accident of some sort like a large can of pumpkin puree falling off a high shelf and landing on someone's head. Lila ran in the direction of the scream. They didn't need any more dead shoppers.

From a distance she noticed several customers and even a few clerks frozen in their tracks. She had a creepy tingle going even before she rounded the end-capped Fruit Loop display leading into Larry's produce area.

There stood Mrs. Mills with her mouth open, and no sound coming out. Mrs. Mills was married to the other Larry, the former Catholic priest. She was a church soloist who had caught his eye at a midnight mass no doubt. A match made in heaven. What's up with the Larry's in this town?

As she approached, Lila snapped a look down each row and there in aisle one, the produce aisle, she saw an empty cart rolling by itself.

Well, hell, it was just a runaway, people, snap

the hell out of it. This ain't no big thing: a slope in the floor, a wild kid giving it a push on the other end. For this we're screaming?

But her neck hairs kept prickling and as she watched it, the cart slowly directed itself, made a turn, sped up, and rammed right into the lemon display. Not only that, the unmanned cart rolled back, and did it again, and again. Larry's lemons bumped and dislodged, dropping onto the floor.

Mrs. Mills backed up, practically knocked Lila over, grabbed her purse out of her cart, and ran out of the store making tiny screaming noises. Who could blame her? Lila spotted Larry at the far end of the department by the watermelons clutching his heart. Wow. If Larry died too, the watermelon sales would plummet. They all hated those damned watermelons and the sooner they were gone the better. The only thing worse than watermelons were pumpkins. Wait, no, frozen turkeys.

She ran for Larry, hoping she wouldn't be called upon to perform CPR, which she again remembered she sucked at.

"Larry, buddy, take a breath." Lila held on to him, afraid he might keel over. Larry wasn't a big man; she could catch him if she had to. He looked at her with big, frightened eyes. He was white as a ghost.

"It's Emily Ruth," he gasped.

Lila couldn't exactly deny that theory. It wasn't every day a cart took off on its own and smacked into the exact orchard bin full of lemons that had been the exact point of death for a woman exactly one week earlier.

She looked at her watch. Wow. Not only that, it was to-the-minute. Ten thirty-six. Lila remembered the paramedics declaring time of death as 10:36 A.M. She got a little dizzy but Lila wasn't a girl who was prone to swooning.

"Well, Larry, if it was Emily Ruth, she's just reminding us how wonderful your lemons are. I'm sure it'll be okay."

"She wants something."

Probably croutons, Lila thought. That Caesar salad she'd been assembling was missing croutons. Although from what she'd learned of Emily Ruth, she probably made her own croutons. We'd just have to see where the cart went next.

But by then the cart had stopped.

Lila gave Larry a hard look, judged him not likely to keel over, and did probably the bravest thing she'd ever done in her life besides give birth to her daughter at age sixteen.

She marched over to the damn cart, grabbed it, and wheeled it outside to the cart rack. Now it was just like any other cart. Unhaunted. So there.

Except, right away, Lila noticed it was *the* cart. The one with the black star she'd drawn to mark which one Emily Ruth had used that fateful morning. But she'd keep that to herself.

By the time she stepped back through the automatic doors the entire population of shoppers had gathered in produce to watch Phil, Larry's produce partner, pick up lemons off the floor. To his credit, Phil didn't restock them. Larry would have surely suffered the remainder of his collapse.

The shoppers stood in small groups and what had started as a whisper grew to a full-fledged murmur, then a rumble. Lila decided to go get a cup of coffee at the deli and wait it out. Pilar was slicing provolone on the big Hobart slicer, so Lila didn't bother her. Never bother a woman on a giant slicer—house rules.

Pilar finished up the provolone then restocked the case with already sliced Virginia smoked ham, then came over to see Lila. Lila poured herself a cup of nasty looking coffee out of the hot pot and took up a perch on one of the stools in front of the coffee counter.

"What's the combination?" Pilar asked in her very sexy Argentine accent. She was trying out new English words and sometimes misplaced them. But then so did Lila, and she was born in this berg. Lila figured Pilar meant *commotion*, but she liked it better Pilar's way.

"The combination is a ghost on aisle one."

Pilar muttered something in Argentine and crossed herself. Lila thought she said "Mother Mary, have mercy on this soul."

Lila thought that was very nice and was again glad she'd taken her one quarter of high school Spanish. Spanish was one class she'd done pretty well in because the teacher had let them walk around a whole lot pretending they were in cafés and on trains, and he was exceptionally good-looking to boot.

"We should pray for this ghost," Pilar said.

"I agree. She's still doing errands and she's dead. That's like . . . *sad*," Lila said. She sipped her bitter coffee and made a face. Pilar reached for the real cream and brown sugar, took Lila's cup, and doctored it up a bit. Lila took a sip and gave Pilar the thumbs-up.

This is what she liked about this place. People looked after each other. The coffee seemed to steady her nerves.

"I'm taking care of her dog," Lila said between sips.

"No husband?"

"*Si*, just an ex. A cold fish," she said. Pilar looked at her funny. That didn't translate well. "*Pescados fríos*," Lila attempted.

"Ahhh," she said, nodding.

The universal language of male imperfections prevailed.

Cold fish is right.

"Even the dog didn't like him," Lila said to Pilar.

"*Si*, yes. Dogs know."

Lila had underestimated how much the ghost cart had shaken her. As she slipped off the stool she had to grab the counter to steady herself. Pilar scooted around the counter side and put her arm around Lila. *What a sweetie.*

"I'm okay."

"*Espírito perdido.*" Pilar shook her head.

No kidding. Lila nodded in agreement. "Lost

spirits" were a pain in the ass. They should have a take-a-number system for the recently deceased. She looked at her watch and it was eleven. She *could* take an early lunch. Get some fresh air. She gave Pilar a squeeze and launched herself off toward the break room. Late break, early lunch, what the heck. Lila's work ethic stunk for the past week.

On the way up the stairs she whipped out her cell phone and autodialed Bonnie at the antique store Bonnie was running for her mother.

"Port Gamble Antiques, Bonnie speaking," Bonnie answered, in her usual way. Lila was so grateful to have Bonnie back in town even though she knew Bonnie might not agree, being stuck in this one-horse historic sea-town taking care of her sick mom. It wasn't the best of circumstances, but her best friend's absence of many years while she went away to college and married, and divorced, were long and lonely for Lila

"You will not believe what just happened. Can you go to lunch early?" Lila asked.

"I've only been here two hours. Oh hell, of course I can. I'll just hang a sign on the door."

"Meet me at Nick's."

"K." She hung up quickly with no further comment. Bonnie liked her dirt live and in person.

Lila grabbed her sweater from her locker and ditched her vest, name tag and all. Tom Boscov looked up briefly. Lila made a girly kind of face and put her hand to her abdomen like she had cramps. He hated dealing with any real woman stuff so he waved her off quickly. She clocked out. She'd make up for it later and give everyone else extra break time.

Nick's Italian Grotto was her favorite real fakey Italian place with red checkered tablecloths, raffia-wrapped Chianti bottles with those drip candles, and stuff hanging from the ceiling tangled with fish nets. Lila always felt like one of those pale green glass fishing floats or the fake grapes were going to drop on her head.

But Nick's lunch specials were superb, and the place was extremely clean despite the fish net. He also had outside tables in the summer, a rare treat for rain-soaked northwesterners.

She parked herself at a deck table after waving to the waitress, a girl she'd known in high school, Debbie. "Little Debbie" Arness. She wasn't little Debbie anymore, but who wasn't fighting off a few pounds.

It had been a spectacular summer. Lila loved the heat. She leaned back in the chair and let the rays soak into her bones. Sunshine: such a lovely feeling.

She popped her head back up when Debbie brought her an iced tea. Debbie knew her so well. She even brought one for Bonnie, knowing they were usually together. Lila waved to Bonnie as soon as she saw her approaching. Bonnie had hiked up the three blocks from the antique store in the summer heat and looked a little pink in the cheeks.

She all but flung herself into the white plastic outdoor chair across from Lila. "Whew! Thank you, Debbie, for reading my mind." Bonnie stripped the paper off her straw and sucked up a large quantity of iced tea.

"Are you ready?" Lila crossed her arms and watched.

"Okay, and it better be good, or bad anyway. If you don't have anything good to say, come sit by me, I always say." Bonnie had a strange second-generation Southern accent underneath her Port Gamble childhood dialect.

"Emily Ruth Griffin is haunting the store." Lila said it flat out. She didn't even have a moment of doubt that Bonnie would believe her. Bonnie was no skeptic when it came to the strangeness of Lila's sixth sense in regard to the dearly departed.

"It's the Strawberry Queen all over again," Bonnie blurted out.

"God, I hope not. She hasn't exactly appeared, but a grocery cart just went shopping all by itself, and it was her cart. I know because I marked it. It was also particular to the lemon bin, where Emily Ruth met her end."

"Have they figured out what killed her?" Bonnie asked. For the last seven days running Lila had fretted whether it was her fault Emily Ruth died.

Lila sipped her iced tea. "The autopsy results aren't back from Seattle, but they're still thinking severe peanut allergy."

"Now, Lila, you see? Cheese Whiz has no peanuts or peanut oil in it unless a peanut jumped into their soybean oil and sullied the entire batch, and then it's still not your fault."

"They're testing the can of Cheez Whiz I was using for possible traces. They're testing the olives too, and the pimentos, and the Ritz Crackers. But that doesn't make any sense. It must have been a delayed reaction to something else she'd eaten or touched—like a fragment on her fingertip or something."

Little Debbie showed up with her sad eyes and stood poised with her order pad.

"Shrimp Caesar," Lila said.

"Seafood fettuccini," Bonnie said.

"You are a horrible person, Bonnie Forbes, consuming something that lovely in front of me when I'm dieting."

"You're always dieting."

Debbie smirked and left them alone.

Bonnie sat back in her chair and got that look she gets when her extremely intelligent brain is rattling something around like a pinball machine. Pretty soon that silver ball was going to come out of her mouth.

"You had Emily Ruth's purse right?"

"Right. Who carries a purse like that? I could put a dog in my bag." Lila hefted her blue and beige striped canvas tote bag off the deck floor.

"And you didn't find anything of interest in that bag?"

"Nothing but the keys to the Jag, a Chanel lipstick, and a very expensive compact. By the way, I still have Emily Ruth's dog. My mother has been dog-sitting her while I'm at work. I haven't heard a word out of Lucas about the dog."

"That just seems really odd to me. Doesn't it to you, Lila?" Bonnie tilted her head. "Something is fishy about this whole thing."

"Maybe that's why Emily Ruth is whacking her cart against the lemon bins. Because you always need lemon with fish, you know." Lila laughed at her own joke.

Bonnie just stared at her. Lila could tell Bonnie had gone to that place in her mind where all the little puzzle pieces were being laid out.

Bonnie was the Nancy Drew of Port Gamble, no doubt about it. All that genealogical research she did for people gave her a knack for solving puzzles. And after all, she was a card-carrying member of the Monday Mystery Book Club. She pulled a green leather-covered notebook and a pencil out of her own generously sized purse.

"I'm telling you Lila, we're on to something here." She scribbled in her notebook.

Lila thought about what Bonnie was saying. "Maybe she's just like the Strawberry Queen. She didn't want to give up her title, and for Emily Ruth she just wants to finish shopping. Unfinished business, you know?"

"Yeah, since nineteen-fifteen she didn't want to give up her title. You did the community a great service having that little chat with her. We haven't seen a wisp of her since." Bonnie smiled across the table at her.

"They're going to want me to get rid of Emily Ruth's ghost, aren't they?" Lila crossed her arms, then uncrossed them as Debbie brought their lunches. Bonnie's looked better. She poured Caesar dressing over her greens and shrimp and fluffed them up. Bonnie put down her notebook and shook an inch of pepper over her fettuccini.

"*Maybe* she's trying to tell us Lucas Griffin killed her." Lila said aloud what she'd been thinking for a week. If that was true, she wasn't too keen on trying to reason with Emily Ruth to stop shopping and get an afterlife if it meant getting into the middle of a murder case.

The Strawberry Queen was just misguidedly trying to get her crown back from whatever unlucky girl was nominated for the honor that year. It had gotten to be a real town joke and only the bravest girls had submitted their name after an almost hundred-year run of the Strawberry Queen showing up to claim her crown back.

Yes, her ghostly appearance in the mirror behind Heather Johnston had caused the girl to faint dead away, but all Lila had done was convince the queen there was an even prettier crown waiting for her in heaven.

Sometimes the simplest things can solve even the most perplexing problems. And she *had* succeeded where the Episcopal minister had failed. But then Father Andrew wasn't exactly comfortable with the whole idea of exorcism. He'd needed two whisky sours before he'd even gotten up the nerve to go into the Johnston's house that day. Father Andrew just didn't understand the mind of a hundred-year-old beauty queen. But Lila did.

"Maybe Lucas did it. *Somebody* did it. I feel it in my bones." Bonnie speared a scallop and sank into her thoughts again. "I just can't figure how."

"It was Lucas. He danced on her grave, I'm sure." Lila stabbed at her salad.

A shadow fell across their sunny table and it wasn't little Debbie. Lila glanced up to see if the umbrella had tilted in the wind. It wasn't the patio umbrella, it was Lucas Griffin. He was still good-looking, despite being a potential murderer.

"I did *not* kill my ex-wife," he said. "You should be looking around to see who her latest lover was. I'm sure you'll find a string of suspects." He leaned in close to Lila. She caught his scent. His eyes flashed as blue as sea glass in the sun. "Don't be spreading that rumor. The woman gave me enough trouble without me ending up in jail for killing her. If I'd wanted her dead I'd have done it years ago before she put the final touches on screwing up my life."

As soon as Lila heard that she remembered the dinner for two in Emily Ruth's cart, and how she'd forgotten to tell Bonnie about that.

Luca started to walk toward the entrance of Nick's but Lila wasn't a girl to let the last word go to a man.

"What about that damned dog, Lucas Griffin?" she yelled after him.

"Keep it," he yelled back.

"Crazy broads," Lucas muttered as he slid into the darkest booth Nick's had. It suited his mood. The only thing good that had happened to him in the last few years was the fact that Emily Ruth had died. Now he could stay in Port Gamble without having to deal with his ex-wife.

Now he could reclaim the house his parents had given to him and his brother and sister.

He bent over the table and put his face in his hands. There must be a special place in hell for men who are glad their ex-wives died.

"*Ahem.*" The waitress cleared her throat next to him.

He looked up and she smiled. "What can I get you, Mr. Griffin?" It was Debbie, one of the locals.

"Full Sail Ale, and a single," he used the local lingo for one order of fish and chips. Not that there was anything remotely Italian about fish and chips, but they'd always served them anyway. He didn't even have to look at the menu. He'd eaten here since he was big enough to sit on a chair, every summer.

Debbie left, sensing his lack of conversational skills no doubt. He had to find a way out of this dark cloud. For the last few months all he'd done was beat himself up for letting Emily Ruth manipulate his brother into giving her a life estate in the Port Gamble house, that lying, conniving bitch. And for the past week all he'd done was beat himself up for being glad she'd dropped over dead.

It was a bad combination when you added in the wounded leg keeping him awake at night and the slow recovery from his stint reporting in Iraq.

At least now he'd get the house back. And maybe there was a chance his parents and sister would see some sense and forgive him for letting some gold-digging local girl steal the family estate out from under his and his brother's nose. Forgive him for bringing Emily Ruth into their family and having his brother end up dead under her influence.

Nothing could make up for her cheating on him with his own brother, but he'd forgiven poor Jason for falling under the evil spell of Emily Ruth long ago—even before Jason had died. If only he'd let Jason know that before that day. Now he'd never get the chance to tell him.

He was buried in *if-only*s.

If only he'd managed to convince his parents and sister she was lying about everything before Jason died with a will that gave Emily Ruth a life-estate interest in the house.

If only his brother hadn't decided to take a run to the liquor store on his motorcycle that night. Probably Emily Ruth's idea, and once she put her mind to something, nothing could change it.

Lucas shook his head and closed his eyes, catching the memory of his brother, sister, and mother and father back when they had loved him and trusted him. Back before he'd misspent his twenties and screwed up his thirties and given them reason to turn their back on him. Back before he'd walked in on Emily Ruth and Jason. Back before his brother had died.

Okay let's look on the bright side. Emily Ruth only had the house for a little while after his brother's death. She couldn't have ever sold the place really, just lived there till she died, which came sooner than later, and, because she died, all the lawsuits to get it back from her were over. No more lawyers, no more contested wills, no more Emily Ruth's dirty looks.

He could move in now and get rid of all remnants of her. He could reclaim the estate that had been in the Griffin family for one hundred and seven years and redeem himself in the eyes of his remaining family.

The Griffin children and grandchildren could now come and play on the beach and gather in the big dining room and all hear the cautionary tale of how Uncle Lucas almost lost the house forever by marrying a townie who drove the entire family to the brink of ruin and beyond, so keep your Bermuda shorts zipped, kids.

Debbie delivered his beer and single, which sent up an aromatic plume of good old English pub food that reminded him he was hungry. He swigged back a good portion of his Full Sail Ale and followed it with a bite of batter-fried Alaskan cod.

Instead of making him feel better, everything just twisted up in his guts. And he knew just why. It was those women out there. He might have gained the estate back but if he ended up in jail for the murder of his ex-wife, what good would that do him?

Hell, he might as well go straight into the lion's mouth or he'd have no peace. He reached in his pocket and threw a twenty on the table, gathered up his plate and beer, and went to confront the town gossips.

When Lucas pushed the outside door of Nick's open with his back and walked over to their table, they both looked like they were going to tip right off their molded white plastic chairs.

"Ladies, I've decided to join you for lunch. Slide on over, will you?" He horned his plate onto their small glass-topped table and pulled up a chair. They scooted, slid, and scrunched their selves and their lunches over. They were speechless. He almost laughed.

"Look, girls, Lila, and what's your name?"

"Bonnie Forbes," Bonnie blurted out.

Lucas took the ketchup bottle from the center of the table and squeezed a big pile of it over his fries. They watched him, still speechless. "I'm a direct kind of guy. I've been through hell with my ex-wife, and I just can't see going to jail for a crime I didn't commit. So I propose we catch this drip of gossip before it turns into a tidal wave."

He popped a fry into his mouth and watched their faces. The redheaded Lila developed an immediate fire in her hazel brown eyes, but the other one, Bonnie, had a cautious, untrusting look. He'd have to watch out for her.

"You've got some nerve, Griffin. You've all but said you wanted her dead. I don't know how you did it, but you probably killed her, and that puts me sitting here with a murderer. Ouch," Lila finished with an exclamation of pain. She reached down to rub her shin. Bonnie Forbes had obviously kicked her under the table.

"What did you want to tell us, Lucas?" Bonnie asked him.

"Just this. I was scheduled to meet Emily Ruth at eleven in her lawyer's office for one last attempt to make her an offer she couldn't refuse and get her out of my family's house." He realized he probably shouldn't have worded it quite that way. "When she didn't show, I went hunting for her downtown. I saw her car in the Market Foods parking lot and when I started into the store, one of the deputies told me what happened, and showed me her dead body.

"The point is, I wasn't anywhere near her when she died. I had no opportunity. I might have had motive, but I had no opportunity. Besides, would I kill the woman over a house?"

Lila Abbott's little red eyebrow arched at him. "From what I hear, there was a lot more to it than the house. Everybody says you are a nogood, cheating, stuck-up rich boy who played around with Emily Ruth, got her knocked up, and left her with nothing."

Lucas leaned forward in his chair. "Oh they do, do they? And do you see a baby anywhere? Is there a child with my blue eyes running around the streets I don't know about?"

Lila thumped back in her chair and crossed her arms. "You murdered her, Lucas Griffin, and no amount of money is going to keep you from frying like that fish on your plate in the electric chair."

He had to laugh. He did laugh. He laughed so hard he felt tears streaming down his face. This girl was completely crazy. That kind of crazy where no actual facts penetrate into the reasonable portion of her brain. The kind of woman you don't want sitting on your jury. She was the kind that flew on emotion alone. He held his stomach and smacked the table with the other hand, trying to stop laughing. Their plates jumped. So did they.

He wiped his eyes with the back of his hand and took a few breaths in. "Okay, okay, you're just killing me here. What about we figure out what really happened to Emily Ruth, and that'll prove my innocence. Most likely she just caught a whiff of Jiff somehow, you know? That allergy of hers was like a death sentence anyhow. The odds of her actually being murdered are extremely low."

Lila could not believe the nerve of this guy. Sitting here, trying to convince them he hadn't killed her. He was guilty as sin, and it was writ-ten all over his face. His *very* handsome face. Maybe he though being handsome would save his ass?

"Why are you playing boy sports reporter at the *Gazette*? Don't you have a sailboat to jaunt around the bay in or some expensive toy to amuse yourself with for the summer?" Lila snapped like a snapping turtle in Lucas's direction.

"I'm downsizing," he snarled back at her.

"Did you notice an EpiPen in Emily Ruth's Jag, Lucas? We didn't find one on her," Bonnie asked.

Wow, sometimes Bonnie was braver than any-one she knew. She imagined Lucas cracking un-der Bonnie's questioning then deciding to kill them both later. She shuddered. She stared and waited for Lucas to answer.

"I didn't really look for it. Now that you men-tion it, it wasn't in the glove box. I can't believe she didn't have one in her bag or in a pocket. She was completely obsessive about carrying several at all times," Lucas answered. He sat back and finished off his beer. His laughter had taken a quick nose-dive into introspection.

"Did she have a lover?" Lila blurted out.

Lucas raised his eyes to her. "Several, I'm sure."

Ah, the rich, they just marry and dally and marry again, Lila thought. Of course so did the not-so-rich, so that wasn't too valid.

"We've been divorced for years. She wasn't exactly the faithful wife." Lucas seemed to catch himself and straightened up to the table. He pushed his plate aside and rose to leave. "But that's irrelevant. She died from an allergic reaction. There's no murder here. So I'm asking you to give me a break. I'd like to stay in town for a while. And after Emily Ruth, I could use a break."

"Speaking of giving someone a break, I don't want your dog, Griffin," Lila said.

"I'll work on finding the dog a home. And it wasn't my dog, Abbott, it was hers. I'll call you as soon as I find her a place."

After Lucas had moved out of sight, Lila clutched Bonnie's arm. She didn't even speak. There was hardly anything to say. Bonnie was also unusually quiet. Lila waited for something profound to come out of Bonnie's mouth. Then Bonnie spoke.

"Want to share his leftover fries?" she asked.

Four

The sun, that rare and treasured element of the late northwest summer, poured down on Lucas Griffin. He could feel the craving for quiet that had brought him here again. Two years as a reporter in an Iraqi war zone had wounded more than his leg. A soft breeze rustled the leaves of familiar birch trees, maples, thick with their summer leaves, and his great-grandmother's Italian plum decked with an abundance of almost-ripe fruit.

That was why his parents had loved the Port Gamble house, too. The sea air, the salty taste of the wind, the driftwood and sand, and most of all the alluringly quiet, soothing rhythm of the sea brought them back again and again, summer after summer. Peace.

He remembered the best times in this house, and the worst of times. Those worst of times all involved Emily Ruth.

Lucas fingered the heavy brass key in his jeans pocket as he walked up the porch stairs. He couldn't dampen the joy he felt when Emily's lawyer handed over the key—and the deed. Her life estate had run out when her life ran out.

So here he was, reclaiming the house that his parents had once entrusted to their two sons for safekeeping, but who had foolishly let a woman steal it away from them. The last time he'd come to Port Gamble had been to collect the body of his brother and have it cremated. Christmastime. Merry Christmas. Of course he'd stayed far away from this house and its occupant—the lovely, evil Emily Ruth.

The good feelings mingled with the pain of losing his brother, and of losing the trust of his parents. His sister and mother would come around eventually, but his father was a hard man.

But he had to try and live in the present. For

once there was a touch of joy mixed in with the pain. Restitution at last.

He touched the glass panes of the French door and looked through the lace curtain panels to the inside. Familiar things caught his eye. At least Emily Ruth hadn't remodeled the place—as far as he could tell.

He used to lie awake listening to the staccato of gunfire wondering if he'd ever see this place again. He'd walk through it in his mind to remember details. Would it all still be here? The family photos or the old dining table that he and his brother and sister had carved their initials underneath on a rainy afternoon when they'd made it into a blanket fort. No adult had ever found those initials, or at least they'd never told him they'd found them.

Secrets. There were secrets tucked in every corner of the house. He put the key in the lock and turned it, then shoved the French door inward. It protested, old as it was, as it did every summer. His dad always meant to plane it down, but he'd never gotten around to it. Maybe he'd do it himself now, since he was here for the rest of the summer. Or maybe the rest of his life.

He'd grown attached to Port Gamble during his hell years with Emily Ruth. He remembered the many hours of walking around town to get a breath of fresh air from his not-so-charming wife during the short time they'd been together. He also remembered how Emily Ruth had drained through his trust fund getting plastic surgery, buying that Jag, traveling to Europe—to buy clothes yet. What an idiot he'd been. Good thing he'd hidden enough to invest and keep himself in a modest income. His old man had taught him something at least. Dad would probably declare him "not a *complete* idiot."

And while they were married he'd never given in to her ideas about changing this house. Everything was just the way he remembered it: the huge beach-stone fireplace, the long, well-used oak dining table with the initials carved in its underside, surrounded with blue woven rattan French bistro chairs his mother had found in Provence and had shipped back here. His mom's favorite blue-and-white striped slipcovered overstuffed furniture still gathered around the fireplace.

It was hard to believe that in Emily Ruth's Jason years, with her unlimited funds—his brother's money and the divorce settlement he was forced to pay her—she hadn't gutted the place and turned it into her own personal "revenge décor." Maybe Jason had kept her from doing it. The last thread of family loyalty his brother might have had.

He dropped the key in the brass bowl on the black wicker side table flanking the entry doors and walked through to the kitchen. These old houses always had the kitchen off somewhere in the back, and when he was a kid his grandmother and mother and several Griffin aunts would turn this kitchen into a kid's wonderland. He could almost smell the clams steaming in the pot, the garlic bread, the apple and blackberry pies, that strange mix and mingle of scents that marked his summers here.

The newer house he'd bought in L.A. had the more open floor plan that people liked now, but he had to admit he preferred this old-fashioned way. When they'd brought everything out to the long table and the whole family gathered together to eat, he'd always felt like the kitchen in this house was another one of those secret, magical places that good things emerged from.

Lucas was struck with how deeply he felt

about taking possession of the house. Sure, he'd known getting it back from his ex-wife had been a fairly burning obsession with him after Jason died, but until this moment he didn't know just how emotionally attached he was to the house. It reached into his soul and soothed the broken parts of him.

Maybe it was more what the house represented. The best of times—with his parents and cousins and aunts and uncles and grandparents, and his brother, who he'd never have a chance to work things out with, if you *can* forgive a brother for sleeping with your wife. *Poor Jason.*

But he still had a chance to make things right with his parents and sister.

He took the stairs to the second floor and walked through each bedroom. He'd been struck by the fact that every room in the house was in perfect order. Not that Emily Ruth had been messy by any means. Still, it was a surprise.

But when he got to the master bedroom that's where Emily Ruth had left her mark. The place looked like a brothel: red satin sheets, red satin and lace pillows and bedding, lingerie hanging on a wall rack, and not the elegant kind of lingerie. The whole room had a *my smutty valentine* look. But clean. Very clean. Wow, she always did go on those cleaning binges.

He could smell her perfume—Passion by Elizabeth Taylor. He'd always disliked it. It was a perfume she'd picked up after they'd split. Not like the elegant Jean Patou's Joy he'd bought her. God, that woman should have come with a warning label.

Actually, the scent of her perfume was quite overwhelming. He backed out the door and closed it. Lucas took a deep breath of nonpolluted air, but her scent lingered like ghostly fingers reaching underneath the cracks of the door.

He'd have to get that room fumigated.

Down the hall he found the room he and his brother used to sleep in. It still had all the original furniture—what his grandmother Griffin called Adirondack style. He'd bunk in here. Maybe it was his way of coming to terms with his brother's weaknesses in regards to Emily Ruth, and his death. He tossed his leather duffle bag on the twin bed he'd slept in as a child.

Lucas ran his hand over his forehead. Well hell, he'd just have to pick up the pieces and see where he landed. He headed back downstairs.

The echo of his footsteps on the bare wood

floors only emphasized the emptiness of the house. Of his life. He decided to air the place out. Each set of French doors that opened onto the porch were more stubborn than the last, but finally he got them all open.

There was probably something to drink around here, what with Emily entertaining so often. He found a fruity Bacardi cooler in the refrigerator. Guess that would have to do until he got to the market.

He walked onto the porch and stretched himself out on the bentwood twig bench with its musty blue cushions and listened to the waves lap against the bulkhead.

The tide was getting high. The sun shimmered on the water. He took a swig of the lemon-flavored Bacardi drink. Not bad, really, for a summer day. He closed his eyes and dreamed of *other* days. Good days. Days on the beach with his brother and sister, digging in the sand with clam shells.

Lucas was startled awake by the yap of a dog—a yap very close to his ear. He had an instant headache. A shadow blocked the sun, and its name was Lila Abbott. Lucas groaned.

"A little birdy told me you'd gotten the keys

to the kingdom back today," she chirped. The dog yipped.

"What birdy?" Lucas growled and righted himself. He was groggy from off-kilter sleep.

"Chief Bob via Emily's attorney, I think. More like a big fat bird," Lila laughed. She had a funny laugh. The dog yipped, which it seemed to do in a sort of punctuating way, as if to emphasize whatever Lila said.

"Did you train that dog to do that?"

"It's your dog. I came to return her. My mom is getting sick of dog-sitting while I'm at work. Schatzie here isn't the most well-mannered miss. Do you have another one of those wine things? I could use a Thank God It's Friday drink."

Lucas snorted. "As in—happy hour?"

"Yup."

"Sure." Lucas got up and Lila followed, letting Schatzie lead the way. Her little nails went tap-tap-tap on the dark wood floors.

"I brought the leftover dog food." Lila placed a rolled-up paper sack on the kitchen counter. "God this place is splendiferous, but still homey. I love it." Lila looked around while Schatzie tried to get into a cupboard.

Lucas looked inside and found expensive dog

food and dog biscuits shaped like cats, and other dog-type items. He gave Schatzie a dog biscuit for nothing.

"You can't just hand those over, you have to make her do tricks. She's very clever. Give me one." Lila held out her hand. Lucas gave her a dog-cat biscuit.

"Here, Schatzie, sit." The dog obeyed.

"Shake hands." Again the dog obeyed, sticking her little paw out, panting with anticipation, alert as a teenager on caffeine overload.

"Now stay, stay." Lila backed away from the dog with her hand up in the air.

"Come." Her slight hand motion brought Schatzie shooting over to Lila. She danced on her little hind legs and Lila gave her the biscuit.

"Wow, you're good with her. Will you sit and stay if I give you a wine cooler?" Lucas chuckled.

Lila followed Lucas back outside and sat on the twig chair facing his bench. "So how long has this place been in your family anyhow?"

"Over one hundred years. My great grandfather built this house. He was one of the original lumber company owners. We made all our money from clear-cutting the wilderness and disturbing the habitats of spotted owls."

"Ah. Makes perfect sense," Lila said.

Schatzie sat down at her feet and sighed, her little head resting on her paws. Obviously the dog was smitten with her.

Lucas watched the strawberry blonde redhead sitting across from him. Lila Abbott was quite pretty. She had an earthy quality he found refreshing. She made herself right at home, pulled up the wicker ottoman, put up her feet, and swigged back her cooler. Her lips looked soft as summer peaches. Luscious.

"So what's the story with you and Emily Ruth, Lucas?"

That luscious summer peach suddenly made him feel pretty damned sour. "Why is that any of your business?" He'd made a personal vow never to talk about Emily Ruth and his brother Jason. The sins of his family weren't for public fodder.

"Well heck, I figure sooner or later it's going to be my business because your dead wife is haunting Market Foods. Since everyone thinks I'm the local spirit exterminator, it's only a matter of time. She gives off a pretty big whiff of perfume in this house, too."

"She saturated an upstairs bedroom with Eu de Slut. It's not a ghost, its lingering sin."

"My God, man, you are harsh. Didn't anyone

ever teach you it's bad manners to speak ill of the dead? If you keep that up everyone *will* believe you killed her." Lila tipped her bottle back up to her lips.

"And if I recall, you are one of them. If you still think I killed her, why are you here?"

"I came to bring your dog back, remember? Besides, after giving my statement to Chief Bob I don't see how you could have gotten to her when she died so quickly."

At this point Lila was wondering just why the hell she'd gotten the idea to go see Lucas anyhow. The dog was just an excuse. She'd gotten pretty attached to it herself, and it was a bold-faced lie that her mother was tired of dog-sitting. Her mother had even made Schatzie a little pink bandanna to tie around her neck.

The truth was she seemed to have developed a slight fascination with Lucas Griffin, the arrogant prick.

This was the sort of thing she'd spent the last seventeen years of her life getting over; a tendency to develop an attraction to the wrong guy. But what girl at sixteen knew who the wrong guy was? Thirty-three? She should know by now. Lila stared into Lucas's clear blue eyes and knew.

Before she could say anything really stupid, Schatzie perked up and started to growl, then yap wildly. She took off into the house through the open French doors and raced up the stairs.

Lila looked at Lucas and they shared a confused moment. Lucas got up and followed the dog, Lila followed Lucas, naturally.

Lucas bolted up the stairs two at a time, limp and all, she noticed. Lila kept up as best she could. He stopped so abruptly in the hallway that Lila smacked into his back.

"Oh, sorry."

He steadied her and put his finger to her lips, then to his own. "Shhhhh," he indicated. Lila felt a little electrical jolt at his touch. She also had another feeling. An old familiar feeling. The prickling of her neck hairs and the rush of energy to her body.

Schatzie was trying to dig under a bedroom door. Lila could already smell the waft of perfume as it curled through the small crack of light between the floor and the door. It curled like a vapor. Then the vapor became more like smoke. Schatzie freaked out and yelped, then peed on the floor.

"The place is on fire! *Damn* it. " Lucas threw

open the door and stepped over the small dog-pee puddle.

"Schatzie!" Lila called the dog to her side and petted her. She knew perfectly well the room was not on fire. The scent of the smoky vapor was not fire-scented. It was Emily Ruth scented.

Lucas stood in the room staring. Behind him Lila watched as the vapor formed a shape. It was so close to him she wondered if it would tap him on the shoulder.

She'd always had this thing where it was more important to her to watch than to let the fear take over.

Lila hoped Lucas wouldn't have a heart attack. She felt herself smile.

"I don't get it . . ." Lucas started to say. Then he turned to face Lila and must have caught the misty shape of his former wife out of the corner of his eye. The scent of her perfume was as heavy as toxic fumes. Lila coughed.

To his credit, Lucas didn't scream like a girl. Lila had seen many a grown man turn into a screaming Mimi when confronted with a spirit. Lucas sucked his breath in and stood very still. His eyes were riveted to the wispy form.

"Emily Ruth Griffin, what the heck is keeping you around, girl? Isn't there some big bright light you should be moving into about now?" Lila asked out loud.

The smoke seemed to turn her way, then to her dismay, started toward her. She'd never actually had trouble with a spirit before, but Emily Ruth wasn't just any spirit. She was a pissed-off ex-wife spirit. The dog cowered behind Lila and Lila kind of wished Lucas was in a different position so she could cower behind *him*.

The vapor came at her *very* fast. Unbelievably, Lila felt the not-so-dearly departed Emily Ruth give her a hard shove of energy. Lila slammed into a slatted bifold closet door directly behind her.

"Hey, just step off, bitch!" Lila yelled. Schatzie growled and barked, but just as suddenly stopped as the smoky vapor hovered over the dog. It almost seemed to Lila like Emily Ruth was petting the dog.

Lucas stood like statue-boy with a shocked look on his face.

Lila put her hands on her hips. "You aren't going to make any friends shoving me around, you know. Get to the point and we can all get back to our lives, and believe me when I tell you there is a better one waiting for you on the other side."

For one brief second the smoke diffused, but it reformed right in front of Lila again, choking her with the perfumed scent. This time the closet door behind her flew open, hitting Lila in the butt as it folded open. Then just as if someone had opened a window, the entire mass of foggy Emily Ruth will-o'-the-wisped to the wind and was gone.

"Good grief, what a drama queen," Lila said. She picked up Schatzie and comforted her.

"Oh my God, oh my God," was all that Lucas could muster. Lila kind of liked this part of her life where she could be the calm one while everyone else lost it. It was a gift, for sure.

Lila came over to Lucas and gave him a friendly bump. "Hey, don't worry, I've seen worse. Well, sort of. She's really pushy isn't she?"

"She? You think that thing was Emily Ruth?"

"Oh come on, you don't meant to stand here and tell me you can't tell that was your ex-wife that just smoked us?" Lila looked at him with her best *How dumb are you?* look.

Lucas shook his head and ran his hand over

his forehead. "I need a drink." He pushed past her and headed down the stairs.

Schatzie growled a few times for good measure. Men. They could see something straight in front of their faces and deny it existed. Lila went to find the upstairs powder room for some tissues to clean up the dog pee.

A claw-footed tub took up a large portion of the old bathroom, with a genuine vintage pedestal sink on one side. She pulled some toilet paper off the roll and went to mop up. While she bent over the floor she remembered the closet Emily Ruth had shoved her against.

Now a woman never shows her closets unless there's something fabulous to see like color-coded linens, a newly organized medicine and sundry section, or new towels. Emily Ruth must have had a reason for doing that.

She could just rummage around in there but that would be rude and her mother always taught her not to poke into other people's belongings uninvited. She better get permission. Lila went back to the bathroom with Schatzie on her heels looking appropriately mortified, and dumped her cleaning tissues down the loo with a follow-up flush. Schatzie jumped. Her nerves were as frayed as her little red-haired fur, poor thing.

"Hey, Griffin," Lila yelled down the stairwell. "Come up here and go through the closet with me."

Lucas got up from the table, swigged down the last of the wine cooler, and stomped up the stairs to the woman hollering at him. Women, they were always creating problems for him, alive or dead. He loved women, but damn, they were such a pain in the ass.

At least he'd regained his senses. That couldn't have been his ex-wife smoking up the place. It was his imagination. It was *Lila Abbott's* imagination. It just *wasn't* the ghost of Emily Ruth. No way.

"What closet?" he asked when he reached the landing.

"The one Emily Ruth tried to shove me through." Lila pointed to the open doors. "Then left open for everyone to see. Women don't let other women see their linen closet unless there's something special in there."

"I love your theories on life, Abbott. Search away. Maybe we'll find the smoke bomb that rolled by us."

"Are you seriously going to dwell in denial? I took you for a more broad-minded individual." Lila started handing Lucas neatly folded white towels.

He stacked them on the floor. "Just because you think that was the ghost of Emily Ruth doesn't mean there isn't some other explanation," he said flatly. "In journalism we learn not to take things at face value, but to find out the hard facts."

She handed him more towels, this time dark navy blue. "Hard facts, huh? Never mind your ex is haunting Market Foods every Monday at ten thirty-six in the morning, we'll just ignore that hard fact."

"Fact? A cart rolled across the floor."

Lila tsk-tsked him and gave him a stack of flowered sheets. "It was *her* cart. I marked it with a permanent marker the day she died. In my experience there are two basic reasons spirits hang around. One is just misguided focus, like our Strawberry Queen. She was just stuck in a sort of loop, you know? Like reruns of old sitcoms on the nostalgia channel."

Lila Abbott was in her own loop in his opinion. She kept handing out linens, talking, reaching back into the closet, talking more. Lucas almost laughed. She was a loopy redheaded automated advice device and closet-clearing machine.

"The other is remorse. Maybe Emily Ruth feels bad about being so mean to you." Lila stopped and looked him in the eye.

"Shoving you up against the closet doesn't look like she's too contrite to me. It looks like she's the same pushy bitch I've come to detest over the last two years."

"Ah-HA!" Lila pointed her finger at him. "So you admit that *was* her."

"Not till I sober up."

"One stupid wine cooler hasn't had any effect on a guy like you, Lucas." Lila turned back to the closet, which was almost empty now, and looked in the corners of the bare shelves. "Well hell, what did she want us to see? That her towels are all folded in perfect thirds?"

"Those aren't her towels, they are Griffin towels. See the G monogrammed on them?" Lucas snarled.

"What's up there on the top? Hold me up." Lila hoisted herself on the bottom shelf, her one little white tennis shoe balancing on the edge.

Lucas smiled to himself and boosted her up by her cute little jeans-covered rear end. She peered over the high shelf then grabbed at something, which put her off balance. She came down hard, directly into his arms, clutching her prize.

He felt a little off balance himself as he looked into her light-as-amber eyes. He slid her to the floor.

"Thanks," Lila blushed. She was a very pink redheaded woman now.

Schatzie, who had been all but napping in the hallway beside them, suddenly came to life and tried to retrieve the gift-wrapped, ribbon-tied package by hopping up and down like she was on a trampoline, her two little back feet on and off the ground, her two little front feet pawing the air. Quite a sight.

"Off, Schatzie, sit." Lila shook her finger at the dog, which sat down obediently.

"That dog likes you, Abbott. Why don't you just keep her?"

"I'll think about it." She stared at the package Lucas had in his hands. "Let's take it downstairs and open it."

Lucas stared at the box. It had yellow and white baby shower wrap and a frothy yellow ribbon. It also had about a half-inch of dust on it. He sneezed.

"Bless you. Come on." Lila took his arm and headed him for the stairs.

Right away he could feel himself getting mad. Emily Ruth's baby scam had worked so well his own parents had let her stay in the house. It was all part of her pack of lies about him cheating on her, drinking, slapping her. Why the hell had they believed her? Emily was the queen of lies and deceit, telling his parents she was pregnant with Jason's baby, and they'd believed her. That was why they hadn't fought her on the beach house life estate. They were softies for any potential grandchildren. Thank God she hadn't actually had one. If she ever was actually pregnant, which he doubted. She'd covered her tracks nicely by telling his parents she'd had a miscarriage.

Even when he'd told them about Emily Ruth lying, cheating on him with Jason, keeping Jason drunk, they hadn't listened. But worst of all, when Jason was killed, they'd blamed him instead. They said he should have watched out after his little brother. They believed her lies. *Why?*

He knew the answer to that. He hadn't exactly been a good son in his teens and early twenties.

His wild youth had caught up with him: some jail time for possession of marijuana, that stupid car accident where he wrecked someone's fence, dropping out of college for a while. Hell, if he'd had a kid like him he'd have given up, too.

Lucas stumbled down the stairs after Lila. But he'd changed—he'd grown up. He'd gone clean. He'd done community service for his car's damage to property and found out he liked working with the kids at the juvenile detention center in the city. They liked him, too. And the writing projects he'd helped them with had sparked his journalistic soul again. He was glad he'd gotten back to college on his own.

Too bad he hadn't shared any of that with his folks. His father's harsh reaction to his string of arrests had created such bad feelings between them. Not going into the family business probably added to it. His wanderlust life of traveling journalism never did appeal to his father. Maybe if he'd won the Pulitzer Prize, or something, Dad would have accepted that. Travel pieces from Asia and Europe in obscure magazines didn't seem to cut it.

And even when he'd sent them articles he'd written about the war, he hadn't heard from them at all. He should have tried harder to mend it between them years ago.

He remembered how he'd met Emily Ruth during a Griffin family summer in Port Gamble. *Oh, the lovely Emily Ruth, now Lucas will settle down. Now Lucas will stop running away.*

But now here he was, holding evidence of her manipulative, conniving scheme to make sure his parents sided against him. *Damn* that woman.

"Lucas? Are you all right?"

"No. This is just a piece of her lies." He threw the package on the table.

Lila grabbed it before it fell off the edge. "Well then, you won't mind if I open it?"

"And you won't mind if I don't watch." He stalked outside and slammed himself into a porch chair.

Lila shrugged. Lucas Griffin obviously had issues. She on the other hand, had curiosity. So did Schatzie, who followed her everywhere, and now stood on a chair poking her little black nose toward the package. If Lila had to guess she'd say it had someone's scent on it that Schatzie knew.

She read the cute folded hangtag attached to the gift.

To our grandbaby. These belonged to all the Griffin babies.

With love,
Julia Griffin

Wow, that sucked. No wonder Lucas was pissed. His mom obviously bought the whole fake baby thing all the way. Lila went to a stylish faux bamboo desk and poked around for a pair of scissors. She pulled them out of a small drawer.

Carefully snipping the tape off the wrapping, she undid the package and opened the box. Inside lay a sheer white handkerchief linen christening gown with embroidered edges and a G on each edge of the collar in pale blue. A matching bonnet and set of booties were tucked underneath.

Well, at least when Lucas actually had a kid, he'd have the family heirloom now. Maybe Emily just wanted to return this to its rightful owner.

She left everything on the table and went into the kitchen for a glass of water, followed by the dog. The sense of memories and time spent with a loving family permeated the very wainscoted walls of the room. She could almost see the many generations of the Griffin clan cooking, cleaning, and talking in the kitchen.

Behind a glass-doored cabinet she found a couple of old patterned drinking glasses from the fifties. She retrieved some ice out of the fridge and filled them both with tap water. Looked good, smelled good, must be well water. Lila headed for the porch and ol' grumpy Griffin.

"Here, Griffin," she handed him a glass.

"Thanks."

Lila plopped in the chair across from Lucas. Schatzie jumped in her lap, and she let her, giving her a pet as she set the glass down on the side table. "Well, all I can tell you is that Emily Ruth might have wanted to return the family christening gown to you."

"How nice of her," he grumbled.

Lucas looked all broody. It was time for her to exit. She finished her water and stood up to leave. Her big striped bag was still there where she'd left it.

"Hey, look, call me if you want to talk," Lila said.

"Or if I need an exorcist?"

"Not my specialty, but I'm a pretty good translator, I guess."

Oddly, Schatzie had curled up at Lucas's feet. Lila decided to leave the dog. Lucas could use some company.

"Later, Griffin." She turned and walked the length of the porch.

"Later, Abbott." She heard Lucas's voice just before she descended the stairs.

Five

Normally Lila's Monday mornings were "trudgery." That's what she liked to call it. Trudge out of bed, trudge to the sludge she called coffee to get her eyeballs to pry open, trudge into a shower, trudge into her clothes, and trudge to work. She'd drive her "vintage" green Toyota Celica, kept alive by her father with duct tape and bailing wire, she suspected, with more coffee in hand. Caffeine, gotta have that bean.

By the time she got there she'd usually woken up completely and regained the spring in her step, unless it was pouring down rain or foggy or cold. But today the sun was already waiting outside the door of her little historical cottage. Birds were singing, too. It was just so . . . Disney around here.

The road to work was lined with historic white houses with green shutters, clean and crisp in the summer sun, like fresh laundry on the line. She started whistling while she drove: *Zippety-Doo-Dah.*

Maybe this Monday would be just an ordinary Monday. No deaths, no ghosts, no craziness. Emily Ruth had given Lucas back the family christening gown after all. Maybe she was done and had crossed on over. It was already 10:30 anyhow. Lila was on the early late shift tonight.

But today as she rounded the bend from Port Gamble to the stretch of town that contained all the un-Disney stuff including Market Foods, Re/Max Real Estate, and Henderson's Drugs, she stopped whistling.

Folks were either running *into* the store, or *out* of the store. Or both. So from where she saw it, the store was either on fire or there was a big Monday-only sale on potato salad and hot dogs at Market Foods. People around here did love their potato salad.

Lila picked her parking space in the far lot where employees parked and hurried herself out of the car. As she approached the north entrance, Bonnie caught up with her. She hadn't even seen her coming.

"What's going on?" Lila huffed and puffed next to Bonnie. She really should pay more attention to her fitness program. Bonnie was fast, damn her.

"Your ghost is having a hissy fit."

"Why is she *my* ghost? Can't she be Lucas's ghost? Or your ghost?"

"She's yours, just admit it. She's trying to tell you something."

"I thought we'd gotten that all worked out Friday night at Griffin's house." Lila managed to get that out as they ran in the automatic door.

"Apparently not," Bonnie said in her *you didn't tell me you went to see Lucas Griffin* voice. A look went with that.

Tom Boscov looked like his comb-over was going to spontaneously flip the other direction. He couldn't even speak. The best he could do was set down an orange cone in front of aisle two and stare.

Lila moved him aside and looked straight

down the aisle. Now, this had to be the strangest thing she'd seen yet. Cans of Cheez Whiz kept popping off the shelf, and at least four of them were upright on the floor squirting cheese fountains up in the air. When one would run out, another one would fall off the shelf, land upright, pop its top, and start to spray cheese all over the place.

What a mess. Talk about your cleanup on aisle two! At the end of the row were the more curious and brave onlookers—as opposed to those running out the doors of the store.

Then Larry Pierson's figure came through the group. He looked positively stricken. He dove into the aisle and started trying to restock the cans that were just rolling about on their own. He was frantic. He was nuts. Lila went to save him.

"Larry, Larry, let it go. We'll clean it up later."

"Customers won't like this," he hissed.

"Well, duh, we've got a poltergeist in the condiment section. That's just going to kill our sales today. But there are bigger things in life than our sales figures, Larry, so get a grip." Lila grabbed him by the shoulders of his short-sleeved white shirt.

He was about as white as that shirt.

"It's her," he whispered.

"Looks like it, unless we're having a really weird earthquake," Lila said. "You've got Cheez Whiz in your hair. Now go back to produce and get yourself together. I'll take care of this."

"Make her stop, Lila." Larry looked wild-eyed.

Lila escorted him back toward produce. "I'll do my best, Larry."

Bonnie must have gone down aisle three and rounded to Lila's end.

"Larry's pretty shaken up," Lila said. "Neat fanatics don't take well to messy spirits, I guess."

Lila looked down the aisle. Through the spray of cheese she saw Lucas Griffin standing at the other end. Their eyes met. She nodded. Lila felt a shudder move through her and the back of her neck hairs tingled. She wasn't sure if it was from the spirit of Emily Ruth or the sight of Lucas Griffin. Damn, she was attracted to him. Wouldn't you know it? That was probably clear proof he did his wife in.

The Cheez Whiz fountains suddenly stopped. A hush fell over the store. Tom Boscov turned around and started saying, "It's over folks, don't worry, we've got it under control."

As if.

Bonnie pointed at her watch. "Look. Ten thirty-six."

"Time of death. She is getting creative, though, she started earlier," Lila said quietly.

"What's with you and handsome?" Bonnie asked.

"Sparks."

"Oh my God, that's perfect," Bonnie laughed.

"Very funny."

The flicker of movement caught her eye and she turned in time to see Lucas standing at their end of the row. Good thing he hadn't heard any of that. Or had he? He wasn't smiling.

"What does she want, Abbott?" Lucas shook his head.

"Damned if I know."

"You're supposed to be the expert, or so I hear."

"I'm no expert, I'm just cursed with some stupid ability. Some ghost early-warning system or something. Honestly, Lucas, your ex has me stumped. I thought she was done. I thought she'd returned the christening gown and be on her merry way."

"Guess that wasn't enough. That damn dog

barked all weekend. I could smell Emily Ruth's perfume like bad cheese all over the house. I cleaned out her bedroom but it didn't help."

"Why didn't you call me?

A small smile crossed Lucas's lips, then faded. "I needed to be alone. I'm in denial, remember?"

Lucas seemed to be absorbing everything around him in a different manner than usual—as much *usual* as she'd seen so far. He was examining the Cheez Whiz cans, and he even whipped out a digital camera from his pocket and took pictures.

"Hey, Lucas, you aren't going to put my name in some newspaper article, are you?" Lila asked. "I don't know if I'm in the mood to be splattered all over the front page of the *Port Gamble Gazette*."

"I'm just trying to get a more investigative take on this thing," he answered.

"Maybe you *should* write an article about Emily. It would stop a whole lot of gossip," Lila said.

"I'm not going to spill the family dirt in public."

Lila handed him the can of Cheez Whiz she'd

been holding. "Don't be so quick, Lucas, it might be better for you to appear cooperative. Good press can work in your favor."

First he snorted in disgust, then he stared at the Cheez Whiz. "Come over to my place tonight, and we'll talk about it."

"I don't get off till eight." Lila got all goofy like she was making a date.

Bonnie elbowed her. "You've got book group tonight," she reminded her.

"Tomorrow night, then," he said. The elusive Mr. Griffin then turned and left abruptly.

"He disappears faster than his ex," Bonnie mumbled. "And listen up, best buddy, I don't want you alone with him until we've figured out some basic facts, like whether he masterminded the death of his ex-wife. So no more sneaking off."

"Yes, Ma'am. I wonder what he was doing here anyway? He always shows up at the strangest times."

Bonnie looked up at her as if she heard something. "He's in the next aisle grinding coffee. Listen."

Lila listened and heard the whine of the coffee grinder. "How do you know it's him?"

"Deductive reasoning. I listened to his footsteps. But notice that he doesn't seem too shook up at his dead wife's Cheezmania, does he?"

"Dead *ex*-wife." Lila snuck around the end cap display and took a peek just to double-check on Bonnie's deductive reasoning. Sure enough, Lucas was grinding coffee. How could he just coincidentally be here when this big supernatural event happened? Maybe Emily Ruth staged it for Lucas's benefit. *Or* for hers. That made Lila shudder. She ran back to Bonnie.

"Maybe Emily Ruth is still angry about the Cheez Whiz demo that killed her. Maybe she blames me."

"You're the expert, what do you think?"

"Why does everyone keep saying that, just because I solved a few random hauntings?"

"That's more than the rest of us can say. Call me when you have a lunch break. We need to talk about your willy-nilly attraction to unobtainable summer boys who might have killed their ex-wives."

"Am I a willy-nilly kind of woman?"

"Yes."

"I thought I'd go shopping on my lunch break. Want to go to Annie Rose's with me?"

Bonnie looked amused. "Oh, so we can pretty up for the murderer? New dress maybe?"

Lila ignored her. "Are you honestly thinking he had anything to do with Emily Ruth's death?" Lila felt very cross and confused. "More likely it was *me*. I'm going over to the chief's office and get that autopsy report. It's supposed to be in today. We'll see what she really died from."

"Why would they give it to you?"

"I don't know. I'll do a lap dance for Chief Bob and see where it gets me."

"You're bad. Bad Lila."

Lila gave Bonnie's arm a squeeze and went to find a mop. There was no doubt she'd be the one left to clean up the mess. Everyone else was too freaked. The customers remaining in the store were clumped in little pods of carts, whispering, and a few pointed looks came her direction.

"Thanks a whole lot, Emily Ruth," Lila said out loud as soon as she'd passed through the thick plastic strips that hung between the selling floor and the stockroom. "I'm left on cleanup and I still can't figure out what the hell it is you're trying to tell me. You're going have to be more direct, you know?"

As if in reply, a very loud, twisted scream

echoed through the entire cement-floored stock-room. Lila backed up against a pile of paper towel rolls. Now she knew where the term blood curdling came from, because that was one blood-curdling scream. She recognized the screamer, too. Larry Pierson.

Lila ran toward the produce stock area. Honestly, that man. He probably found a moldy zucchini in a delivery.

But when she got to him, Larry was pinned between some apple crates and three very large boxes of peanuts. The shells-on kind that are kept in his area.

Lila hefted the boxes off him, wondering why he didn't do it himself. They weren't heavy. He looked like he was going to hyperventilate so she grabbed a paper bag off the restock pile and handed it to him. "Breath into this, Larry."

"She's . . . trying to . . . kill me." Larry said this between breaths into the bag.

"Oh, for heaven sakes, look here. The bottom section of this pallet is cracked. You just bumped it and the boxes tipped in your direction. Look, I know this has been hard on you, but it's time to put it behind us now. We've scrubbed the floors, your department is spotless, and you've got plums coming in this afternoon, okay?"

Larry nodded okay. Lila remembered she was heading to get a mop. She gave him a pat on the shoulder and went back to work, leaving him to his breathing.

Wow. Peanuts. Emily Ruth's death nut.

Lila rolled the mop toward aisle two. Tom had put another orange cone on her end. She maneuvered around it. She thought about calling Larry's wife after she was done. It seemed to her he was in need of some family support.

It would help if Emily Ruth would leave him alone. She didn't really believe the cracked board on the pallet thing, she'd just told Larry that to calm him down. That hadn't been any accident. "Quit picking on Larry, Emily Ruth, you're going to give the guy a heart attack," she whispered under her breath.

Speaking of family, her darling daughter Mallory was overdue for her midmorning phone call. Lila figured she better resign herself to an afternoon call, but the whole idea was to check up on the girl and make sure she wasn't partying late into the night before her college classes even got started.

The only reassuring thing about Mallory going to college so early is that her longtime year-older friend had joined her and they were allowed to room together. They'd redecorated the dorm room already and were taking digital photos and sending them to Lila via computer. It all looked very innocent so far. When would she ever stop worrying about her extremely bright and capable daughter? Never.

Lila slapped the mop down on the sprays of Cheez Whiz. This stuff was a bitch to get off the floor. Good grief, it even bleached the color off the tiles a little bit. Maybe it *had* killed Emily Ruth!

Dropping her little girl off at the Stanford University dorm had been the hardest thing she'd done so far, besides giving birth at sixteen. Her parents had been there, and she'd bawled like a baby on the way home, her mom handing her Kleenex, her dad keeping the station wagon on the road.

Empty nest syndrome. But she was only thirty-three, and Mallory, brainy girl who just had to shoot through high school in record time, was only seventeen. Too young all around. Lila sniffled a little and wiped at her eyes with the back of her hand. Okay, no getting nostalgic for the teenage unwed mother years, you dope.

After all, Mallory had been a very smart girl and stayed away from all such tactical premarital sex errors, so she had nothing to complain about. She just missed her, that's all.

And now here she was, mopping up after a ghost. No life.

Tom Boscov peered sideways down the aisle as if he might see something even stranger than before. When she looked straight at him, he gave her a big thumbs-up and took off like a cartoon coyote.

The scent of coffee drifted past the scent of floor-cleaning detergent and made Lila perk her head up. She jumped and sucked her breath in. Lucas Griffin was three-feet close with a half-pound of Starbucks Breakfast Blend in a green plastic carry basket, as well as a six-pack of beer. Beer, breakfast of champions.

"Your friend thinks I killed my ex-wife."

"Wow, you can sure come and go like the wind, Griffin. Try not to scare me like that. I've got enough things that go bump in the night to keep me entertained right now. And as for Bonnie, she's the suspicious type. She just likes to look at all the angles.

"She came back to Port Gamble to spend time with her sick mom and run the family business. I'm lucky to have her around," Lila babbled. She babbled when she was nervous.

"Do you think I killed Emily Ruth?"

"How could you have killed her? You weren't even here." Lila got that whole combination creepy/attraction feeling again.

"Chief Bob called me this morning. He said she had died from her peanut allergy. They're going to conduct a coroner's inquest. Apparently they're considering foul play."

"That doesn't make any sense. Why investigate an allergy death? She died from what we all figured she died of. The only missing element is where she got the peanut in the first place, which was probably my fault." Lila got that other feeling—the horrible feeling again. She was now officially haunted by the thought she'd somehow killed Emily Ruth. Maybe Emily Ruth was haunting *her*, not Lucas.

"Seems there was quite a bit in her system. Also the fact that she was so meticulous about carrying her EpiPen with her made the county guys suspicious. Plus that missing element, like you said—where did she come into contact with it?

Also the county sheriff wasn't too happy about how Chief Bob handled the initial investigation and now Bob is on the rampage to compensate for his sloppy police work earlier. He told me not to leave town."

"Speak of the devil." Lila stared past Lucas at the figure of Chief Bob in full uniform moving toward them.

"Well, isn't this cozy," he said. "You two known each other long?"

The entire insinuation of her relationship with Lucas hit Lila like a twenty-pound Copper River salmon slapped between her eyes. Big, wet, and slimy. *Damn.*

"We barely know each other, Bob. Mr. Griffin here came in for some coffee, and as you recall, I work here," Lila snapped back at Bob but she could feel the heat rise in her cheeks, and like any good redhead she knew she was flushed with nonexistent guilt. Damn, why did her face do that? It was like *The Telltale Heart.*

Chief Bob hooked his thumb through his belt loop and took up what Lila called a "stance." Cocky bastard.

"Well now, you know Mr. Griffin well enough to pay a visit to his house last night, don't you?"

"The dog, Chief. I went to return the dog."

Lucas could chime in here any time, for pity sakes! Lila gave him a look. He stayed silent, the big jerk. Men were just such a pain in the ass.

"I came to tell Miss Abbott here that she should stick around town and not take any sudden trips. The department is going to start requestioning everyone involved, as I already mentioned to you, Mr. Griffin."

"Oh for pity sakes, Bob, I already gave you a statement. Are you boys so bored you need to invent a murder investigation?"

"Certain facts have come to light that indicate we'd be negligent not to pursue the matter."

"You want to share those facts?"

"Not particularly. The county boys are breathing down my neck and I've got no choice. We'll be in touch, Lila." Chief Bob touched his hat and sauntered off toward the bakery aisle. Hot pursuit, Lila thought.

"Wow, you do color up, don't you." Lucas laughed.

"Could you have maybe opened your mouth and defended us?"

"What's to defend?"

Lila wasn't sure she liked that, but it was sort

of true. "You know what he thinks, don't you?"

"That we planned the entire thing together and somehow got away with murder?"

"Yes, that little thing." Lila put her hands on her hips.

"Why would we do that? I didn't need to kill her to be with another woman."

"Maybe I wanted the family estate back and drove you mercilessly with my feminine wiles until you agreed to plot her death. Kind of that whole Lana Turner kill my husband for me thing. So why didn't you say anything?"

"Hey, you're good at this." Lucas was staring at her; his blue eyes had an intensity that made her blush again. "My motto when it comes to police is to answer only what is asked of you and provide no extra information they can twist into something it isn't."

"Spoken like a rich boy who's had lots of lawyers do his dirty work for him." She flipped away from him, more for her own sanity than to be rude.

He grabbed her arm gently and pulled her close. "Unfortunately, I *am* finding myself attracted to you." He was close and his words were hot against her cheek—against her ear.

"That's such a bad idea on so many levels right now." She looked up at him and caught that same intense look. It made her very unsteady. He let her go.

"Later, Abbott."

"Later, Griffin," she answered softly.

Well hell, pretty boy sure ruffled up her morning. Lucas took a right toward produce and she got back to her Cheez Whiz project. You'd think Emily Ruth would be throwing stuff at her about now. Did Emily Ruth still have feelings for Lucas, she wondered? She'd treated him like crap, that was for sure, according to him anyhow. And Chief Bob's previous gossip stream.

What did Chief Bob mean by *certain facts* coming to light? She was going to have to talk to Bob alone as soon as possible. She was the queen of getting the truth behind *certain facts*. People just felt compelled to tell her stuff.

What else could there be? She already knew about the whole peanut-substance thing, but it was just so obviously accidental. Otherwise, it would have to be her, Lila Abbott, that did it, and she knew darn well it wasn't.

But she'd had a feeling all along that something really bad was going on, so why should she be surprised? Emily Ruth wasn't flinging fits for nothing.

Lila hit a particularly thick spot of orange goo and splattered Cheez Whiz across her white sneakers with the mop. Shoot, here she was cleaning up after these damn summer people even when they were dead.

And worse than that, here she was lusting after a summer boy: scourge of all evil, source of all pain to townie girls. She must be insane. She was going to go home tonight and wash Lucas Griffin out of her hair, along with the Cheez Whiz. Then she'd go to her every-third-Monday mystery reading group and immerse herself in the discussion of books.

This all came from reading too many mystery novels. It gave her an unnatural curiosity about death and murder. And a kind of blasé attitude about the whole thing, as if everything would be solved in two hundred pages and they'd all go back to their little lives.

But Lila had a feeling that Emily Ruth's death wasn't going to be so easy, even with her weekly hints and big pushy shoves. If there was one thing Lila had learned about restless spirits it was that if you didn't solve their problem they tended to get very pissed off and noisy, and up the intensity.

From where she was standing, smack in the middle of the Cheez Whiz, surrounded with empty cans, Lila figured things were only going to get worse.

When Lucas turned the corner to grab himself a bunch of bananas, he caught sight of Larry the produce manager making a thin dash toward the back room. If he didn't know better he'd say Larry might have been eavesdropping. But, hey, it was a busy store and the guy was sort of a nutcase, so most likely he was just doing his job in his own weird way.

What *did* concern him was that the chief had seen him and Lila talking so soon after the whole don't-leave-town thing, but he sure as hell didn't want to let on about that concern in front of Chief Bob, or even in front of Lila.

It did complicate his growing fascination with Lila and all her various personality quirks. But when had his life been anything but complicated? He'd made it that way by the choices he'd made.

Lately he felt like he was in some kind of altered universe. Not only had his ex dropped dead, he'd seen things he didn't believe in happen right in front of his eyes. Most of his thoughts ran toward trying to find some kind of strange scientific reason for the Cheez Whiz cans exploding or the way Lila had been pushed backward by *thin air* upstairs at his house.

It was the reporter in him. Fact checker. And here he was in this tiny historical burg writing police blotter bits and obituaries and pieces about the local football team's new sophomore wonder-boy quarterback and how good he looked in practice. Journalism at its finest. Lucas chuckled out loud thinking of his former cutting-edge war articles.

But, hey, this was keeping him occupied and getting the juices flowing again so he could take out that novel he'd been writing for the last six years and finally finish it. Now he could turn it into a true-crime novel.

Rest was on the top of his list too, and this whole thing was making it darn hard. He knew he should be doing more physical therapy to get his leg back in working order, and way less stress was the prescription the doctors had given him; recovery for the mind as well as the body.

Instead he was up to his neck in a ghost story.

He had to admit there was something more than wind or heat or coincidence at work here. And it also looked like Lila was the only person in town who could figure it out. He'd seen some strange stuff overseas, but this was . . . personal.

Lucas grabbed his bananas and decided to pick out a bunch of melons to make a summer breakfast—something healthy besides coffee now that he had a place to live and a kitchen to cook in. Maybe some bread, too. And some cleaning supplies, and all that household stuff, since he didn't have to be anywhere until this afternoon's high school soccer practice. Damn, he was going to need a cart. He grabbed one big watermelon and turned to head toward the carts up front.

Out of the corner of his eye he caught Larry staring at him through the clear plastic strips that hung between the stock rooms and the selling floor. That guy was really strange.

Six

 "Lila Mae Abbott, get in here and help me with this veggie platter. These are *your* guests, you know." Roselyn Abbott hollered from the kitchen.

"Coming, Mom." Lila made a face at Bonnie. Bonnie laughed, then made a gesture that said, *Better get your butt in there!* Bonnie was the queen of nonverbal gestures and Lila figured they'd been doing that since they were in the seventh grade behind their parents' back.

The cool dark pink and burgundy of the front parlor gave way to the blazing hot, bright yellow kitchen. Historic houses weren't much for temperature control.

"Mom, I told you not to bake, it just makes it hotter than heck in here," Lila said as she fanned herself. She settled in next to the vegetables and started arranging the iced radish roses on the platter her mother had already started.

"Don't deny me my fun, Miss Killjoy, I know how your group loves my pies and even the Key Lime needs to have its crust pre-done. It's been hours. The heat'll dissipate."

Bonnie came in the kitchen. "What can I do to help, Mrs. Abbott?"

"Oh, call me Rose, Bonnie, for heaven sakes, I've know you since you had pigtails. Pick up that stack of plates and put them on the table, will you?"

Bonnie came over and stole a radish rose off the tray.

"God, it's sweltering in here," she said. She sucked on the iced radish.

"You know how your folks say the same things over and over again, like when you wake up and it's overcast and gray and they say, 'It'll burn off.' Or when it's ninety-five in the kitchen and they say 'the heat will dissipate'?"

"Yup." Bonnie smiled at Rose Abbott and got a look in return.

"You girls just carry these things out to the front table and we can all get out of here." Rose wiped her brow with the dishtowel she had draped over her shoulder, then made a twist-and-snap attempt toward Lila's rear end, but missed.

"Ha, missed." Lila stuck her tongue out. But she knew full well if her mother had really meant to give her a towel snap, she would have met her mark. Lila had the welt memories to prove it, all in good family fun of course.

"Run, Bonnie, she's got the towel!"

Bonnie faked a terrorized run through the swinging half-door of the kitchen into the front dining room, balancing the stack of dessert plates.

"Don't you drop those, Bonnie Forbes," Lila's mother called out.

"The kitchen looks nice and cheery, Mom, the paint really helped. It was fun packing everything up, too. I mean, hey, we found Grandma's old dishes, and that great cast iron skillet, you know how I've always wanted a good one, and there it was, right under the Tupperware."

"There's always treasures in old houses. You know what they say; one man's trash is another man's treasure."

"They do say that." Lila's mind jumped to Lucas's house and the closet incident, and the christening gown. "Say, mom, you knew Emily Ruth's parents, right?"

"They moved away, but I did know them for many years."

"What do the ladies say down at Lottie's when you're getting your hair done?"

"I never listen to gossip."

"Oh *brother*, Mom." Lila finished her veggi tray. "This is me you're talking to. Did you know Emily Ruth Griffin married Lucas's brother after their divorce?"

"I did hear talk about that. Why are you so interested?" Her mother gave her the eyebrow.

Lila wondered just how much news of the Griffin saga had filtered into the beauty parlor. "What *did* you hear about Emily Ruth?"

Rose Abbott heaved a sigh. "Well, if you must know, I heard at church that she'd taken a fancy to Prentice Cortland, you know, that gentleman that summers here and recently lost his wife?"

"You mean that lecherous sixty-year-old guy with more money than God?"

"Watch your mouth, young lady, God does not have money. He doesn't need money."

Lila stifled a laugh at her mother's defense of God's income. Prentice Cortland. Was that who Emily Ruth had been having over for dinner?

"I also heard you'd been up to the Griffin house and that you've got a ghost on your hands. Want to tell me more about that?" Her mother wiped her hands on the vintage red-and-white floral apron she'd worn since before it was vintage. Wow, they really *did* get the news at Lottie's.

The doorbell rang and she swooped up the veggie tray. Saved by the bell.

"I'll fill you in later. Thanks for cooking, Mom, it's lovely, as usual. Come and say hello to everyone."

Bonnie had already opened the door for the Nash sisters, Earlene and Raylene, and Mrs. Jenny Gardiner, who was from Devonshire, England, originally and had on a yellow polka dot dress that turned her into a bit of a caricature when teamed with the short brimmed straw hat with matching ribbon perched on her head. She was a dear, though, and brilliant as a Sherlock when it came to solving mystery novels. She *always* won the who-done-it contest, damn her, beating them all to the punch.

Behind Jenny Gardiner was Jenny's best

friend, Denise Schramke, the lively Irish woman who often got into the most heated discussions with Jenny. So heated, Lila was left wondering why they were friends, but their common European roots seem to bind them together.

"Right this way, ladies, we'll grab a plate and head for the front parlor. There's lemonade, too."

"Bloody hot, isn't it?" Earlene Nash fanned herself. Earlene had picked up that phrase from Mrs. Gardiner. The Nash sisters were fraternal twins, both thin as sticks, both wearing T-shirts that referred to the mystery book conference they'd attended. The *Kiss of Death* conference, both in turquoise spandex bike shorts, both dripping in costume jewelry, both about sixty, or as Earlene liked to say, sixty and fifteen minutes younger in her case.

On their heels the screen door opened with a springy sound and Jerry of Jerry and Jasper's bookstore, Port Gamble Books, came in, natty in his bow tie as usual. Jasper preferred sci-fi to mystery, so Jerry was their main supplier of reading material and kept a healthy mystery section in stock.

Bonnie flipped the fan on high in the front

parlor. Jenny held her hat and perched in front of it on the piano stool. "Ahhhh," she uttered a long sigh of relief. The fan fluttered her blonde bobbed hair.

"Okay, everyone, let's get settled." Lila herded everyone to the dining room and poured glasses of lemonade. She had a real hunger to discuss the solving of their latest read, *More Bitter than Death*, by Dana Cameron. Any crime that didn't involve the Griffin family would do at the moment, just so it resolved. Besides, she had a sense tonight wasn't going to be any old Mystery Monday, and the day had been weird enough already.

"Did you hear Chief Bob was questioning everyone in town about Emily Ruth Griffin's death? Did he question you yet, Lila?" Leave it to Jenny to dive right into the local scandals.

"Yes, but he's questioning everyone again," Lila answered. Immediately she wished she hadn't said that.

"What in heaven's name does he think he's looking for?" Earlene moved into the room balancing her plate of carrots and radishes with just the smallest puddle of ranch dressing. No wonder she stayed so thin.

"Something about the autopsy and some other things made him think she was murdered."

"As if the Port Gamble sheriff's department could handle an investigation that delicate. They probably screwed up half a dozen things at the crime scene as it is." Denise Schramke entered and found herself a place on the burgundy velvet sofa with its huge clawed bird feet clutching clear glass balls.

When she was a kid, Lila used to be afraid that the sofa was going to come to life and sprout giant wings and chase her with those claws.

"They think Lucas Griffin killed her to get her out of his family's house," Jenny piped in.

"He had plenty of other reasons to kill her besides the house," Lila muttered.

Bonnie looked at her with big, best-friend eyes, as if to say *Shut up!*

Jerry's bow tie fairly quivered at the prospect of solving a real crime. "Good grief, do you think Lucas Griffin killed her? How did he get her to have an allergic reaction like that, out of the blue, without being with her?"

"That's the trick, isn't it? How to get her to ingest the stuff somewhere far away from the murderer, and with an allergy as severe as hers, that's no easy task. Also she'd have to be devoid of any curative measures—antiallergenics and such adrenaline shots, right?" Jenny's English accent added a rather sinister note to her speculations.

Lila got one of her spine chills. Lucas had so many reasons to hate Emily Ruth. I mean, who could forgive someone for sleeping with his own brother. And had he forgiven that brother? That brother . . . *that died?*

Her plate tipped and a radish rose rolled off, onto the Oriental rug and under the piano bench. She jumped like she'd sat on a tack, set aside her plate, and crawled on her knees to retrieve the radish.

Oh God, oh God, was Lucas taking revenge on his brother and Emily Ruth? Was he some kind of crazed serial killer?

She hit her head on the bench. "*Ouch.*" Lila backed out backward.

"Lila?" The upside-down face of Bonnie came into view.

She rose up and smoothed out her black-and-white checkered sleeveless blouse and black Capri pants, or pedal pushers, as her mom called them, and tried to look calm. She tucked her stray curls back into place. "I'm fine, just fine," she said, rubbing the top of her head.

But she wasn't fine. She listened to the buzz between all the members of the Monday Mystery Book Club and it became like the hum of a summer mosquito droning in her head. Maybe Lucas had a dark side that no one had ever seen. Maybe he had a dual personality. Maybe Emily Ruth was trying to warn her!

Bonnie leaned over Lila. "Hey, girlfriend, let me get you a refill of lemonade. You must have hit your head harder than you thought." Bonnie took Lila's glass and sort of joggled her back to reality with a few shoulder shakes. Her friend was prone to spacing out at unexpected times, but she looked pretty pale at the moment— paler than her regular pale redheaded self.

Bonnie picked up Lila's glass and walked into the dining room to get more lemonade and some ice. Lila was supposed to be the one with the sixth sense but Bonnie felt like this whole Lucas Griffin thing was going to get very, very bad before it got better.

There were a few things about the case that nagged at her. The chances that Emily Ruth died accidentally were low. The woman was obsessed with having her safety precautions with her, and the contents of the food she'd eaten off Lila's tray had to be the items that contained the offending peanut substance. The truth was that if there were foul play, it would appear that *Lila* was the main suspect, not Lucas.

But of course that was ridiculous and Bonnie knew it. Before two weeks ago Monday, Lila had hardly noticed Emily Ruth, or Lucas. And Bonnie intended on letting the chief know that tomorrow when she went in to be questioned, which kind of made her stomach hurt thinking about it. She was sure Bob wanted to question her about Lila's character, and she didn't want to say anything that might make things worse.

Bonnie carried the lemonade back to Lila, handed it to her, and sat back down. The background conversation had shifted to Prentice Cortland, the late Emily Ruth's latest suspected love interest, and how his former wife had died under mysterious circumstances involving a drunken boat party. Hopefully they'd move on to Dana Cameron's book soon and forget all this local intrigue. But people love local intrigue.

Bonnie knew only one thing for sure right now, and that was that Lila Abbott was going to need all the friends she could get in the coming months.

"Thanks for helping, Bonnie," Lila said as she stacked the last of the washed pink Depression-glass plates in her mother's cupboard. Her mom had gone up to bed long ago, probably to read. This was Dad's night to play poker with his buddies at the Port Gamble Yacht Club. They didn't exactly own a yacht, but a regular-sized powerboat qualified you for membership in this neck of the woods.

It was great to see her dad enjoying his retirement from the grocery business. It'd been lucky for her he'd still been the manager of Market Foods and could get her a job there when she was a young mom.

She was just plain lucky to have parents like Del and Roselyn Abbott. Lila wasn't sure she'd be as understanding if Mallory had come home pregnant at sixteen. Fortunately she hadn't had to test that theory, and hopefully her daughter would make it through college with the same brilliance and grace she'd managed so far.

"I guess that shiftless rich boy that knocked me up must have had good genes on his side. Otherwise why would Mallory be such an egghead?"

"This is what I love about you, complete stream of consciousness comments that bear no relevance to whatever it is we're doing." Bonnie put her hand on Lila's shoulder with a best-friend pat.

"Oh, you know, the usual, how great my parents are, and were, and how lucky I was to get a kid like Mallory." Lila tucked the dishtowel she'd been carrying over her shoulder into the old-style white porcelain towel bar hanging on the wall.

"It couldn't have anything to do with the fact you were a great parent, now, could it?"

"No one is a great parent at sixteen."

"True. But you did pretty damned well despite it all."

"I guess." Lila shrugged. "Let's go over to my place. I have something I want to show you."

They hung up their aprons and Bonnie grabbed her big summer tote bag full of books and genealogy projects. "Ready?"

The night had barely turned to a reddish

shade of dark even at ten o'clock in the evening. "I love these summer nights," Lila whispered, just in case her mom had gone to sleep early. Her parents' bedroom window was open and the narrow stretch of lawn between their house and Lila's little cottage made their voices echo.

Lila stepped onto her porch and opened the door, flicking on the inside light. It was the house of hand-me-downs, but Lila still loved it.

"How's the Forbes family breakfront doing?"

"I can't believe we painted it white."

"It's having a better life, remember? Besides, it can be stripped anytime."

"Speaking of stripped, what's going on with your love life? I feel like we've been so wrapped up in all this Griffin goop we haven't had a chance to talk."

"Hector at the bakery asked me out again," Bonnie said casually.

"A good-looking man that can bake, that's not a bad thing." Lila led the way to the kitchen for their traditional Monday-night glass of wine after the book group. They'd stopped indulging in alcohol during the meetings on mutual agreement that it made them all stupid and unable to analyze and review the books properly.

"Look, a nice two-thousand-seven boxed Chardonnay." Lila pulled the box out of the fridge and took two wineglasses from the cupboard. She dug up a couple of ice cubes from her plastic tray and dropped them in.

"We're so pedestrian, cubes in our wine," Bonnie said. She took the glass and downed a large swig.

"Yes, we are. Back porch?"

"Cooler, for sure."

While Bonnie walked to the back door, Lila stopped and pulled Emily Ruth's appointment and shopping list she'd kept out of the blue willow ginger jar on the kitchen counter. She'd never broken that habit of squirreling things away, despite many hours spent looking for where she might have hidden the keys to the bike lock or the button off her daughter's coat.

She had a Mallory moment thinking of the little red plaid jacket with the black corduroy collar she'd gotten her daughter when she was five, going to kindergarten. Mallory, in that coat, her red knit hat tied under her chin, with a pompom on top, yellow boots and blue jeans, would go down in the cuteness files forever. There was a photograph of her wearing that—somewhere in the photo stacks.

You'd think a psychic would be able to find the missing button from her daughter's coat. But apparently a ghost would have to tell her where it is for that to work.

The screen door slapped behind Lila as she walked onto the porch to join Bonnie.

"I miss Mallory," Lila said.

"I bet. You two have been joined at the hip for the last seventeen years. This must be really hard."

"She's too young to start college."

"True, but she sort of used up high school here, didn't she? She'd been going to community college for over a year with that running-start program you put her in, so hey, you know she'll love college. She's such a knowledge sponge."

"I should have had more kids. For that matter, I should have gotten married and done the whole kids, family thing." Lila felt that old pang in her for what she'd missed.

"Woulda, shoulda, it's not too late for any of those, you know." Bonnie gave her the standard reply. They'd had this conversation before.

Lila leaned back in one of the old white wicker chairs she kept on the back porch. Another

Forbes family hand-me-down. When Bonnie's mom downsized and moved into assisted living after her stroke, Lila had been given the leftovers. The chair creaked comfortably as she settled in.

Bonnie's tiny apartment over the antique store could only hold so much, and some things Bonnie just didn't want to sell at the store. Oh, who was she kidding, her best friend wanted her to have a better life and made up excuses to give her things like . . . furniture.

It *had* been an adventure these last seventeen years, but not an easy adventure. She'd let her own life slip away like a quick, hot summer that fades into cool autumn nights before you've even gotten to the beach to play in the sand.

The frogs were out in full voice tonight, an invisible chorus of croaking creatures.

"Wow, a regular concert," Lila said.

"What is it you wanted to show me?"

"So impatient. Here, I took this out of Emily Ruth's cart and kind of forgot about it. It's her appointment schedule and shopping list."

"You kind of forgot about it?"

"Stashed it in the ginger jar the day she died."

"Kind of a large piece of evidence, you know?"

"Maybe." Lila handed Bonnie the folded up note. Bonnie unfolded it and studied it for a while.

"It's her Outlook schedule. And she had a dinner date at six thirty."

"Ol' Prentice Cortland I'd venture, according to my mom," Lila pointed out. "And look here; after she went shopping she was supposed to meet Lucas at his attorney's office, just like he said."

"So I guess he was telling the truth about that part. Have you shown this to anyone else?" Bonnie asked quietly.

"No. For some reason I'm compelled to keep it hidden. Maybe it will come in handy later. Maybe you can break into her computer and see what else she'd scheduled herself for: 10:36 A.M. Meet Death." Lila giggled despite herself. Must be the wine. Bonnie was a computer whiz. Probably from all that eBay buying and selling she did.

"I'm not going to be able to hack into Emily Ruth's computer for a while."

"Why?"

"I'm going to Canada on a buying trip. Mom

had arranged to meet up with a string of antique dealers for this big furniture and collectible blitz. I think it's a good idea. The store needs an infusion of new goods, and now is the time. I've hired Jenny Gardiner to watch the store. That woman sure knows her English china. I'm leaving tomorrow."

Lila felt like crying. "Why didn't you tell me?"

"I didn't want you to think about it too long. I knew you'd feel rotten, what with Mallory gone, too."

"I'm a big girl. I can take it. You've left before." Lila sniffed. "You'll be back, won't you?"

"Yes, I'll be back in about three weeks. Maybe four. I'm adding in a side trip to do some genealogy research for a client."

"Three weeks, that's nothing. I'll be here, probably in jail, but you go have fun."

"That's the spirit."

They sat silently for a while, drinking wine, listening to the frogs sing. Lila felt a deep ache in her chest. She wasn't completely alone, she had her parents, and other friends, but Bonnie was her confidant. That's what she got for keeping her life so small. Small town, small circles.

"Well, hon, I'm off to the Port Angeles boat rooster crow early tomorrow so this is it. Give me a hug. I'll send postcards." She put her empty glass down and stood up.

Lila stood up too and gave her friend a good hug. "Bring back a nice Mounty or something will you? Get laid by a Canadian while you're up there."

"I'll do my best. Bye, sweetie. You're going to be fine. I'll call." Bonnie walked off the porch, turned and gave her usual parade-queen wave. Lila waved back, smiling.

Then she was alone.

She picked up both of their wineglasses and chugged down the remaining portion of her own, then walked inside.

Through the screen door she watched Bonnie walk over the open field behind their houses toward the opposite street, home of Port Gamble Antiques and Bonnie's upstairs apartment. Lila suddenly felt the need to get out of this town for a while. Maybe she'd take a vacation. Lord knows, she had enough sick days stored up.

Who was she kidding? She had a daughter in college. Mallory had gotten some great scholarships, but she still needed cute clothes and there were payments on the new laptop computer to make.

But honestly, her checks from the uppity family that wanted to cover up Mallory's birth pretty much paid for all that, so she was probably free for the first time to do some traveling, treat herself. She just wasn't used to thinking that way. She kept thinking the checks would stop when Mallory hit eighteen, but lucky for her, that was a year off and she'd saved up quite a bit over the years just in case. Her dad had taught her that.

Maybe she'd join Bonnie next time she went gallivanting off on an antiques road show. Maybe she'd take a cruise.

Maybe she'd meet someone.

Lila went into the kitchen, put the dishes in the sink, poured herself a glass of water, then walked up the narrow stairs to her bedroom. The wine and the heat had combined to make her drowsy.

She struggled to get her bedroom windows open. They'd swollen in the heat, as usual. She should have done it before the book group tonight because it was stuffy as hell in here.

She stripped off her clothes and made a slam dunk into the hamper next to her small closet, missing. Someday she was going to have a house with huge closets. Not that she cared about clothes that much, she just wanted to walk into a big closet and see her hats and handbags happy at last, instead of stuffed into her miniature closet.

And her collection of vintage mystery books and her boxes of tourist junk from every little adventure she and Mallory had ever taken: Sea World coffee cups, a stuffed goeduck toy from Orcas Island, the Mickey hats from when her parents had taken them all to Disneyland, one with MALLORY and one with LILA embroidered on the back in yellow thread. While Lila brushed her teeth, she imagined all her various scarves, which she liked to tie in her hair, hanging on some fancy scarf rack.

Good thing she'd caught a shower after work. She was so tired her head was fuzzy.

It was just too damn hot to sleep in anything. She slipped between the white sheets naked and rolled the thin blue woven blanket up over herself. Her new habit was to wait till she was exhausted before she went to bed so she didn't lie there and worry about Mallory and feel the emptiness of the room across the hall.

Tonight it was a deeper emptiness. Bonnie was leaving town. Having a best friend to tell secrets and dreams and worries to was better than paying two hundred bucks a week to a therapist. It had kept her sane over this transition time with Mallory leaving. Now she'd have to keep sane all by herself for three or four weeks. Not an easy task.

Then there was that other emptiness. The one where she wished she'd put more effort into finding a good man, who would be lying next to her right now. Who would be her other best friend. Who would be her lifelong lover.

Lila fell into the dark pool of her tiredness and let herself sink to the bottom. She actually dreamed she was swimming in a cool black-watered lagoon, and the rhythm of her imaginary strokes put her farther under, into the deep, endless blackness of sleep.

The sound of a body falling to the floor. The sound of a bracelet against the linoleum, an odd dull tinkling. The eyes of Emily Ruth staring blankly, no life behind them. The sound of a heartbeat, thud-thud thudded in her dream. Dozens of lemons roll oddly, slowly around the body, then bushels of them, then a flood of lemons, bright unnaturally yellow lemons surrounded the dead body of Emily Ruth.

Lila was dripping water as if she'd just stepped out of the sea in her dream. She wore a white cotton nightgown, but it was drenched and a river of water droplets made small streams appear behind her like a long wedding train, almost as if they were attached to her.

And then Lucas appeared, a dark shadow in the dimness of the unearthly light. His footsteps made no sound and he moved toward her, past Emily Ruth's body. Behind him a glow of yellow lemons rimmed his figure, yellow light glowed brighter and brighter. Then she couldn't breathe.

Then, *she couldn't breathe*, and the unthinkable sensation of someone's hand over her mouth moved Lila into a full, terrifying awakeness. She screamed against the pressure of that hand, a muffled, horrified, scream.

"Shhhh, shhh, don't scream. I'm sorry to scare you. I don't want the chief to see us together. It's me, Lucas."

"Are you out of your *mind*? Get *away* from me. Get out of here!" Lila scrambled away from him and backed herself into the far corner of her room. He couldn't exactly blame her. He hoped to God she didn't have a gun in her bedside table.

She was stark naked and scared to death. But what else could he do. Chief Bob had a man watching his house, and he needed Lila Abbott in the worst way, right this minute.

Actually the more the moonlight played on her pale naked skin the more he felt a need of a different kind rise up in him. But it would be incredibly bad timing on his part to mention that.

He looked around. "Here." He grabbed a thin robe off the end of her bed and threw it to her. "Don't freak out. I had to see you. They're watching my house but I gave them the slip. If they think we're together they'll blame you for the murder."

"Together?" She pulled the robe on but was amazingly uninhibited about letting Lucas have a fairly long look at her beautiful, full breasts before tying it closed.

"I'm sorry, I'm having a really, really bad night," he said.

"Oh *you're* having a bad night. Poor thing," Lila snarled.

"Emily Ruth is making me nuts. She's banging on the walls and the entire house reeks of her perfume. The dog is completely out of control, barking her head off. You've got to take Schatzie back before she has a nervous breakdown. I locked her in her carrier before I left. I hope Emily Ruth doesn't let her out and make her bark again. That could wake up the deputy who's sleeping in his car in front of my driveway."

"So what, you broke into my house and scared the crap out of me to ask me to dog-sit?"

"Come on, Abbott, I couldn't just knock on the front door. And I don't want any record of phone calls to you. What other choice did I have?"

"How about anything but putting your hand over my mouth while I was dead asleep and making me think my life was over?"

"I'm sorry. I'll make it up to you. I'll send you flowers," he said flatly.

"That'd clear everything up. And then they'd think we were an item for sure. Be sure and send lilies, they're my favorite."

Lucas sat down on her bed and motioned to her. "Sit down and just talk. I can't get any sleep at my house. I think Emily Ruth is trying to scare me to death; I don't mind telling you

I'm not used to this supernatural crap and it disturbs me to the core. And believe me, I've seen a whole lotta strange stuff in my time."

Lila gave him a dirty look but she slid onto the bed with her back against the footboard. The curly iron bed creaked under their weight. She sat opposite him and pulled her robe closed tightly.

"She even haunted my dreams tonight. I fell asleep for, like, an hour and dreamed a whole truckload of lemons buried me alive in my bed. They fell out of the ceiling."

Lila laughed. "She does have a sense of humor, doesn't she? I had a similar dream."

"You did?" Lucas rubbed his hand through his hair. This was without a doubt the weirdest stuff he'd ever dealt with, and he didn't have a clue what to do about it except to steal into Lila Abbott's bedroom and have a midnight consultation. He glanced at her clock. It actually *was* midnight.

At least Lila was lightening up and hadn't tried to call the cops or shoot him—yet. He took in her curvaceous body thinly veiled in the cotton robe. Her red hair was wild. Her room had a slight lavender scent, a refreshing break from the oppressive Passion perfume that haunted his every waking and sleeping hour at his place.

"You've got to help me, Abbott. Do an exorcism or séance or whatever it is you do. Get this woman off my back. I'm begging you. I'll pay you."

"Do you swear to me you didn't kill her?"

Lucas laughed out loud. "And if I did, would I say, 'Yes, I swear I didn't kill her'? Come on, Lila, I swear it wasn't me, and I have a really bad feeling one of us is going to take the fall for her murder. If it was a murder. All they found is peanut butter in her throat. Somehow peanut butter got into her mouth from that cracker you fed her.

"Not that anyone *wouldn't* want to kill her. Her hobby was screwing up people's lives. Who knows what she'd gotten herself into. Shoot, I guess she *was* murdered, because I know you didn't do it, and I didn't do it, so who managed to get peanut butter on that cracker, and who the hell made sure she didn't have an EpiPen with her?" Lucas leaned toward her. "Where did that tray come from? The one with the crackers and cheese you were handing out?"

"Listen, I sat there and squirted that cheese

onto those Ritz with my own hands. There is no way someone could have tampered with that food. I—I only left it for a second, and that was before I set everything up. I popped the top on that Cheez Whiz myself and opened up that box of Ritz. Even if I delivered the poison, I didn't mean to kill her." Lila put her hand over her mouth. Her eyes teared up a bit.

"You didn't. I know that. You know that, but the chief is going to question you again, and this time not so nicely. He pulled me in yesterday after I saw you. He asked me specifically if we had a relationship. My guess is they're moving toward some sort of conspiracy between you and me to do her in." Lucas was toying with the idea of running his hand over Lila's smooth leg and pulling her over to his end of the bed. She looked like she needed comfort. God knows, he needed . . . something.

He tried to dismiss that thought. At the moment he felt like he was drowning in lust instead of lemons, a very odd side effect to their unplanned midnight meeting.

"Shhh, Listen," Lila put her finger to her lips. She heard the distinct sound of car tires driving past her house. She got up and stood to the side of her window. A slight breeze stirred the sheer white curtain. It was a patrol car. She knew perfectly well there wasn't much of a night route for the Port Gamble law enforcement. This was out of the norm for them.

"Jesus, I hope they didn't see me leave the house," Lucas whispered.

"Well, you can't leave here now—and darn, I was just about to throw you out."

Lucas moved behind her, where he couldn't be seen and watched as the patrol car rolled slowly and deliberately past Lila's cottage. He held his breath. He could feel her next to him holding her breath, too. He could also feel the heat from her body and smell the scent of her hair.

Lavender.

There was a long, quiet moment in the dark, in the golden glow of moonlight. Then he reached over and ran his hand from her shoulder to her elbow, softly, smoothly, unexpectedly.

Just as unexpectedly, she turned to him. He put his arm around her and pulled her closely to him. He lifted her chin with his other hand

and kissed her full, pretty lips. To his amazement, Lila Abbott kissed him back. Softly at first, then something passed between them—some deep mutual understanding of what they'd just done—and then she let herself go.

He fell headlong into his driving sense of need for her and pulled her up against him. He was met by kisses that seemed to need him, invite him, tease him, pull him into her like a whirlpool. Kisses that went on and on.

Finally he slipped her robe off her shoulders and ran his mouth down the silky smooth skin, down her neck, over her bare shoulder and over to her full, voluptuous breast. He could feel her breathing speed up, and she gasped when he slid his tongue gently across her nipple. She grabbed hold of the window frame and leaned against the wall, her head back, a soft moan escaped her lips.

He pulled the belt and the robe slipped off. Lucas let her body drown him in its loveliness. His hands roamed across her curves as he let his mouth explore her, returning to her kiss, which was now hot as a fire and hungrily responsive to his deep, probing embrace. *Damn*, she was amazing. She was delicious. She was everything he'd imagined in the dark flashes of his attraction to her. He wanted her. He wanted her right now.

Lila devoured the sensuous, intoxicating touch of Lucas Griffin like a woman devours a particularly amazing slice of chocolate cake. One layer at a time, licking the frosting off the top. He was such a perfect combination of forceful and gentle. And at this moment, that was exactly what she needed. She held his strong, broad shoulders as he made her whole body ignite with desire. She gave in to his mouth and leaned against the cool frame of the window, helpless to keep herself from falling under his moonlight spell.

It had been so long, so long, since a man had desired her, held her, touched her. She felt a rush of emotion as he moved her into a beautiful, long, drawn-out climax that just rolled over her like a wave of hot water. Hot. So very hot. She felt herself throb against his touch and watched, eyes wide open, as Lucas stayed the duration, rode the wave with her, his body revealing the intensity of his arousal.

She moved him away for a moment and undressed him. His beautiful, sculpted, athletic body shone from the heat and the moonlight as he assisted her in removing his shirt and shorts. She ran her hands over his chest and every caress made her ache. She smoothed over every inch of his sides, and as she eased off his underwear she felt the scar on his leg that had left him with a limp. She lightly touched it and moved back up to the strong muscle of his upper thigh. *Wow, Lucas Griffin was built strong.*

He picked her up in his arms and pulled her into a dream state. But as he lay her down on the cool white sheets of her bed, she recalled all the reasons she shouldn't let Lucas Griffin make love to her. They drifted away when she felt his body long and lean against hers and his hard, huge, seriously amazing erection that made her smile through her momentary pause. He also paused. She knew why.

"I'm on the pill, and disease free," she whispered in his ear. She couldn't get pregnant, she'd been on the pill for years to control her nasty periods, and probably, secretly, on the off chance that someone like Lucas would come into her room in the middle of the night and sweep her away with his demanding kisses and smooth, naked, muscular body.

"Likewise," he whispered hoarsely, "except for the pill part."

That was as much as she managed to think before Lucas took her to another level of pleasure and she reached over to touch him, caress him, and heard him groan with a deep, growling arousal. They played, they touched, they made each other crazy until all she wanted was to have him inside her.

When he finally pulled her so close their breath was one breath, she was lost in him so completely it was as if she couldn't tell where he began and she left off. She raised herself against him and allowed him to move into her slowly, so slowly she came when he finally thrust himself deeply into her. She stretched her arms above her head and cried out with pleasure.

He held her there, stroking into her, so amazingly good, so sensuous. Lila felt like she'd never really been made love to in her entire life until this moment.

Lucas could tell that Lila was a woman who had forgotten what it was like to be made love to. It was like discovering a new, secret island that no one had set foot on for a century. It was wild and jungle-like and he took the time to tame her and bring her back to her primal memories of what it was like to be desired.

He was shocked at the amount of emotion that pulled from him as he was caught up in the passion and playfulness of their lovemaking. When he finally entered her he felt like he'd come home. His heartaches, his emptiness was, for this moment in time, completely removed and in its place he found himself safe in her. She brought him to the edge of his need, then pulled him back, only to make him twice as driven to lose himself in her.

She'd come to him awkwardly, but after hours of patient, soft, hard, lustful, wild, tame, explosive, rhythmic pleasure in each other, she had become his equal in every way. They let themselves go into the emotion of what they'd fallen into, and when he finally climaxed deep inside her he felt—actually *felt*—his whole world shift. His guarded, walled emotions were torn open and this redheaded, curvaceous creature put a spell on him—a spell that made him feel alive again.

As they lay together in the quiet he propped himself on his elbow beside her and watched the light play over her naked, glistening body. Her hair was curled and pale red against the white pillows. Her lips were red and swollen from his kisses, his sucking on them, his devouring her mouth with his kisses.

He felt himself throb thinking of her. He was drunk with her. He stroked her waist and over her hip and stared at her open, golden brown eyes. She was a beautiful, amazing woman. She just didn't know it.

"Lila, Lila," he whispered in her ear after many hours. "I have to go."

Oh, she'd heard those words before. Those words said by the very few men she'd taken to her bed in the last seventeen years. It wasn't easy when your only opportunity was when your daughter was at a sleepover, because she'd never even *think* of having a lover when her daughter was in the house.

Come to think of it, she'd said those words before, herself, a few times, and left a few lovers in their historic apartments in the middle of the night and gone home to her own place to be there for Mallory in the morning. It wouldn't do to think your mother was catting around at night while grandma was baby-sitting.

"It'll be light soon and I need to get home before they can see me." His deep, tender voice made her ache. She turned to him and pulled him close against her body. She wanted to remember this feeling for a long time. Because when Lucas Griffin went out her door or her window, or whatever, she'd probably never see him again. Not like this anyway. He gathered her close, then kissed her cheek, her lips softly, then pulled himself away from her.

"Now we're in for it," he laughed quietly. He stood up, then went to find his clothes, pulling on the various pieces she'd taken off of him. "Lila, bring Bonnie and a few chaperones to the house tomorrow if you can and help me get rid of my ex-wife. That sounds really odd doesn't it?"

"Bonnie is out of town, but I'll think of something." Lila's voice was hoarse—probably from yelling out his name all night every time he made her climax. "Be careful, Lucas. Go out the back way." She pulled the sheet over her naked body. She could see the hint of morning muddying up the dark sky. "Hurry," she said. She watched him.

He stopped next to the bed and leaned over to touch her cheek with his fingertips. "I better get out of here before you tempt me again."

Lila smiled as he quietly left the room.

When she heard the back door downstairs close, she pulled herself into a curve and wrapped the sheet around herself. Lila reveled in the sweet, sexy aftermath of having Lucas make love to her. She let herself sink into it like a dream. The rest of her night was undisturbed by visions of Emily Ruth, by rolling lemons, or clunking bracelets.

Seven

Lucas let his eyes adjust to the dark and moved quietly from shadow to shadow. It was a long ways and he took to the old trails he'd known as a kid, back in the woods behind the white houses with green shutters that lined the streets of Port Gamble. He heard night birds and rustling that quieted when he passed. His footsteps were softened by the mossy trails.

When he reached the cutoff that would expose him, he walked quickly. His house was accessible from the beach without passing his sleeping deputy. A dog barked as he passed one house, then Lucas slipped down a stairway to the beach beside one of the old summer shacks. He held the rail and moved fast, the night slowly fading into morning around him.

The beach was deserted and he heard the water lap quietly against the gray rocks. What crazy thing had he done, falling into Lila Abbott's bed? What now?

Lucas climbed the stone steps his grandfather had worked into the cliff behind their house and reached the gravel path. His leg ached from the effort. He should do this more, it might help. The crunching sound of his own steps made him nervous, and he moved over onto the grass as quickly as possible.

His grandmother's garden was abundant with summer blooms, and he caught the scent of lavender on the sea breeze. Actually, this garden went three generations back, so who knows who planted that lavender, but it reminded him of Lila now.

A sound startled him. He jerked his head to the side and saw the flash of a shadow. It put him on guard and he moved quickly up the back stairs to the expansive porch and through one of the French doors he knew was the easiest to open. If there was one thing he learned overseas, it was how to move quickly in and out of danger. And something didn't feel right.

He saw a shadow flicker inside the house. Somehow he knew it wasn't his ex-wife's ghost. As he pulled the door closed behind him a light switched on and illuminated the entire living room. Schatzie started barking, still in her kennel.

"Rough night, Lucas?"

"Chief Bob. How nice of you to let yourself in and make yourself at home." Lucas tried to be casual. "Did you make coffee?"

"I usually wait till four or five A.M. before I hit the caffeine, but I've got a pot down at the station. What do you say we go down there and have a nice donut and that cup of coffee and discuss your night-crawling habits?" Chief Bob was comfortably stretched out on Lucas's mother's blue overstuffed chair, an ottoman under his feet.

"Why not?" Lucas replied dryly. He started to look around the house and what he saw made his guts twist into an even more creative knot than they already were. Emily Ruth's belongings, which he'd packed into a cardboard box to give to Goodwill, or burn, he hadn't decided which, were strewn all over the room, up the stairway, and across several pieces of furniture. *Damn that woman.* Lucas staggered to a chair and stared at the mess.

"I'm kind of surprised you'd want to keep all your ex-wife's dainties hanging around, Lucas." Chief Bob plucked a pair of bright blue panties off the side table and held them up to the light.

"I don't suppose you believe in ghosts, do you Bob?"

"Depends on the circumstances. Don't get too cozy, we're leaving now." Bob's words were punctuated by growls and barking. Lucas could hear talking and footsteps in the kitchen.

"Let me take the dog out of the kennel."

"I'll have Peterson take care of it."

"She bites."

"I'll warn him. Let's go, Lucas. I've had a long night."

Lucas stood up. As he and the chief stood there, a wave of Emily Ruth's perfume hit like a slap and the room went ice cold. Lucas looked at the chief to see if he smelled it too, and felt the cold. A look passed between them and Lucas raised his eyebrow. "She's not too happy about me packing up her stuff I guess."

Chief Bob didn't comment. "You first." He pointed toward the kitchen. "We're parked out back."

Having sex with Lucas Griffin was probably the dumbest thing she'd done in seventeen years. And this time she had zero excuses. It's not like she was young and stupid and drunk on Annie Greenspring's Pear Apple wine.

She must have a sign on her head. Any rich summer boy that just blows into town and wants some local girl to dally with then drop flat, apply within.

Lila let a smile flicker across her lips. He certainly did dally with her. And he certainly did apply within.

She snuggled back under the covers and wallowed in the loveliness that Lucas had made her feel last night. She might as well enjoy it because she'd never see him again. He was probably on his way to the airport to skip out of town on this whole murder investigation and just stopped in here for a quick romp with an easy girl.

The only thing that was surprising was that he didn't leave his dog. Because these summer boys just loved to leave a little package behind. Something that required you to be responsible for it for the rest of your life while they skipped out and went back to prep school or ivy league college and forgot you ever existed, except for a little check sent by their parents every month. Not that those little checks hadn't helped keep Mallory in piano lessons and yellow mud boots.

She rolled the sheet up with her foot and twisted it around her leg. If it weren't for Emily Ruth Griffin, she'd be partially contented right now. It was obvious that Chief Bob had come up against the county sheriff and come up short in his death investigating style

They were probably all over him, and if she knew Bob he'd be doing intensive backpedaling to cover his own errors. But he was barking up the wrong tree if he thought she had anything to do with the death of Emily Ruth. It was just too ridiculous. She'd have to have some words with ol' Bob. Mallory's mom cannot go to jail for a murder she didn't commit.

Lila turned sharply to her side and pushed

angrily at the blankets on her bed. The early summer morning light pierced through the lace curtain and made a copycat shadow on the wall of her bedroom.

Heck, she might as well get up early and get ready for work. Maybe she'd call Bonnie on her cell before she crossed over the water to Canada. Best friends always had to know about new developments in each other's love lives. If you wanted to categorize a one-night stand as a love life.

She tried to remember the last time she or Bonnie had said the magic words *"I've met someone special."* Although, Bonnie had been much more actively involved than she had. And a nasty breakup it had been, too. Peter the Great she'd called him. Once he'd won the prize and conquered a woman's heart, he'd apparently become bored of his prize and moved onto the next heart.

Bonnie had definitely had a few bumps along the love-train tracks. They had that in common.

Lila flung back the covers and planted herself on the cheerful floral carpet that shielded her bare feet from the wood floors. She snatched the unanchored sheet off the bed and wrapped it around herself, still plagued by a modest nature, even though she was the only one in the house.

After a quick shower she wrapped herself in a towel and rubbed a circle in the bathroom mirror. She noticed she looked completely hideous and wondered why Lucas didn't jump out the window instead of just bolting out the door.

She wrapped another towel around her wet hair, dropped the body towel and wrapped her old yellow cotton robe around herself, then padded barefoot down the creaky narrow wooden stairs.

In the kitchen she went into autopilot: setting up coffee, scrounging for a decent piece of bread to make her usual toast-and-cheese breakfast. But this morning she felt the emptiness of her house more acutely than usual.

Maybe she'd tell Lucas to let her have the dog. She kind of missed the little monster. And it could be a connection between them.

Why did she just assume he'd be on the next train to anywhere, anyhow? Maybe he'd stick around and they'd have a proper summer fling.

Oh, *that* old thought. The one she entertained

for at least a year, writing letters to the boy who had donated to the conception of her daughter. Those letters that moved from heartfelt to hysteria and her telling him he had a child on the way.

Now that she was older and wiser she knew his family probably shut the door behind him and—how surprising—they never summered in Port Gamble again. She'd all but forgotten about Bobby Stanton and his seductive brown eyes and his wet, amazing kisses that led her to give herself to him in a tree, in his car, and mostly in the boathouse of his parent's summer place. She should probably ask Lucas if he knew them. Or not ask. That would be better.

The phone rang its out-of-place electronic ring and made her jump. She sometimes wished she still had a vintage phone to go with her historic cottage, but with a teenage girl in the house the old black dial model desk phone didn't really cut the grade. Maybe she'd dig it out of the storage and use it again now that she was alone. *Alone*, she let that word clank around in her mind as she fumbled for the phone.

Caller ID said it was Bonnie. Wasn't she on a boat to Canada?

"Hey, Bonnie, miss me already?" Lila cradled the phone under her ear as she poured the spittling coffee into one of her blue willow cups before it was done perking.

Bonnie's cell was a little scratchy. "The chief picked up Lucas Griffin last night. I happened to drive by as they took him into the station house. How's that for a fluke. If I hadn't been up so early I wouldn't have seen. I would have called sooner, but I had to make my ferry and there's no cell service for, like, miles between us and Port Angeles."

"Shoot." Lila clunked into the built-in breakfast nook backward and sat down hard. She put down her coffee cup.

"I figure they are heading your way, Lilabelle, so get out of your pajamas and into your old sweats. You don't want to look too femme fatal. Also don't say anything and I mean *anything* without a lawyer present. Do you understand? I'll call Bernice Jensen and put her on standby. She helped me out with something once. She's weird, but a good attorney."

Lila felt a cold chill run through her veins. "I understand. Bonnie, there is something you should know. Lucas came over in the middle of the night after you left. I ended up in bed with him."

Bonnie kind of laughed nervously. "Obviously that must be the pending charge against him. Contributing to the delinquency of an idiot."

"Oh, so funny." Lila had put her coffee down and stood frozen in an adrenaline rush of massive proportions.

"Just get ready. And do not forget my words. Say nothing without an attorney present. *Nothing*, do you hear me?"

"Say nothing. I hear you. Why do I need an attorney if I didn't do anything?"

"Honey, those are the last words of many an innocent person before they slam the cell door behind them. Hang in there, Lila. I'll call Bernice. I'm sorry I can't be there." Bonnie actually hung the phone up without another word. Hung up!

Lila's hand shook as she tried to steady herself into a sip of coffee. Coffee would help. It helped everything. She kept sipping as she went up the stairs to get dressed. Times like these she wished she were a more organized person.

She set the coffee on her dresser and rummaged for some decent clothes that didn't scream *"I knew you were coming to arrest me so I spiffed up a bit."* A nervous laugh twisted out of her. She threw off her robe and let it drop to the floor. Old habits die hard.

Jeans. Jeans would be good. She pulled on her favorite jeans and hoped they'd zip up without a battle, which they did. She found a clean light blue T-shirt and even a bra—the sporty kind. Maybe it would help if she looked stacked and innocent, but comfort was the only thing on her mind at the moment.

It was clear to her she was free-flow thinking to avoid the big fat purple elephant in the room. That she might be arrested for suspicion of murder any minute now.

She tied a pair of Reeboks on in case she decided to try and outrun the law.

At times like these, she knew she could count on her parents. They'd stood by her through her pregnancy, ignoring all the town gossip, acting as if it was just one of those things that their sixteen-year-old daughter should have a baby out of wedlock, and they'd stand by her no matter what.

She finished her coffee off with one gulp and

thudded down the stairs, grabbed her purse, then ran out the back door and over to her parents' house. She knocked three times then went in. Her parents weren't much for locking the doors if they'd already gotten up, and ever since her dad had turned sixty and retired, they seemed to get up an hour earlier every year.

Shocking of her mother to marry a man ten years older than her. But they always seemed to be having a great time together.

"Yoo-hoo, Lila, we're out here," her mother called. They were out on the back porch reading the newspaper having coffee and mom's blueberry coffee cake. She always got a flat of blueberries from Larry at the market when they hit their peak, then froze them for her pies and muffins and coffee cake.

God, that smelled good. Lila sat down at the old drop-leaf table that used to be inside and helped herself to a square of cake, just like it was any other morning.

"Bonnie says I'm about to be arrested or detained or something," she blurted out between bites of cake.

Her father lowered his newspaper. "Whatever

for? Did you forget to pay a parking ticket?"

"No, they think I murdered Emily Griffin."

"Well, that's just silly," said her mom. "Why would you want to kill Emily Ruth?"

"In their eyes it would be to have Lucas and his family's estate all to myself or something classically greed-and-passion oriented. Is there any coffee left?"

"Sure, dear, get yourself a cup from the kitchen. And bring the pot in here—give your dad a warm-up. Want a warm-up, Del?"

"Yes, please." Her dad nodded.

Lila stood up and walked into the kitchen. This was going better than the time she told them she was four months pregnant at sixteen. Her mother had cried, her dad had put his arm around her and hugged her till she thought she'd pass out. Maybe they'd become adapted to crisis. Which was her fault, she was sure.

She took one of her mom's mugs from the odd collection in the cupboard and poured herself another cup of coffee. It had Mickey Mouse on it, and the year in gold letters, from that same trip to Disneyland she'd thought of the other day. Mallory must have been about seven. She was truly one of the luckiest people ever to have such great parents. She knew other women who didn't have such great childhoods.

Funny to think of it that way, what with her childhood being as short as it was.

She carried the pot out and gave her dad a re-fill.

"We've decided to hire you a lawyer, hon," her dad spoke as she refreshed his coffee.

"Thank you. Bonnie is digging someone up and said not to say anything to the police without an attorney present."

"She's right about that. Maybe you should turn yourself in before they come and take you. Might save some time," Dad said.

"Not before you've eaten a good breakfast, though," Mom added, and cut her another piece of cake. "Can I make you some eggs?"

"No thanks, Mom, my stomach is jumping. This is enough."

There they were, pretty-as-you-please, eating blueberry coffee cake on the back porch, drinking coffee out of Grandma Abbott's Royal Doulton cups and a Mickey mug, waiting for her to be hauled off in a squad car. Maybe she should just go down there and get it over with. They certainly didn't have a thing on her, aside from delivering the fatal Ritz cracker to the woman, and *er*, sleeping with her ex, who just happens to hate Emily Ruth's guts.

"It's all just circumstantial evidence," Lila said out loud.

"Yes, it certainly is dear. We've seen enough CSI to know that circumstantial just doesn't cut the mustard," her mom chimed in.

Lila loved how her parents never even asked if she actually killed Emily Ruth Griffin. Hey, maybe Chief Bob wouldn't bring her in. Maybe Bonnie was wrong.

The crunch of tires on the driveway that ran between her house and her parents' gave her a chill up the back of her spine. Then the sound of car doors closing, and the heavy footsteps of a man—no, two men.

"Morning, folks." Chief Bob came around the side of the porch. "Saw you out here as I drove by." He took his hat off. His deputy stood off in the distance.

"Normally, Bob, we'd invite you to join us for coffee, but surely you don't expect us to be hospitable when you've come to take our daughter away in a squad car."

"Sorry, Del, we need to ask her some questions."

"Two big fellows like you to pick up one small gal like me?" Lila joked her way above the butterflies that were storming her stomach.

Del Abbott got up from his breakfast. "Tell you what, Bob, I'll bring Lila down in the Ford and meet you there. It's better than my daughter being driven through town in the back of a police vehicle."

"I guess that's fine, seeing as I've known you folks for so many years, but don't be making any unscheduled stops."

"I *am* out of nail polish remover." Lila stared at her short, barely polished nails nonchalantly.

"See you in fifteen minutes, Miss Abbott."

Lila wasn't used to being called Miss Abbott—particularly by Bob Boniford. She looked at Bob. He looked tired. Then she stared out into the yard and felt her emotions well up. She didn't have any more snappy comebacks. The grass was brown from the summer heat. She could feel the temperature rising as the sun glared down from a cloudless sky.

"I'm not talking to you without a lawyer present, Bob, so order up some lunch for me, won't you? We're in for a long morning."

"See you in fifteen minutes, Lila." Bob put his hat back on and nodded to his deputy. They went back down the alley between the houses and got back into their car. Doors closed, engine started, backed out, and then they were gone. The neighbors were going to talk.

"I'll get my keys," her dad said.

"You stick to your guns, Lila. Don't let anyone bully you. I'll get you a bottle of water out of the fridge," her mom offered.

Lila patted her mom's hand. "I'd like that," she said.

When her parents left the porch, she put her hands over her eyes and rubbed her forehead. She didn't even know what to say to anyone. Her thoughts swirled in circles.

She looked up and saw someone standing out in the field behind the house. Probably neighbors coming to see why a police car pulled into the Abbotts' driveway.

She really wanted to stop causing her parents pain. It grated on her. She got up from the table and went toward the steps to head the nosey neighbor off before she got to their porch.

The nosey neighbor was still in the same spot. Lila stared out at her. The nosey neighbor was floating six inches off the grass. It was Emily Ruth Griffin. On a Tuesday. In broad daylight. Lila felt that strange shift in perception she got when she was seeing something other folks couldn't see. She stared at Emily Ruth, who seemed to be trying to say words, but no sound drifted across the space between them.

And then Emily Ruth vanished like a mist. Lila smelled lemons.

"Ready?" her dad called from the porch door.

"Almost," Lila answered without turning around. Just once she'd like to see a vision or get a ghost that laid it all out plain as toast with butter just what the heck they wanted her to do or say or look for. Was everything on the other side a big mystery? Because she was getting mighty sick of being the psychic hotline for the indirect dead.

Lila went back up the porch steps, pulled her white jacket off the chair, and put it on. She always got a chill from encounters with the recently deceased.

Eight

Lila wondered if Bonnie was out of her mind. This was her lawyer? Bernice Jensen had on overalls and a V-neck T-shirt. She took off her straw hat and nodded to Lila. She then removed a pair of green striped gardening gloves, which she stuck in her back pocket.

"Is my client under arrest?"

"Now, Bernice, this is just a little friendly chat. There's no need for all this formality."

"Lila Abbott?" Bernice stuck her hand out to Lila. "Did you answer any questions?"

"No. I had a donut." Lila shook Bernice's hand.

"I need a moment alone with Miss Abbott. How about some of your horrible coffee, Bob? I brought you a carton of my raspberry jam. It's at the front desk. I take my coffee black."

Raspberry jam. That would explain the red stains on Bernice's fingertips. Lila caught herself biting her nail and stopped. She looked down at her own peeling pink nail polish and short, chewed on nails. The polish was supposed to keep her from chewing them.

How the heck did she get into this mess?

Well, duh, she went near a genuine trouble-on-wheels summer boy. You'd think she would have learned from experience, and from every other townie girl she knew who ended up with her heart broken and her life a mess—or worse, dead, like Emily Ruth.

She twisted in the uncomfortable chair waiting for Chief Bob to leave the room. Even when you know you didn't do anything, there was something about sitting in the chief's office that made you feel guilty. Like going to the principal's office. Which she'd done plenty of times.

Back in school, Bonnie had been the quiet type—still waters, all that jazz. Lila had always been the rowdy one. Bonnie had been pulling her behind out of the fire for quite a while now. She owed her one.

Redheads with a tendency to turn beet red for no reason at all should never be involved in anything shady.

"Now, they haven't actually charged you with anything, and assuming you kept your mouth shut so far, we're fine. Because let me just clue you in on the ways of small-town cops. Any of that buddy-ol'-pal stuff Bob tries to pull on you is just another way of gathering information. Even a casual answer to a casual question can look quite different on their report. And I happen to know that Bob is trying to salvage his reputation with the county law enforcement boys after doing such a sloppy job on this case. It was the county coroner that put in for the investigation, you know."

Wow, Bernice might have on overalls, but she was a fast-talking dame for sure.

"Bonnie filled me in on the basics. Is there anything you want to add? Oh, and if you actually killed her, never tell me." Bernice took a pen out of her overall bib and started taking notes on a yellow legal pad inside a leather folder.

Thank heavens Bernice was a charge-ahead

kind of gal. Probably a good thing about now. Lila just wasn't sure how much trouble she was actually in.

"You should probably know I slept with Lucas Griffin last night." Lila felt her face color up. "But before he showed up in the store on the day Emily Ruth died, I barely knew him. We just ended up with some weird attraction to each other. It won't happen again." Lila took a breath in then heaved a great sigh.

"Why not? Was he bad in bed?"

"Hell, no. He's just out of my league."

"Interesting. Listen, Miss Abbott, right about now you're going to want to develop a seriously strong sense of self-esteem. If you go around thinking you don't deserve any better than this or that, you might end up in prison. It's important to start thinking positively and visualizing your freedom." Bernice pointed to her own head with her index finger and thumped at her temple several times. "Lucas Griffin is no better or worse than you because he comes from money. It's all in your head." More thunking.

"So my friend Bonnie keeps telling me. You should probably also know that Lucas sort of snuck into my house last night and scared the crap out of me, which probably didn't look too good with him skulking around town in the dark and all. But he just didn't want the deputy who was watching his house to follow him, and he really just wanted to have an emergency consultation regarding the ghost of his ex-wife. The sex was—unexpected."

Bernice smirked. It wasn't a bad smirk, just a lawyer kind of smirk. "The ghost of his ex-wife. I heard about that. She's taken to appearing in the grocery store every Monday morning?"

"At exactly ten thirty-six. Time of death. But also at Lucas's house, completely random times." Lila sat back against the hard chair. She'd certainly told Bernice Jensen more than she'd planned on.

"And you're sort of the local can-do gal in regards to these ghostly appearances, aren't you?"

"I'd love to say otherwise, but I have some sort of ability to deal with it. Some people are good with dogs or horses, I'm good with the dead," Lila laughed.

"That'll come in handy. But for now, let's just see what kind of questions Bob has up his sleeve and play to being cooperative. Tell me everything that happened the morning Emily Ruth Griffin died and I'll tell you what to include and what not to include. Go."

Lila rattled off the whole Death-on-a-Ritz scenario and every time she'd seen Lucas after that. When it all came out of her, it didn't sound that great. She'd gone to his house after the murder, they'd been seen several times together, and then the latest, their midnight madness.

"Wow, that all sounds really bad, doesn't it?" Lila asked.

"Depends on how you spin it." Bernice had been scribbling madly the entire time. She peered over a pair of half-mast black reading glasses with flowers painted on the edges. "I'm trying to decide whether you should stay away from Lucas or see him all the time. It might be more natural-looking for you to continue your relationship in the light of day."

"I'd have thought to stay away from him," Lila said.

"What fun would that be? One of the biggest problems here is they haven't caught the real killer. They're casting out the wide, easy net because they've got nothing. You've really got no motive at all, so all they have is opportunity, which is extremely weak. Too weak for them to arrest you, so it's obvious you're only here as a person of interest and for further questioning. Do you have any idea who might have killed Emily Ruth?"

"Not a clue, but she is trying to tell me. I've just been too busy to listen. And she's also not too great at getting her point across. She's very stuck in metaphors."

"Maybe a nice old-fashioned séance is in order. I'm not opposed to it." Bernice pushed away from the desk. "We'll need to go over some more details later, but here's what we'll tell ol' Bob for now. . . ."

Bernice fine-tuned Lila's story for the next ten minutes then called Chief Bob in from the other room.

An hour and a half later Lila got up from the bare wooden table and steadied herself. She'd probably learned more from being questioned than they had from questioning her. Bernice stepped out of the room for a moment while Lila picked up her things. She returned with a small bottle of cold Coke. Not even diet. Lila remembered the police station kept an old-time chest cooler stocked with soda bottles. Very historical.

One for her, one for Lila.

"Wow, you *are* a good lawyer."

"I only indulge when I'm on a case. Otherwise I stick to green tea and spring water. I have to keep my girlish figure. Go take a rest, but I want to see you in my office at three. We have lots to talk over."

Lila smiled to herself about the girlish-figure crack—Bernice was a sturdy gal. She'd proven to be a real hard-ass too, slapping Bob down at least ten times with, "*I'm instructing my client not to answer that. You're fishing, Bob.*"

Lila walked outside into a blaring sun-scorched morning. It made her eyes hurt.

"Hey, Abbott," he called to her. Lucas was leaning casually against the side of the police station building, trying to look less stressed out than he felt.

"Hey, Griffin," she called to him.

"Lila." He walked over to her, and when he got very close he looked into her eyes to see what was left of the night before.

"I see they didn't lock you up," she said.

"Not yet anyhow. You look beat."

"I should get to work."

"I called Tom Boscov and told him you'd be late. He seemed quite cooperative. Come on, I'll take you to lunch."

"I'm always up for food. You called my boss and told him I'd be late?" Lila asked.

"Why not. What could a little more town gossip do to us? How about takeout?" He pulled her close to him. He could feel her hesitation. "We could grab a picnic and sit on my porch. Or in my bed."

"My lawyer Bernice wants me to come to her office this afternoon."

"Bernice, what kind of name is that for an attorney? Now, my attorney, his name is Stanley."

"Stanley and Bernice. We should get them together." Lila was leaning slightly away from Lucas's encompassing embrace. If he let go, she'd probably fall over.

He gathered her closer. "I'm sorry you had to get involved in this," he said. "But we've started something and I don't think we should stop seeing each other just because Chief Bob thinks we conspired to kill my ex-wife, do you?" His voice was soft against her ear.

She pulled back again. "Let me get back to you on that one. I have to think about it."

He kissed her forehead. "Think away. Come over and we'll talk about it." Talking was the last thing on his mind when it came to Lila Abbott. He pulled her back to him and kissed her lips, hard and long, right in front of the chief's office window. *Go ahead, take a picture.*

She sort of shoved him away after getting a good kiss out of it.

"Chicken." He grinned at her.

"That's me, Miss Chicken, and I even have a ghost to go with me."

"We've got to find out what Emily Ruth is trying to tell us. I have a few ideas, based on my interrogation in there." Lucas nodded toward the chief's office.

"My head is too fuzzy. I will agree to lunch, though, but not in your bed, and not in some isolated romantic woodsy setting. Out in public."

"Nick's?"

"Sure."

Nine

Lila stretched out like a cat in Lucas's guest-room bed. She felt so small beside his long, tall naked self. He kissed her neck as he tucked her into the curve of his body, her back to his front.

"Mmmm, that was the best lunch I've ever had," he said softly.

"You are a devil, Lucas Griffin. I have a lawyer to meet in a half-hour. And didn't you say something about a sporting event? The Port Gamble Goeducks, was it?

"LadyHawks. Girl's soccer. The Goeducks are the girl's basketball team." He ran his fingers lightly over her hip, up her waist, and over her breast. She felt that good throbbing sensation— or was that him, pressed so close to her she could feel his arousal start up all over again. She turned herself around and faced him.

"No, no, no more of your sexual advances, mister. I'm going to take a shower." She wriggled away from him.

He grabbed her back and kissed her. Their bodies got all tangled up in that kiss. Hers didn't seem to be listening to her. His *sure* wasn't listening. She could hear Schatzie's little doggie snores beside the bed. She'd been all over Lila when they'd gotten there—and so had Lucas. The pooch seemed content to let them roll around in the covers without disturbing them. Actually she seemed a bit bored by the whole thing.

"Now stop that. These sheets are just too fine and I'll end up frittering the day away if you kiss me again. Why are we in the guest room anyhow?"

"Haunted master bedroom." His voice reverberated through her body as he pressed his lips against her neck.

"Damn, we'll have to fix that, Lucas, but right

now I need to see a woman about staying out of jail." She slipped out of bed and gathered her clothes off the floor where he'd strip-searched her.

Lucas groaned. "All right, all right, we're off to our various responsibilities. I wouldn't want to shirk my editorial duties and not report on the upcoming Port Gamble girl's soccer team."

Lila turned and looked at him oddly. "Why are you working for the *Port Gamble Gazette*, Lucas? Why are you even in Port Gamble?"

Lucas knew that sooner or later he'd need to tell Lila a few things about himself. To be honest, Emily Ruth's death had been a great diversion.

"I'm working at the *Gazette* to keep my skills up," he said as he slid out of bed. "I came back from a stint over in Iraq working for Associated Press. I took a piece of metal in the leg from a car bomb. I got a little too close to the action, I guess." Lucas pulled on his clothes.

"Anyway, I came back to the States just in time to find out my brother had been killed. I was in Port Gamble to attend to my brother's funeral. That was around Christmas. I spent some time with my family, then returned at the beginning of summer to Port Gamble to get this house back from Emily Ruth, a very long and time-consuming process. My brother left her a life estate in the property, or so she said. I contested the will, and as you've no doubt heard, the judge ruled in her favor. Fortunately, she expired. Null and void."

"You just can't talk like that, Lucas, people will think you really did kill her." Lila was standing naked with her bundle of clothes clutched in her hand. The dog woke up and yipped one short yip. Lucas agreed. Lila was as beautiful in the light of day as she was in the moonlight.

"To tell you the truth, it never occurred to me to kill her. I just figured I'd brought this bad luck into the family and would have to live with the consequences."

"And now that it's all settled, what now? Are you planning on going back to L.A.?"

"I'm not sure."

"I guess that's honest." Lila headed for the bathroom door. He could feel her upset.

Lucas walked after her. "I'm sorry Lila, I've had to deal with disposing of Emily Ruth's remains. Shipping her ashes off to her parents, that sort of thing. I haven't thought about much else, besides not getting arrested, and well . . . *you*." His voice rose to a shout on his last word as she slammed the bathroom door in his face.

"Women," he muttered. He threw on his shirt. Talking about Emily Ruth's cremation had given him the creeps. He kept expecting her to come walking out of a wall or something.

He heard the shower running and decided to cut his losses. He'd had a great afternoon delight with Miss Lila Abbott of the Port Gamble townie girls, but he needed to remember not to get his foot caught in the door. He'd only mess up her life, anyhow. He wasn't sure where he was headed.

"Come on, Schatzie, you can score a treat."

The dog stared at him and kept her position waiting by the bathroom door.

"Fine."

Lucas headed for his old room and some fresh clothes. He'd be out the door before she got out of the shower.

She was being stupid, Lila decided. She knew perfectly well that Lucas Griffin was only here for the summer, so it shouldn't be any big surprise to her that he planned to leave.

Lila indulged in the lavender-scented soap she'd found in the bathroom. Probably from his last conquest. And the little bottle of shampoo from the Hilton Hotel. Who knows where this guy had been. She'd just wash that man right out of her head. He'd been fun. A great roll in the hay. That's all. Heck, for that matter, she could just keep enjoying his company and his kisses and his flattering attentions for the rest of the time he was here, as long as she didn't take it too seriously.

Then she'd get back to her life. Maybe take that cruise. She'd always wanted to see New England and the East Coast. Talk about your arts and crafts, she'd heard those baskets over there were the cat's meow. Her mom would love that. Maybe she'd go with her mom.

She'd tell Lucas she was sorry for sounding huffy. It's not like he'd made any promises to her, they were just having a nice romp together.

She shut off the water and stepped out into the pristine but old-fashioned bathroom. The towels were white and clean and thick just like a luxury hotel. Like the time she'd stayed in a couple of those with her parents and Mallory. Hey, she'd traveled a little. Phoenix, Disneyland, Seattle, Portland, San Francisco. That's not *nowhere*. Those were interesting towns.

She turbaned her wet hair in a towel and wrapped another one around her body.

"Lucas," she said as she opened the door into the guestroom. "I'm sorry if I sounded weird. I'm no teenager, I know the score here. . . ." It didn't take but a second for her to figure out she was talking to thin air.

She listened but didn't hear him nearby. Lila slipped the towels off and dressed quickly. She grabbed her sneakers and padded downstairs barefoot. Schatzie followed her, her little nails clicking on the stairs.

"Lucas?" Her voice echoed in the empty house. She walked through to the large kitchen, and into the big sunroom dining area.

"Wow." She looked around the place and realized how completely cool it was. A big farmhouse sink—the real kind—took up one wall and had a cheery blue-and-white woven gingham sink curtain below it. Just like the old days. The fridge and the stove looked very vintage, but when she opened the fridge it was completely modern inside. Huh, go figure. She helped herself to a bottle of water and shut the door. *Heartland*, it said on the door front.

Very "Lifestyles of the Wealthy and Wealthier." She popped the water top and took a drink. Obviously, Lucas had taken a powder. Either he was mad, or he didn't like to stick around for the afterglow. This was twice he'd bolted out the door after they'd had sex. Well, once if you didn't count dodging the local deputy. There were extenuating circumstances there.

Maybe it was because she'd gotten tough over the years or because she'd decided that Lucas was just a fling, but Lila made up her mind not to get all crazy about it.

She looked around a little more and saw Schatzie's water bowl on the floor, which she refilled. Schatzie seemed grateful, and lapped it up. Lila gave her an affectionate head scratch.

"Is he treating you well, poochie?"

Schatzie seemed to smile.

Lila walked back out into the living room dining area and shook her head at the clothes strewn all over the furniture and floor. She picked up a silk blouse. If she were the jealous type she'd wonder, but these were obviously Emily Ruth's. They still had her perfume on them. She gathered up a pile of things and put them back in the cardboard box that sat next to the sofa.

Then she spotted a note on the long oak table, along with a set of keys.

"Lila, I'm off to the girl's soccer practice at the high school. Thank you for a very special afternoon. Here are the keys to my Jeep. I'd give you the Jag, but it's due to go in the shop. I don't trust it. Emily Ruth wasn't much for car maintenance. We will reconnect later," Lucas had written.

"Later," she said out loud. Well, hey, she had a lawyer to meet, and she *had* left her car at her house.

He could have walked to the high school. It wasn't very far, really. Nothing vital was very far from Port Gamble. It was a small circle of quiet. Only the area with Market Foods started to become unhistorical and they'd manage to tuck that slightly out of town.

She took the keys and picked up her purse from a fancy black wicker chair. Wow, if you sleep with one of these old-money types you get to drive their car. That sounded familiar for some reason.

Suddenly Lila felt a cold chill run through her. Schatzie came out of the kitchen and whined, leaning against Lila's legs. The dog shivered, her long red hair shaking along with her shiver.

A waft of strong scent came rolling down the stairs like someone had burnt the toast enough to make the smoke alarm go off, but it was that nasty perfume of Emily Ruth's instead.

"Yeah, yeah, yeah," Lila hollered. "You better figure out how to tell us what it is you need, because I'm going to have your ass sent to the hereafter as quickly as possible, Emily Ruth. And while we're at it, thanks for screwing up a perfectly good man. He's obviously got commitment issues, thanks to you."

At that moment a very large blue-and-white porcelain vase flew off the mantel and barely missed Lila's head. It crashed onto the floor and shattered. Schatzie ran for the kitchen, barking.

"Bitch!" Lila screamed. She followed Schatzie into the kitchen and scooped her up from under the sink. No way was she leaving the poor dog in this house. She left through the kitchen door and it slammed behind her.

Bernice's office was actually quite elegant with a large arrangement of late summer dahlias—a full-on riot of color on a side table and very chic retro fifties upholstered chairs with orange, black, and gray geometric patterns. Not your usual turn-of-the-century historic décor, even though the building was one of the originals. There was also a photo of Bernice standing next to a *gi-normous* pumpkin.

"Did you grow that?"

"Yup, I've won six years in a row. The flowers are mine, too. A woman needs a hobby besides the law."

Schatzie yapped at nothing.

"Sorry, I had to bring my dog." Lila held the traumatized Schatzie in her lap.

"Don't be silly." Bernice opened her desk drawer and brought out a large dog biscuit. Schatzie perked up her little ears and took the biscuit. Lila put her down and she stayed close to her chair, munching her treat, which was a bit oversized for her, but made her happy, so hey.

"It's Lucas's dog really. It *was* Emily Ruth's dog. I don't know how I ended up with her, but that seems to be the way of things for the last few weeks."

"Dogs are very comforting. She'll help you through this time. You should hang on to her. No telling what she knows."

"Tell me Bernice, why does the chief think Emily Ruth was murdered? It looks more like some kind of food tragedy to me," Lila asked.

"I spent some time on that today and here's what I've got. First, the evidence they gathered up from the store—the items you used in your demo—showed traces of peanut butter. Somehow several of the cheese-and-crackers were contaminated. It is *possible* that some sort of fluke of manufacturing took place at the Cheez Whiz factory, and I had my secretary, Rolly, go pick up every can of Cheez Whiz on the shelf at the market and see if any other cans had traces of peanut butter. That would be the luckiest break you ever got."

"Well, that just has to be it, because I can't think of anything else." Lila sat back in her chair.

"The fact that her EpiPen was missing has Chief Bob and the county sheriff all curious. And she wasn't wearing a medical bracelet either."

"Bracelet? Did she wear a bracelet?" Lila flashed on her dream of the clunking bracelet. "Wow."

"They think so. Do you know anything about that? Did you find it anywhere?"

Lila felt herself blush. "No."

"Lila, give me anything you've got. I'll need it. I managed to talk Bob out of detaining you in jail as a person of interest, but he's very focused on you and Lucas. Shortsighted if you ask me. They've only done one sweep of the crime scene on that day, and he's been trying to explain that decision away. Finding a suspect will make him look better."

"I dreamed about her bracelet."

"Do you know where it is?"

"No."

"I'm having Rolly do a second look around the area she was killed—I mean where she died, to see if it came off."

Lila shook he head. "Gosh, I never even thought of that. It could be under a fixture or something. I keep trying to figure out what she's saying but nothing has been very clear."

"Who?"

"Emily Ruth. She threw a vase at me today. She's got a bad temper."

"Normally I'd figure you were off your rocker, but your reputation precedes you, Lila, so I believe you. Emily Ruth's ghost is getting very frustrated with everyone for . . . something. This will be a different case for me, that's for sure."

Bernice scribbled some notes on her yellow pad.

"Anyhow," she went on, "to answer your question, there is something Bob is holding back from the autopsy report, and I've got to find out what that is. He knows something, but he's not talking."

"So, they *do* think she was murdered? Boy, I've got to tell you, if you think it through, whomever it was would have to be really clever. They'd have to know her schedule, and what she was allergic too, and basically it *had* to be someone she knew."

Bernice looked at her. "Yes, I figured that much out. That doesn't make it look too good for your boyfriend, Lucas."

"He's not my boyfriend, he's just a summer fling."

"Duly noted. Summer fling." Bernice wrote that down on her pad, smiling.

Lila hesitated. She'd been trying to figure out if she should really trust Bernice. Bonnie had ground it into her head that loose lips sink ships when it comes to your life and a murder investigation.

"Bernice, remind me exactly what our relationship is all about?"

"My job is to defend you against any charges the District Attorney may come up with, and short of that, protect your rights during the investigation. They might never charge you, for all we know. I proceed with the premise that you are innocent. And I believe you are, but again, don't ever tell me differently."

"And if I tell you things, you are bound by some code to keep them confidential, right?"

"Correct, but if you have information that you should have told the police, or some evidence, don't tell me about it. We'll both be up on charges. Things like that should, well, appear somewhere they can be found, if you get my drift."

Lila reached into her purse and felt for the paper that she'd found in Emily Ruth's cart. This probably wouldn't be a good time to produce it, with all the warnings, but the whole Prentice Cortland deal *was* important. She had an intuitive feeling about it.

"Well, it's not like the police took much notice, but I saw the contents of her cart the day she died. And I'll tell you this, that girl had a dinner date. She had wine, candles, steak, all the fixings for a Caesar salad. Rumor has it she was making a play for Prentice Cortland. You know, the widower? Summer people? His young third wife fell off a boat and drowned not long ago."

"Thanks; I'll look into that. It kind of sounds like the department missed a few details in their investigation. I'm thinking my idea of investigating on our own is a wise one."

Lila was thinking she better hightail it to work and make sure ol' Rolly finds the infamous shopping list. Or she could just say she found it herself—tomorrow. After all, she did work there. Good thing Lucas had called her in sick today. This looked to be a long-winded interview.

Lila's mind wandered to Lucas. What the hell did she think she was doing with him anyway? Well, they were tied together for better or worse now, so maybe together they could figure out who killed Emily Ruth and get both of them off the hook.

She and Bernice went over the entire episode of Emily Ruth's death with a fine-toothed comb for the next two hours, including extremely personal details about her own life, and every possible connection she might have to the Griffin family, past and present.

By the time it was over, Lila was exhausted. It was seven o'clock in the evening and she was completely wiped out, not to mention starving. She took Bernice's gift of a freezer carton of raspberry jam with her and climbed back in Lucas's Jeep, Schatzie in tow. She'd run the Jeep back over to his house and hope he was home to take her back to her cottage, because she just wanted to crawl into bed and sleep.

She'd had to do a refresher course in driving a stick shift on the way over to the office, with a few grinding gears and popped clutches before she got her groove back. This time after she got the Jeep started and going, she was doing a fair job of it. Lila drove past the historic Port Gamble graveyard and gave a little shiver. She always felt like folks were waving to her from the barely legible tombstones. Just sitting around shooting the breeze next to the old headstone, waiting for her to see them.

She turned up the radio and pushed the buttons till she got stuck on an old Hank Williams song, *I'm So Lonesome I Could Cry*. Oh, brother. That made *her* cry. She started bawling and wiped her eyes on her sleeve. That made the Jeep jump around the road, so she slowed down. Schatzie howled when Lila sobbed. What the heck was wrong with her? Post-traumatic lawyer stress probably. Maybe it was because she'd talked about her life and when you do that it sounds really small. It's a small life after all. That made her start singing the Disney song with her new variation.

She rounded the bend and headed out of town, with the pretty little white houses and their green shutters to her right and the Puget Sound to her right. A wind had kicked up and the water had whitecaps on the surface. Gulls cried and swooped down to the mud flats to pick up crabs.

The pretty white historic St. Paul's Church stood waiting for another summer weekend wedding. It was a constant stream of brides and grooms during the summer and into September. Every girl in Port Gamble dreamed of coming down those front steps with her veil flying in the wind. A secret they all kept tucked in their historic cedar chests.

As she passed the last historic house a dark, sleek car pulled out behind her. It wasn't one of the local cars, and it wasn't the law, as far as she knew, but she checked her speedometer just in case.

The leaves rustled overhead with the increasing winds. The late August sky was tinging to dusk more quickly these days, and a dark sky moved quickly into place. That cloud cover meant only one thing—it was going to rain. And only the locals knew that after a hot spell, the roads became very slick after the first rain.

She better watch it, she didn't want to ram Lucas's Jeep into a madrona tree. The thought made her smile for some reason. And she noticed a wave of anger rolling around in her, just like a storm brewing. Wow, she had some attitude problems. And a real mixed bag of emotions toward Lucas.

The dark car was getting a little too close for comfort. If it were one of Chief Bob's deputies, she'd give him a piece of her mind if he stopped her, after shoving her down the road. Lila sped up.

The rain started. Big fat drops fogged up the windshield. She fumbled around for the wipers and the defroster. Damn, this Jeep thing wasn't too intuitive in the controls. And *damn* that car, it was getting too close for comfort. Lila started to get a little . . . scared. And she didn't scare too easily. Schatzie seemed to sense her tension and huddled next to her.

She tapped on her brakes a few times to warn the idiot behind her that this was no time to play macho Nascar man. Peering out the slowly defrosting windshield, she searched for the turnoff to Lucas's house. Wow, it had really gotten dark fast.

The idiot behind her got closer. Damn, what did he think he was doing? Lila noticed she assigned the driver a male identity without really being able to see who it was. Well, hey, the women she knew didn't drive like this. She looked in her mirror to see if she could read his license plate, but the Jeep was too high, and he was *too close*!

She took a deep breath and tried to relax, but it didn't work. The dark car loomed behind her. She tapped on her brakes again. A huge noise immediately followed that action—the noise of the dark car's bumper hitting her rear end.

Lila had that automatic response of slamming on her brakes, but that just made everything spin out of control and instead of backing off, the car behind her slammed her again. Lila screamed and tried to control the Jeep.

The road sign to Lucas's house loomed bright in front of her and she made a sharp, screeching right turn off the main street. Lila glanced in the mirror and saw the dark car speed by. But at that point she'd run out of road luck and slid into the ditch, the Jeep pitching sideways. She was Jeep-deep in blackberry vines and salal bushes. Schatzie yelped as they slid into the brush.

"Crap!"

The seat belt had kept her in place, but when she popped the belt she lost her holder and slid up against the dirt-side door. The dog had wedged herself under the seat.

Then she saw headlights. This time she panicked. She pulled herself back over and locked the door, then started honking the horn. Someone would hear. This was a quiet street. A dog nearby started barking. So did Schatzie. Yap-yap-yap, sharp punctuated barks.

The car pulled up next to her and left its lights on, blinding her so she couldn't see it well. Besides, the windows were completely fogged up. Lila kept honking the horn.

Someone knocked on the window and scared the crap out of her. She screamed in fright. A flashlight beam blinded her.

"Lila? Are you okay?" Lucas's voice was muffled through the glass.

It was the best voice she'd heard in a long time. She rolled down the window with great difficulty.

"Oh God, Lucas, I'm so glad to see you. I'm so sorry about your Jeep. Someone ran me off the road!"

"Are you hurt?"

"I don't think so. Just shaken up."

Lucas popped the door lock and opened it wide. He reached in and pulled Lila out of the Jeep, which was at a very steep angle. Schatzie managed to crawl up the floor and she jumped right into Lucas's arms. Lila was cradled in one arm, the dog in the other. She let his warmth comfort her.

They were both shivering. The rain pelted them. Lila didn't have much to protect her from the elements.

"Come on, get into the Jag with me."

She'd heard those words before, but she was too frightened and tired to care right now. He walked her over to the passenger-side door and opened it for her. After she slid in he handed her the dog.

"I'll be right back." He closed the door.

Lila shivered and closed her arms over her

chest. Schatzie jumped into the back seat and found something familiar—a blanket that must have been from her old dog days as Emily Ruth's Jag dog. She whined a bit, but after doing three circles she fluffed down into the blanket.

"Good girl," Lila whispered.

Through the windshield as the wipers thwapped away the rain, she saw Lucas turn the lights off on the Jeep and lock the door.

Lucas looked around the Jeep and felt sick. He could see slashing dents in the back where a metal bumper had scraped the blue paint with black paint. Not just one dent.

He was glad he'd pulled her away, because there was a steep ravine not four feet ahead, with no guardrail. Lila had almost bought the farm, or at least come pretty close.

He wasn't keen on the women in his life getting bumped off one by one, even if the other one was Emily Ruth. He felt a rush of emotion, and to his surprise it was directed toward Lila. Lila with the red-blond hair and local ways and ability to train dogs and apparently talk to ghosts. He slipped on the new mud and caught himself against the Jeep.

Lila needed looking after, and he was going to make sure she let him do that. First things first, he'd get her out of those wet clothes and into a warm bed.

Worried as he was, that made him smile.

Ten

Lila grabbed Lucas and tried not to scream. Something had scared her witless and wide awake from a very nice, solid sleep. Lucas wasn't much better off, but he *was* good at holding on to her. They clutched each other and the sheets as an ever so slight motion caught their attention and they both looked up to the ceiling, simultaneously.

"Holy *crap*," Lucas yelled.

"Wow," Lila echoed in a whisper.

And there she was, floating above the bed, hovering on the ceiling, Emily Ruth in all her ethereal finery.

"Don't move," Lila said in a hushed voice.

"That's just not a problem," Lucas said hoarsely.

Emily looked pale, actually transparent, but not dangerous. Lila stared with curiosity as she regained her old fearless nerves. Truly she'd only seen a few full-blown apparitions.

Emily Ruth stopped looking not dangerous. She slowly lowered toward them. Lila noticed both she and Lucas tried to sink deeper into the mattress, to no avail.

Emily opened her mouth and a horrible, wailing cry filled every inch of the room. It made the thin woven linen curtains at the window flap like crazy. The stench of Passion perfume made them both choke for air. A blue willow ceramic vase tumbled off the dresser across the room and crashed to the floor. *Man, that was the second nice vase she'd busted up. Emily had learned one trick at least—vase busting.*

Lila stared into Emily Ruth's ghostly face. Emily Ruth stared back, unblinking, and apparently, unforgiving.

"What do you *want*?" Lila yelled. "How about a big fat clue? Can you write? Shall we get a chalkboard?"

As the last syllables of her words came out, Emily Ruth vanished like powder. As a matter of fact, a fine white powder drifted down on Lila and Lucas. Lila touched it. It was chalk dust. *Oh, such a funny ghost.*

For such a determined spirit, Emily Ruth was having a whole lot of trouble with communications. From Lila's experience, though, it did take some time for someone trapped in the twilight zone between earth and heaven to learn how to make things happen and get everyone's attention. Really, Emily Ruth was learning pretty fast.

Lucas leapt out of bed and threw open the windows. The sea air mingled with the after-scent of Emily Ruth and eventually won out, refreshing the room. There was still a strong wind dipping the branches of the fir trees to the right of the roofline. As she sat up in bed Lila could see the murky dark water of the sound stirred by wind.

He stood by the window, breathing in the fresh air. He ran his hand through his tousled hair, obviously freaked out, and Lila took in the scenery. Wow, he was cute naked.

* * *

"I don't mind telling you Lila, this sort of thing really scares the hell out of me. I've run behind battles, I've faced all kinds of danger. But the undead ex-wife is really hard to take. We've got to find a way to get rid of her." Lucas walked back over and sat on the bed.

"Come back under the covers." Lila threw the bed sheets open and beckoned him to join her.

He looked at her and smiled a sexy smile. "You have interesting timing, woman."

He slid in close to her, warming her with his body heat. Warming himself as his arousal sprang to life. She tasted as sweet as summer watermelon. He devoured her. There was something about making love to a woman the fifth or sixth time that was incredibly good. Like a newly discovered path that takes you to a wonderful beach, and the next time you take it you know the footing and which branches to duck under, and how beautiful the beach is at the end of the trail.

He let himself forget for the next hour that his dead ex-wife's ghost had just appeared above the bed, because, hey, he was a guy.

Lila was speed-checking at her checkout counter. It was a little game she played when things got busy or she was trying not to think about something, like who ran her off the road last night or why her lover's ex-wife appeared over the bed. Today it was both.

All the checkers agreed that, aside from the usual *five o'clock I forgot to figure out what's for dinner crowd*, and the standard holiday weekends, there was absolutely no pattern to the odd phenomenon that occurred when everyone in the store got finished at the same time and came to check out in a wild mob. Chaos theory.

So here she was on a Wednesday morning, fresh from Lucas's bed, speed-checking, seeing how fast she could run Libby's creamed corn five-for-a-dollar on special over the scanner window. Nelson, the seventy-five-year-old former naval engineer grandpa who worked in the store to have contact with folks, was catching like a champ and bagging as fast as she could dish it.

Nelson made the squirmy two-year-old boy in the cart laugh with his funny noises, which was quite a relief for the mother trying to juggle her purse and wallet and run the credit card through the card swiper while keeping one hand on her monkey-boy so he didn't jump out of the cart.

All the time Lila was doing her thing, she kept a wary eye for out-of-the-ordinary occurrences at the store today. It seemed like Emily Ruth had moved beyond Mondays and had become much more active.

A shiver ran through her as she chucked Mrs. Speers frozen peas at Nelson. She looked down the check-stand rows at her fellow workers. Cindy, Vicki, Susan, Fran, Lani, Nancy, Ann Marie, and Fred all seemed to be in their own grooves of moving the rush of customers out the door. *Ah, the checker chicks.* They were the best. And Fred, too.

She'd organized a bowling team and had Checker Chicks put on the back of cool bowling shirts about four years ago, and they were kicking those "Kiwanis Kewtees" butts so far this year. The checker boys, Fred, Stan and the others, were great during the baseball season, but the bowling team was strictly female.

Anne Marie, the wine expert and assistant to the assistant manager, was having an involved conversation with a good-looking guy. All the good-looking guys liked to go through Anne Marie's aisle and talk wine with her. Of course it did have something to do with Ann Marie's great figure and easy-on-the-eyes good looks.

Summer guys looking for a summer fling. The checker chicks all knew better. Lila's own life was a cautionary tale whispered during coffee breaks. And right now she was violating her own cautionary tale by being with Lucas.

But she knew what she was doing. She did, she did, *really* she did.

"Whoa, slow down, Lila, those pickles are loaded and dangerous!" Nelson called to her from his bagger station.

She looked up and saw Mrs. Speers staring at her in amazement. Lila loved it when the universe sent her messages. *Slow down. Take things slow with that man!*

"Nice checking there, Lila," Mrs. Speers said. She finished punching buttons on the pay station and the receipt popped out of the register.

"Thanks for coming in, Mrs. Speers." Lila smiled and handed her the long receipt.

She looked over to the next customer. He looked familiar in a way, like she'd seen him around town but he wasn't a townie. He had salt-and-pepper gray hair and a sort of nautical outfit on. Tennis shirt, dark blue blazer, white slacks, rich.

That was obvious by the caliber of his groceries. Sun-dried tomato and basil pesto spread, a fresh baguette, an assortment of those fancy olives from the salad bar case they'd put in for the summer people, then champagne, and not the cheap stuff, four bottles of Roederer's Cristal at $270 a bottle. To top it off, a box of their most expensive truffles and an orchid from the floral department, boxed and ready, pretty as a prom date.

Lila passed each one carefully over the scanner. Wow, Anne Marie must have stocked a good year or something. And salt-and-pepper dude must have a date. He was very Cary Grant, maybe a little shorter, and the older Cary Grant, who was still dashing but way too old for Audrey Hepburn in *Charade*. What were they thinking when they cast that movie?

Lila had taken to watching late-night movies since Mallory left. She and Mallory had done their share together, especially anything spooky like *The Sixth Sense*, which creeped her out way more than Mallory, of course, and all the Hitchcock movies, like *Marnie* and *Vertigo*, their favorites. After Mallory left, Lila had been staying up way too late watching anything she could find.

Until now . . . and Lucas. Lucas was taking up her movie nights.

"Looks like some lucky girl is in for a treat tonight," Lila whistled. Of course that was completely against the rules, but, hey, this was Port Gamble, not Mercer Island, and Tom Boscov was doing paperwork upstairs. Even so, Lila had a bad feeling creep over her and wished she hadn't said it.

She got a flash of memory and realized this guy had been there the day Emily Ruth died. She'd seen him in the crowd, comforting someone.

Cary Grant smiled at her and ran his credit card through the machine.

Lila pulled the sales slip and her fingers went cold when she read the name. Prentice Cortland.

Prentice Cortland. Emily Ruth's unconfirmed dinner date on the day she died. But why was he in the store? Had they been shopping together? She hadn't seen him at all till after . . . after her death.

Wow, he sure recovered quickly from his interest in her, didn't he? Three weeks later and he's hot to trot with some other poor unsuspecting girl.

He could be the murderer! Her hand shook a little as she handed him the slip to sign.

"Thanks, Mr. Cortland, we appreciate your business," she lied. She stared at him and tried her damnedest to take in every detail.

He glanced at her. "Thanks," he said. Leaving the slip, he grabbed his bagged groceries and left quickly.

Lila had seen enough crime TV to know that she should keep that slip and get his fingerprints. She slipped his signed slip carefully in her vest pocket.

Lila slammed down the CLOSED sign on her aisle and called to Becky across the way to cover for her. Everyone looked at her like she'd lost her mind, but Becky walked over from video and reopened the register. Becky was wise to Lila's current situation.

She walked out the store doors behind Cortland, being very sleuthlike, and watched him. He'd already jumped in his car and started it up. Heck, he practically ran her over as she crossed into the parking lot. A black Porsche. Black car! How strange was that? She only saw the back end of the car so it was impossible to tell whether it had dents in the front bumper. It was hard to believe anyone would use a pristine black Porsche to ram someone off the road, but still, this was extremely odd and coincidental.

Back inside, Lila made a beeline for the storage bag aisle, found a snack-sized ziplock carton, generic even, tore it open and slipped the signed receipt into a fresh plastic bag. She dropped the box on the floor. *Clean-up on aisle three.* She was in too big of a hurry.

Lila ran upstairs to get her cell phone out of her purse. She popped her employee locker and grabbed it out of its special place. For once in her life she actually wanted to talk to Chief Bob. But weirdly, she dialed a different number instead. Lucas's cell phone.

"Hey, there. You left early. I didn't even get to make you breakfast." Lucas had reached over to an empty bed this morning. Lila wasn't a girl to get to work late.

"Are you at the newspaper office?"

He heard the panic in her voice. "Yes."

"Can you look up all the details about the death of Prentice Cortland's last wife? Or even the one before that? I just ran into him at the store. He drives a black Porsche, Lucas."

"No one would use a Porsche to hit a Jeep off the road." Lucas said what she had thought out loud.

"What is that, a rich-boy behavior code? Maybe he knows we've been snooping around and maybe he knows I think he had a date with Emily Ruth, and, well, I don't know, he was just really creepy!" Lila blithered. "Lucas, he was here the day she died! *In the store*. I saw him myself."

"Wow. That's something. Okay, you're upset. But reach into that talented intuitive sense of yours and see what you find. Do you really feel like he's the one? While you are doing that I'll do some snooping in the archives. I promise I'll get as much information as I can."

"Well, thanks, I guess. I'm starting to be very confused about my intuitive sense. You're muddling it up with all this . . . *sex*." She whispered the last word.

Lucas smiled as he talked. "Sorry to muddle you up. I can't seem to help myself. Can I make you dinner after work?"

"I don't know, that ex of yours is really nasty. And stinky, too. How about we catch a couple of bowls of chowder or a salad at Nick's. Just dinner. I need some space."

"I can't sleep alone with Emily Ruth prowling around, throwing vases," Lucas kidded. But he wasn't too far from not kidding.

"We'll see. How come I keep saying no to you and end up in your bed later?"

"Because I'm cute and I used to be rich?"

"No, that's NOT why," Lila yelled into the phone.

"Because you haven't had sex in like a zillion years and you're remembering how much fun it is?"

There was a big pause on the other end of the phone.

"That's it," she said slyly. "Let's change the subject. I'm not too fond of the floating former wife myself, Lucas. I think we better solve her problems before she gets really crazy. How about I invite my little circle of strange friends over and try for a contact séance? It's a shame Bonnie is out of town, but there is nothing I can do about that."

"I guess so. Shall I bake?" Lucas joked.

"Not necessary. We'll have a potluck dessert. These people can dish out the brownies with the best of them."

"Shall we say eight-ish?" Lucas asked.

"Sounds perfect. I'll round them up."

"See you for a quick supper at Nick's at what, six?"

"Yup."

Lucas signed off and shut his cell phone. Lila made him smile more than any woman he'd ever known. She was so honest and brashly innocent, but strange as hell. The honest part was the best part.

He stared out the window of the historic offices of the *Port Gamble Gazette.* The morning was still steel gray and the seaside reflected that color, with its gray rocks and gray water. The marine layer, they called it around here. By noon the sky would turn sunny, but it would never get into the scorcher zone if the morning started out like this.

Who would try and run Lila off the road? He was damned glad she didn't get hurt, but that was no ghostly occurrence, that was a real live person who felt like Lila was getting too close for comfort. Who could that person be?

Her theory that Prentice Cortland, the intended date and recent widower, had anything to do with putting peanut butter in the Cheez

Whiz on the off chance Emily Ruth might pick it up and eat it and die was pretty farfetched. But what else did they have?

He slipped into research mode and Googled Prentice Cortland. Links to articles regarding the death of his young wife came up. It looked like there was no trial, just an inquest. Just like Emily Ruth's death.

Cause of death for Mrs. Cortland was drowning and a blow to the head from the fall. Not necessarily in that order, Lucas thought. The story detailed that the wife had been drinking heavily and gone up on the front deck, lost her balance, and fell overboard without being noticed. Loud music, loud engines, classic stuff. But honestly, from his days of boating with his set of boaty rich friends, it was highly possible for someone to fall overboard. Not as likely that no one noticed, but apparently the coroner was satisfied.

Holiday boat party. Kind of cold out there for a Christmas bash, but part of the reason she'd drown had been her heavy mink-trimmed down parka sucking her under. That and some kick-ass eggnog apparently.

That was just about the time Jason had died.

A skip to the back pages found the obituary

for Cortland's first wife, Cornelia Cortland, who died of a heart attack, the article said. She was in her sixties. Kind of young for a heart attack, but it wasn't out of the question.

Looks like old Prentice got over it quick, re-marrying within three months of her death. *Wow*.

Heck, if he was some kind of serial killer he'd branched out with Emily Ruth and killed her before he even married her. Lucas had no idea how many times they'd dated, but he knew they'd been seen together around town.

And if he wasn't a serial killer, the dude had a very strange run of bad luck, that was for sure, which only got worse with the addition of Emily Ruth into his life. But the fact of Cortland being Emily Ruth's 6:30 date on the day she died had not been truly established.

He printed out a few articles to show Lila and got back to his legal pad scribbling style of writing up the local football team's roundup from watching their early practice this morning. The boys looked like they were shaping up pretty well. These small-town schools could surprise you sometimes if they snagged a young, inspiring coach who had that win-lust.

Maris, the newspaper office manager, dropped a stack of papers on his desk and breezed back to her office. He thumbed through them. Birth announcements, lots of weddings, and some obituaries. When did he get to be Dear freakin' Abby, anyhow?

Well, it was this or go back to his old footloose, freelancing ways. Until his leg healed a bit more he better just enjoy the rest and try to write nice about Mrs. Manke's ten-pound baby boy, the promising junior quarterback, and the girls' volleyball team.

Something caught his eye. He flipped back a few pages and read:

Pauline Pierson died Saturday, July 29, 2006. A memorial service will be held at the Port Gamble Lutheran Church Thursday afternoon, 4 P.M., August 23rd. Mrs. Pierson was born in Savannah, Georgia, in 1966, and moved to this area as a young bride in 1986. She is survived by her sister, Mrs. George Fellows of Port Angeles, and her husband, Lawrence Pierson.

Someone had faxed in a very complete obituary for her.

Pierson. That name rang a bell. Lawrence Pierson. Something Lila had told him, lying in his arms in the moonlight, recounting all the gossip about Market Foods and everyone who worked there. Great stories, really.

It was Larry, the produce guy. That was it. Larry Pierson. The one who eavesdropped, kept his area spotless, and was very, very, high-strung.

Lila never said anything about knowing his wife died, and that was before Emily Ruth. Maybe he was just a really private guy. The article didn't say what the cause of her death was.

All these dead wives. Lucas leaned back in the wooden swivel chair and stuck his pencil behind his ear. There was a real rash of dead wives in this town.

He decided to do a little statistical analysis of how many women had dropped dead in the last year in Port Gamble. The more he wondered about why they'd earmarked Emily Ruth's death as no accident, the more he saw the sense in it. Chief Bob and the coroner and the county sheriff might be right. The absence of her EpiPen *was* highly suspicious.

He just couldn't figure out why she'd go out without that. Her blood alcohol test was zero so she wasn't hitting the Bloody Mary's for breakfast, so why would she have made such a slip.

Or did someone take it out of her purse?

And out of the car? Which reminded him, he needed to pick up Emily Ruth's Jag from the shop. He'd intended on selling it but thought about giving it to Lila. He'd noticed Lila's car was a complete pile of crap.

But a Jag was sort of high-maintenance. Like Emily Ruth. Well, he could always fix it for Lila later if she needed it fixed. If he was around. Was he going to be around? Would he be here if Lila needed the car fixed? Where the hell was he headed anyway?

He'd have to figure out how to make a living. The sale of his house in L.A. would keep the wolves away from the door for a while, but he didn't earn much as a small-potatoes reporter. The beach house he'd put back in the family trust. He sure as heck wasn't going to ask his father for money. Those days were over. He'd used almost all of his remaining trust fund paying the back property taxes on the beach house. He had some things to straighten out, that was for sure.

From everything she'd told him it wouldn't be the best thing for Lila Abbott to have another man take a powder on her. But he did have a career to think of, beyond the Seen and Heard and Local Sports section of the *Port Gamble Gazette*.

And Lila seemed firmly entrenched here in Port Gamble.

He better think all this through very carefully before he hurt someone he was getting to care about very much.

Lucas straightened up and went to work on his statistics. He wondered what the statistics for selfish rich boys leaving behind brokenhearted local girls were.

Eleven

Raylene and Earlene were way too anxious to get the dead on-line, like you could log on and IM to the other side. Jenny Gardiner had been to all manner of séances back in England, and was a member of a very exclusive British society for the study of psychic phenomenon. Jerry from the bookstore looked nervous, but swore he was game. His partner, Jasper, had come along and looked quite excited. Denise Schramke looked nervous, but she'd insisted on joining the group. Lila caught her crossing herself a few times. A patron saint or two wouldn't hurt about now, in Lila's opinion.

The long pine dining table that stretched across the south side of the room groaned under the weight of potluck dessert. The sisters had outdone themselves with stacks of double-chocolate brownies, and Lila's mother seemed bound and determined to create as many dessert items as possible out of the ripe late-summer blackberries they'd picked together and frozen: cobbler, pie, her famous coffee cake, and one amazing blackberry soufflé.

Lucas had contributed beautiful Bartlett pears from the tree in his backyard and some kind of great cheese with port marbled through it, and a bottle of port, which looked like it came out of a fancy wine cellar.

Lila whispered to him, "What did you do, find the liquor cabinet finally?"

"Exactly. I found my grandfather's secret stash in the basement. Quite the vintages down there."

"You went into the dark and spooky basement?"

"In broad daylight, but let me tell you, the spooky part of this house is upstairs, not downstairs," he said softly. "And the sooner we get this over with the better. I want Emily Ruth evicted so I can finally get some peace."

"Okay, nobody eats till we get this whole phone calls to the dead thing handled." Lucas blocked the way to the desserts. "We can have coffee later, too."

"A glass of port would be lovely, all around, though, don't you think? Just to get our nerve up and all?" Jenny Gardiner pointed out.

"Well, yes, I suppose that's true." Lucas unblocked the table. "Port all around, then?" He started pouring the deep red-gold liquid into the loveliest glasses Lila had ever seen. They were etched with old-fashioned patterns. These wealthy people, they had all the right stuff.

"And you just can't have a glass of port without a nibble of chocolate on the side, and a little slice of pear. Those pears are lovely, Lucas. Are they from the property?" Jenny slipped past Lucas and went in for a glass dessert plate, piling on a bit of this and that.

"Yes, it's a very old tree out back on the west side. My great-grandparents put in an orchard many years ago."

Lila was stifling a laugh at Jenny's ability to just schmooze her way right past Lucas's little

control-freak moment, get him to completely change his mind and end up pouring port.
Women, you just had to love them. The others
followed suit, but didn't load up too much; a
brownie here, a pear there, just the basics, heavy
on the port.

"Once you're braced, gang, I've got chairs
over here around the round table." Lila gestured
to a glowing, polished round table with enough
room for all of them. Boy, how she missed Bonnie. Bonnie would just round out the group so
nicely. Lila got that lonely feeling again. The
empty-nest daughter gone, best friend flown
the coop feeling.

Lucas took Lila's hand and tucked it under his
arm. That felt good.

"Let's get settled. I'll bring you whatever
you'd like."

"Thanks, I'll just have a sip of that port and a
glass of water, if you don't mind. I'd like to keep
my wits about me," Lila said.

Lucas let her go and pulled out a chair for her
to sit down at the séance table, nearest the inside
of the room. "I'm with you there," he said. "Wits
in tact."

He retrieved her water and a pretty glass of port with just a touch poured in.

"Thanks." Lila took a small sip. It was amazingly mellow but strong at the same time. It gave her a strange feeling. Or was that the impending night's activities?

"Okay, ladies and gentlemen, let's gather and talk about what we're going to do. Believe it or not, I've never done this. Jenny, you've been to a few of these, how do they usually go?"

Jenny settled in across from Lila and deposited her plate and wine. "Well, sometimes the host would use an Ouija board, but we've all found that those tend to attract a flighty level of spirits. Mostly the more talented mediums would just set about to contact the person in question and make a rather direct request."

Lila had to laugh. She wasn't sure if Emily Ruth could be qualified as a flighty spirit, but she sure was a pain in the rump. "Direct it is."

Lucas sat down next to her. The others joined shortly, sipping port and laughing nervously.

Lila felt herself slip into a strange space—the one she went to when she was thinking about spirits and the way they occasionally popped into her life. She could smell just the slightest hint of Emily Ruth's perfume. Lucas caught her eye and she could tell he smelled it, too.

"Passion," he whispered.

Lila nodded. She'd kept her promise to Emily Ruth and brought a child's chalkboard and chalk from the store. Kind of a back-at-you, really.

"Let's settle in, folks. Lucas brought us this photo of Emily Ruth to pass around. We can get a feel for what she looked like and connect with a little of her energy."

Lucas took the photo out of a book he'd laid on the table and passed it around. Lila took it first and got an almost electric snap of energy off the image. It was Emily Ruth in better days. She had been quite beautiful, and the photo showed off her great figure. She stood on the beach in the typical Northwest garb of a swimsuit and a sweater. Her sleek hair was pulled up into a bun on the top of her head. She was shielding her eyes from the sun, looking at the camera, which Lila guessed had Lucas behind it at the time.

She stared at the image, trying to imagine Lucas and Emily Ruth as a couple. They must have had some good times for him to marry her. Well, the good times were over now, that was for sure. She glanced at Lucas.

"She was very beautiful at one time," he answered her unasked question.

"I'm actually starting to feel sorry for her. She was really misguided," Lila said.

"I have moments of that. Then I have other moments. Moments involving my brother's funeral." Lucas took a hearty swig of his port.

He remembered his parents' sadness that day, and how they'd somehow blamed him for not looking after his little brother. He felt a wave of emotion that ranged from sorrow to anger at Emily Ruth. She'd barred herself in the beach house and hadn't even bothered to talk to the family.

His family had all stayed at a friend's home by Sea Crest Country Club instead of in their own house. Lucas had done his best to talk to his parents and sister, but everyone was so upset it wasn't successful. They couldn't even get Jason's belongings out of the house.

He'd found them packed in a box in the basement when he'd explored down there the other day. How could he have ever loved Emily Ruth?

He took a draw of his port and pressed his hand against his forehead. He'd brought her into the family and it had cost his brother's life and the respect of his parents.

Lila noticed how upset Lucas was. She sensed it was thoughts of Emily Ruth and all the havoc she'd caused. She'd really like to rid him of her once and for all.

Lila passed the photo on and toyed with the colorful paper napkin Lucas had put out for her. She folded it into triangles. She could feel the hairs of her neck prickling. It's one thing to endure the random antics of a resless spirit and quite another to invite her to port and pears.

The photo came back in Lucas's possession and he put it in the center of the table. There was a fat candle with three wicks they'd found in a cupboard and Lila leaned in to light all the wicks with a long skinny lighter just in case Emily doused the electricity. Lucas had also built a lovely fire, since the late-August evening had taken on a northwest chill.

Would Emily Ruth behave and try and get some information across to them, or would she be a drama queen and scare the crap out of everyone?

Probably the drama queen option.

Which the ghostly Emily Ruth did, immediately. The room darkened before Lila could even speak. Everyone gasped. Lila calmly finished lighting the candle. The three wicks flickered in the darkness, along with the soft glow of the fireplace.

"Take it easy, everyone. Let's join hands." Lila was going by stuff she'd seen on television. Shows like *America's Most Haunted* and old movies like *Blythe Spirit*. She just wasn't in the mood to be possessed or anything, so Emily Ruth better watch her boundaries, that pushy bitch, or she'd shove back.

"We are all in a circle of protection, and no harm can come to us. We're here to help the spirit of Emily Ruth Griffin communicate whatever is troubling her. We're here to help Emily Ruth get an afterlife."

A few giggles went around the circle.

A gale-force burst of wind made all the French doors fly open. Their sheer curtains billowed and danced. Lila was facing those doors and she saw the tiny sliver of a moon over the water far out in the distance. The rain had let up, and a clear dark sky shimmered over the bay. She felt her usual chill of recognition.

A waft of *Passion* perfume made several people cough. "Oh, my," Jenny Gardiner said softly.

Schatzie yapped from the safety of the dog kennel in the kitchen.

Lila felt a touch on her shoulder and took a quick breath in. Then the candle was slowly, ever so carefully, blown out, wick by wick. The breath of spirit curling over her shoulder like a butterfly fluttering softly. The flames snuffed out, leaving them in a pitch-black room.

Everyone was very, very quiet.

Leave it to Emily Ruth to fling open the doors and act like she was on the Broadway stage. That woman really missed her calling. When the lights snuffed out Lucas sighed. What a display.

Lucas felt Lila give him a kiss in the darkness. Her lips were cold. He'd have to warm that girl up later. He squeezed her hand.

Then the most ungodly sound made him jump like a schoolteacher sitting on a tack. The scritching, screeching sound made him drop

Lila's hand and cover his ears. Others made groans and cried out, dropping hands to cover their ears. It continued for about ten seconds, then stopped.

Suddenly the candle sprang back to life, all three wicks flaming up at once. When he looked to Lila, what he saw wasn't Lila. It was Emily Ruth's face floating over Lila's face. She smiled a very wicked smile at him, then looked positively . . . sad. Or guilty or something like that.

Lucas yelled out loud, without thinking. The sound just slipped out of his mouth. Everyone else jumped and the twins let out a short scream each. He wasn't sure if they'd seen the same thing he had.

The superimposed face vanished like a shadow. Lila looked at him with a dazed expression. He grabbed her by the shoulders and looked deeply into her eyes. It was her, all right. He examined her and saw she was holding the small chalkboard and a piece of chalk.

Lila looked stunned. She stared at the chalkboard and dropped the chalk on the table. It rolled away.

Suddenly all the French doors slammed shut, again startling people. They were clutching each other at this point. Jerry was fanning himself with a paper napkin. Jasper was adjusting his bow tie nervously. Then he patted Jerry on the back in comfort. Mrs. Schramke crossed herself and sat back in her chair looking stunned.

The electric lights sprang back up all at once, and several bulbs popped loudly—two of the wall sconces blowing completely.

Boy, talk about your power surge. Emily Ruth was a spike all on her own.

"Are you all right?" Lucas asked Lila, still holding her.

"I think so, I just went all blank."

They both looked at the chalkboard and there, in a very scripted style, was a design or a letter or something. Lucas took the board out of Lila's hands and turned it this way and that. The scribbling looked very familiar.

"What is it?" Earlene sounded shaky, and didn't seem as anxious to forge ahead into the unknown as she had previously, in Lucas's observation.

Lucas looked at the chalkboard again. Well, there wasn't any denying it, and there were six witnesses, so he better just face it.

"It's the letter *L*," he said. He held it up for

everyone to see. "And it's Emily Ruth's hand-writing."

A collective gasp went round.

"What does it mean?" Raylene asked. "It could be anything. It could be Lila, or Lucas, or Liverworst, you know?"

Lila had been rather quiet, and Lucas was watching her stare at her chalk-dusted fingers. She'd been the one that wrote it, but it was Emily Ruth guiding her hand.

Boy, Lucas had to remember after this to count his blessings when things were just quietly normal. Like having dinner at Nick's with Lila. They'd really had a great time just talking about Port Gamble history, about her job, and about anything but the murder of his ex-wife and who might have done it.

He put his arm around her and pulled her closer to him. "Jerry, can you get that bottle of port, please?" Lucas had seen Jerry turn seven shades of pale and figured the guy needed something to do, and a little nip wouldn't hurt Lila about now either.

Jerry jumped up and walked across the room quickly, retrieved the bottle, and returned to pour a bit in everyone's glass. Lucas handed

Lila her small glass and helped her take a sip. "There you go, that'll help. Steady there, girl."

"My heavens, that was the most dramatic demonstration I've ever seen. I once saw a misty cloud that felt as if it had a very human essence at a séance in Salisbury. What ever do you think she means, with the L? She's not pointing the finger at Lucas is she? I mean, I'm fairly clear it wasn't you who poisoned her, Mr. Griffin, even though you did have a nasty opinion of her and a bad tendency to express it in public. I trust Lila's judgment on this matter completely." Mrs. Gardiner chattered nervously.

"Thank you, Mrs. Gardiner." Lucas gave her a semi-sarcastic look. But the woman was obviously in a state. Who could blame her? He was most concerned about Lila, who still looked pale, and was very quiet.

The port Lucas gave her made her snap out of her fog. She'd had the oddest feeling, like someone had used her hand for a puppet. Lila stared at the chalkboard. It wasn't how she made her L's that was for certain.

She raised her head and looked at the people at the table, who were all excitedly talking to each other. Suddenly she wanted to be alone with Lucas.

"Hey, folks, it looks like the show is over. Let's get to the important part—dessert! My mother will grill me for an hour if I return any of that pie. Lucas made coffee and I'll pop the tea in the teapot for you, Jenny."

After letting poor Schatzie out of her kennel for everyone to fawn over, Lila hustled around and got everyone moving. She poured herself a strong cup of the Earl Grey tea. It smelled so good. So much preferable to the scent of Passion perfume. To that she added a piece of her mother's blackberry-blueberry pie. Lucas had one too, and he raised his eyebrows to Lila in serious approval of the pie.

"Mmm," he mumbled. When he'd finished his bite he added, "Can you cook like this?"

"When inspired," Lila replied. She dropped a blueberry down her shirt-front. Her nice white button-up stretchy cotton shirt. It left a blue dot. She'd just never be one of those perfect girls. Of course it would help if she didn't eat standing up. She sat down at the long table and settled into enjoying the pie with an amazing fork—the

Griffin family sterling silver no doubt. And this was the summer-house stuff.

Finally after a good hour, everyone decided to go home. They'd carpooled and each expressed gratitude they wouldn't be driving alone in the dark.

"That was much more exciting than Mystery Mondays, and now we have a real *live* mystery on our hands," said Jerry as he shook Lila's hand with two hands and he and Jasper headed out the door.

Lucas was over by the big beach-rock fireplace adding a couple of logs.

"Alone at last," Lila yelled, then ran toward him and threw herself into Lucas's arms, laughing.

He caught her and held her close. She thought maybe for a moment she'd overstepped herself. A strange idea when she thought of it. They'd been having intimate, revealing sex for days, but throwing herself into his embrace seemed too . . . clingy.

He made it funny, backing them up to the table and pouring them two small glasses of port with her in his arms. Then Lucas pulled her over to the big overstuffed blue-and-white ticking sofa near the fire. It melted under her like the down stuffed thing it was. The big, comfy couch.

He gathered the cashmere blanket that was usually folded over the side and wrapped it around her. "Can I get you anything, Lila?"

"This is good. Warmth. Calm," she murmured. Her body naturally curled into the large pillows and she burrowed in for comfort. Lucas sat beside her, balancing their glasses.

Schatzie, who had been cowering under the kitchen table, jumped on Lila's lap and snuggled in with the two of them. The dog heaved a sigh. Lucas handed Lila a glass and scratched Schatzie on her head.

"It's been one creepy night. I don't want to freak you out, but I saw Emily Ruth's face sort of floating in front of yours. Not like she was actually in you, but just outside of you. I don't mind telling you that seeing her face instead of yours isn't high on my list of things I want to experience." Lucas pulled her feet onto the sofa and slipped off her sandals with one hand while taking a sip of port. Very dexterous of him.

"I felt like she borrowed my hand to write that

letter. Couldn't she have just finished the word? I mean L for crying out loud. That's you, Lucas, or me, Lila with an L. She's got to get more specific! Like, *Lucas, I've been murdered by Prentice Cortland who 'done in' all his wives*. You know? Like *spell it out!*"

"This is your area of expertise, sweetie, not mine. Have you ever seen a ghost be so unclear?"

"I've read about it. Really, I've read where spirits hang out for a hundred years waiting for someone to get that they want to be buried under the apple tree back home in Indiana, not at Grassy Knoll Cemetery in Cleveland. So I'm thinking some ghosts are better at communicating than others.

"Kind of like people," Lucas said.

Lila went all quiet because she was thinking about how Lucas just called her sweetie. She wasn't sure whether to mention it or just enjoy it. Being wrapped in cashmere, sitting on his lap, sipping port, watching the fire she was leaning toward enjoying it. She also wondered how she ended up here.

"You sure are easy to be around, Lucas, I mean, don't get the wrong idea, but it's nice.

This is nice," Lila blurted out. She immediately regretted it.

"Back at ya, Abbott," he said, and toasted her. They clinked glasses and Lila felt warm all over. Schatzie closed her eyes and leaned her head on Lila's stomach.

Twelve

Monday morning the shit hit the fan. Or rather the Cheez Whiz hit the floor. And the windows and the walls. Lila figured they'd really stirred up Emily Ruth and somehow her ability to move and shake was at its peak during the corresponding hours of her death. But she must have started early today. It looked like a lively Monday for their recently dead customer.

Tom Boscov was sitting in a chair next to the video counter, crying. Actually sobbing in that grown man sob kind of way. Pilar was standing calmly beside him with a box of Kleenex. One of those boxes with little kittens on it. She'd set up a paper sack and Tom just kept drawing out tissues, bawling into them and tossing them in the paper sack. Then he'd try and talk and point to different parts of the store, which only served to make him cry again.

Pilar said soothing things in Spanish. She was just the kindest person Lila knew.

Maybe Emily Ruth didn't liked Lila driving her car. Lila had driven Emily Ruth's yellow Jag sedan to work. It had given her the willies all morning thinking of Emily Ruth's final shopping trip. Lucas had picked it up from the shop Friday and given her Jag driving lessons. It was just so, so funky to be driving around in her car, the car of the rich. Lila felt like a traitor to her townie roots.

These were the thoughts she was having standing next to Tom, still in her jeans jacket, holding her dinner cooler, wanting this to all go away. She also wasn't ready to walk down the condiment aisle and find out if Emily Ruth managed to complete her graffiti statement she'd started on the windows.

L-L-L, the infamous scripted L done up in Cheez Whiz graced the storefront windows, the floor of the produce department, and, well . . . God knows where else. She must have been practicing her L's since the early hours of the morning.

It wasn't going to go well for her if Emily Ruth had managed to spell out Lila on aisle two. There was a photographer from the *Gazette* poking around. Every few minutes a flash would create a splash of light. Great, they were going to print pictures of this mess in the local paper. Then it would be trial by gossip. Who knows, it might make the tabloids, although so far nothing in Port Gamble had ever grazed anything larger than the *Seattle Times* weather page regarding the big storm of December 1989.

But what if it were L for Lucas? Oh my God, Lila felt ashamed of herself for thinking of herself first instead of Lucas. That L just stuck with her like it was her own name. Even last night she didn't really think Emily Ruth was trying to spell out Lucas.

Lucas, with whom she'd spent a very intimate, wonderful weekend hanging around the Griffin beach estate, not talking about anything but breakfast or beach rocks or Griffin family stories, or her daughter Mallory.

Oh, how the lowly single-mom-grocery-clerk had gotten comfy at the rich folk's house. Of course the beach house had a real air of casualness to it, and it wasn't too hard to relax in all that casual comfortable rich stuff.

Oh my, yes, they'd been a freakin' Hallmark movie, walking the dog on the beach, frolicking in the kitchen with bakery treats, bacon, and eggs, which Schatzie had a particular taste for, and even doing laundry, since she'd been out of clothes. Lucas had even built an outdoor dog run for Schatzie with a shelter and a bed. They'd filled it with dog toys for when they were both away. They'd talked about getting Schatzie a pal. *That* was a scary conversation.

And then the late-night cozy fires. Those romantic fires in the big beach-stone fireplace.

This morning they'd had coffee and blueberry leftovers from her mom's bake-a-thon before Lucas left for the newspaper office. So domesticated. So easygoing. She'd gotten herself ready for work without even thinking of what day it was. She had felt contentment.

Maybe that's how Emily Ruth felt when she and Lucas were there. But that's not what Lucas had told her. She'd been restless and *dis*contented. Hard for Lila to imagine at the present time.

The ghostess with the mostest seemed to have

taken a small weekend break from haunting them at the Griffin house. She must have been saving it up for her Cheez Whiz graffiti moment today.

If Lila didn't know better she'd say Lucas seemed to be settling in, not making plans to leave in the fall. Saying little slips like . . . *we'll go to the Harvest Dance together in October as a pair of scarecrows*.

Of course it could be *LIAR, LIAR pants on fire* Emily Ruth was spelling out.

Lila got her courage up, handed Pilar her lunch, and stalked down to aisle two, her handbag slung over her shoulder, bumping her in the hip as she walked.

Nothing new here, just a sort of penmanship lesson where Emily Ruth kept practicing her L's. Lila tilted her head and walked the edges of the artwork, following it all the way into the produce department straight to, of course, the lemon bins. There, an intricate pattern of lemons and Cheez Whiz decorated a large portion of the produce department. But things got a little freakier at that point—the lemons were cut in half and sort of oozed juice in rivulets that puddled up against the Cheez Whiz letters, and . . . oh God, poor Larry.

Fran came from floral and stood beside Lila.

"I have never in my life seen anything this weird, Lila. I keep thinking someone must have done this—kids or something. But when I got here at six this morning, most of it was done. Pilar had watched almost the entire thing from five to six and well . . . the cans were still floating in midair—one at a time, as she drew the letters. Then at ten thirty-six everything just stopped. The cans dropped, and that was it. Maybe we're all hallucinating. Maybe there's acid in the water cooler or something. You do see this too, don't you?"

"I do. Where's Larry?"

"He's not here. Chuck is covering. No one has seen Larry today, but he's on the schedule. He probably cracked when he saw this, wouldn't you say?"

"I'd say. Poor guy. Well, this isn't some cleanup for amateurs. We're going to need a crew in here."

"Hold it, Lila, we're going to take some photos first." The photographer had walked down toward them without Lila even seeing him. "This is evidence now, you know. The chief is going to want to see this."

Speak of the devil, Chief Bob ambled passed the banana bins and headed her way.

"We've got to stop meeting like this, Chief," Lila joked.

"Being as I represent the law, I can't just blurt that out where anyone can hear me." Bob eyed Fran, who was all ears. "But it sure looks mighty spooky to me, off the record. Even so, this time we're going to do a little experiment. Me and my deputy would like to gather up all these Cheez Whiz cans and run them for fingerprints."

"Wow, that should be interesting." Lila crossed her arms and thought about that. Would Emily Ruth's fingerprints show up? Would someone else's? Could someone be one of those master illusionists that could make things fly around? They might find their *murderer* if the prints matched some deranged magician or something. "Well, you don't need my permission, help yourself. I was just telling Fran we'd have to hire in a crew for this mess. It's way bigger than last time. By the way, Bob, whatever became of the Prentiss Cortland connection?"

"Turns out he was seeing her and was even in the store when she died, purely by coincidence. He was talking wine with Ann Marie when it happened and didn't even know she was on the opposite end of the building. His story checks out, and it doesn't look like he had any motive at all. That's all we've got so far. Sorry, Lila. But we're going to do a secondary crime-scene sweep, so no cleanup crews for the day, please. We're having our own man take some more pictures, too."

"You mean the *Gazette's* photographer isn't good enough?"

"We look for different things. Like that name on the wall in the stockroom."

Lila's skin went all clammy. She didn't even ask whose name it was, she just ran to the back and through the plastic strips into the produce stock area.

Up on the back wall, dripping slightly, were large Cheez Whiz letters spelling out "LUCAS."

"Oh, *no*," she cried out. She stared at the writing on the wall. Her stomach flipped. Tears welled up in her eyes, blurring her vision of the orange accusation. That *bitch*. That spiteful, hateful dead woman. Lucas didn't kill her, Lila knew that deep in her heart. If Emily Ruth Griffin was alive right now, she'd kill her herself.

She wiped her eyes on her blouse sleeve.

"Pretty specific this time, wasn't she?" Bob was standing very close to her

She hadn't heard him enter and she jumped slightly, startled.

"Don't sneak up on me, Bob. We don't know that it was Emily Ruth that did this one; it could be someone alive and nasty. And if it were her, I don't know why she wrote it, but the woman was just as bad alive as dead."

"I noticed you were driving her yellow Jag this morning."

"So what. She's dead. She doesn't need it. Not that she's mentioned anyway. She didn't spell out JAG on the wall, did she?" Lila got all snippy. "By the way, did you ever track down the black car that tried to run me off the road?"

"Whoever it was they must be hiding the vehicle well. None of the body shops in town or in our area have had anything resembling that car."

"They could have caught the ferry into Seattle or driven the long way around to Olympia, you know. It's hard to miss a dented front fender with bright blue paint scrapes on it."

"We're still investigating."

The police photographer came in with the *Gazette* photographer on his heels. Behind both of them came Lucas.

He stopped in his tracks when he saw the wall. "Wow."

"Yeah, she finally got the last word in." Lila made light of it and poked Lucas in the ribs with her elbow. Then she did the stupidest thing, she burst out crying. Lila Abbott did not cry in public. Bob handed her a handkerchief, which made her ill to think about accepting. She waved him off.

Lucas gathered her up in his arms and held her.

"Don't worry, Sweetie, she's just being mean. It's not important," Lucas whispered to her.

"I was . . . supposed to . . . send her to *hell* by now," Lila said through her sobs. She couldn't seem to control her outburst of emotion. It welled up like a tidal wave. She sobbed against his clean white shirt.

"Shhh, watch what you say, Lila. The chief, here, will get the wrong idea. You mean convince her ghost to take a hike into the light, right?"

"Right," Lila hiccupped. Lucas could feel Lila getting herself more under control. She took a few deep breaths in, then stepped away from him and wiped her eyes on her shirtsleeves.

"I don't know what's wrong with me. I guess this is all starting to get on my nerves. I need to get out of here for a few minutes."

"Do you want company?" Lucas asked. He hadn't been with Lila that long, but the woman had nerves of steel as far as he'd seen. To see her cry was extremely unusual.

"No." Lila turned and ran through the plastic strips of the doorway, leaving them swinging in her wake.

"Chief, we need to talk." Lucas stared after her.

"No kidding," Bob replied.

"I'm not a guy that jumps right to otherworld-ly conclusions. And on my way in I was noticing a few things. One is my ex-wife's penmanship. She had a very distinctive script and the efforts in the aisles match it pretty well. But not this one." Lucas turned and gestured to the cheesy wall art. "This one isn't hers."

"Is that so? I can't tell you how relieved I am to have any kind of hard evidence to deal with. I'm getting gray hairs in places I've never thought of from this case."

The photographers had both been busy taking pictures of everything, including Lila's break-down. Lucas would get that picture away from Carter at the *Gazette* office later. Now, how the hell was he going to report on this incident if he was involved? He'd been sent to fill in for the out-sick feature writer. That would be conflict of interest. Unless he did it like . . . *his* side of the story.

But he wasn't much for exposing himself to the public at present. He'd have to call Brenda Stark and get her to cover this story, even if she did have the sniffles.

Lila ran down past the creative lemon and cheese art, out the automatic doors and into the sunlight. She took a deep breath of fresh air. It didn't help. She felt like the sky was pressing down on her.

Why was everything her problem? She was always going around fixing everyone's messes. Even people who weren't alive anymore. She just worked here. She just checked groceries and greeted customers. She wasn't a counselor for neurotic produce managers or a professional ghost buster or even a *wife* stuck with her husband's mess of an ex-wife. She'd known damn well when she got messed up with Lucas Griffin it would only lead to trouble.

She wanted her quiet life back. She wanted to see her daughter and her mom and dad. And *damn* her best friend Bonnie for being gone at a time like this. Lila felt herself about to have a damn-busting cry. Must be hormones or something, but she wasn't going to stand out here on the sidewalk where everyone could see her. She reached in her shoulder bag for the keys to the Jag. She'd just sit in the car for a while. It was in a quiet spot at the top of the parking lot where no one went very often.

Lila walked to the car and quickly rounded to the driver-side door, holding in a sob. But when she got to the side she noticed something.

"Damn, damn, damn!" She leaned against the car and smacked her fist on the roof. The front tire was flat as a pancake. No doubt Emily Ruth's handiwork. Or maybe she'd just run over a nail leaving Lucas's house. Or maybe her mysterious pursuer in the black sedan was back.

Now she was mad. Mad always trumped a crying fit. She took a Kleenex out of her purse and madly blew her nose, walking to the parking lot trash can to throw the soggy tissues away.

Keys dangling from her fingers like a wedding ring, she went back to the jag. She was no helpless female. She'd change the damn thing herself. Lila found the trunk lock and figured out which key opened it. This wasn't one of those new models with the lock buttons on the key. Lucas had bought a classic for Emily Ruth. A 1996 XJ Vanden Plas with the sleek Jag body, before Ford took it over, as he said yesterday.

There were blankets over the well where the spare was stored and she pushed them away so she could peel back the carpet and get to the spare. There was a tire iron on the side and she pulled on it, but it was stuck. She pulled harder and it popped out, making her stumble backward.

When she looked down in the trunk again something caught her eye on the side where the tire iron had been. Something bright orange. She reached in and pulled out . . . a can of Cheez Whiz. She dropped it like it was on fire.

Flipping back the blankets she ran her hand under the side carpet. There were at least four more cans, some empty, some not. Lila ripped away the black trunk carpeting. Half a dozen more cans revealed themselves. And there was something else. She felt the panic rise up like a lump of lead out of her chest and into her throat.

There was a jar of Creamy Jiff peanut butter. And there were maybe ten hypodermic syringes. She looked closely at one, without touching it. It had no needle, but an opening like you might use to give your cat medicine. Several had peanut butter inside of them. And glittering in the sun, pretty as you please, lay Emily Ruth's gold metallic alert bracelet. The bracelet of Lila's nightmare.

Her hand flew to her mouth. Her heart pounded and she felt faint. She shut the trunk and inched over to the driver-side door. Unlocking it she slid inside, safe for the moment in the cool white upholstered hiding place.

My God, my *God*, what did it mean? She leaned back against the seat. A thousand thoughts ran through her head. All the way from the possibility that she herself had a split personality and was insane but didn't know it, that she killed Emily Ruth—or that her other personality did

No wait, she remembered everything about her life today—coffee, blueberry cake, great sex with Lucas, feeding the dog, not necessarily in that order. And she had no blackouts or signs of orange-stained fingers or any of that.

Could Lucas really have killed her? She twisted her light red hair into a dreadlock on one side. Could her lover be a murderer? Emily Ruth had really done terrible things to him. Terrible. And he had hinted at blaming her for his brother's death—driving him to drink. Then there was his precious house, which he loved, and which was the only thing left connecting him and his parents and sister. His only thing of value since they cut him off.

No, no, it just couldn't be true. Someone was setting him up. Maybe even Emily Ruth. But ghosts don't usually open trunks and put such things inside them.

The car had just gotten back from the shop, for heaven sakes. Surely if he was the killer he'd be smart enough to take out all that . . . *evidence* before he handed the car to a mechanic, or even more so, to his new girlfriend.

Lila looked into her own eyes in the rearview mirror. She saw fear there. She wasn't a girl that did fear. If she told the chief about all this stuff, they might think Lucas was responsible.

But surely even Chief Bob wasn't that dumb. This was a setup, plain and simple. There may be a ghost in aisle two, but there was a real live person who killed Emily Ruth. And for the first time Lila was completely convinced that someone really did kill her. And whoever that was maybe wasn't too fond of *her* either, trying to run her off the road like that. Maybe he didn't like her chatting with the murdered ghost.

This could actually help clear Lucas—and herself. This stuff might have fingerprints on it. Oh great, she'd touched one. Well, they could take her prints and compare them to anything else they found. Maybe on the *trunk* even.

Oh wait, she and Lucas had washed the car in one of their domestic scenes just a few days ago. *Damn* it. Even so, there was probably something good for them to work with in there.

She opened the door and went to find the chief.

Lucas was standing outside talking on his cell phone.

"Lila"—he excused himself for a moment from whomever he was talking to—"Are you okay? I wondered where you went." He caught her arm.

"I've got something I want you and the chief to see. Follow me."

Lucas finished his call and followed her over to Bob.

"Bob, you need to see something. Walk to the back parking lot with me," she said.

Bob nodded toward the door and followed her. Lucas wasn't sure what to make of Lila's behavior. Maybe someone had a fender bender in the parking lot and she witnessed it. He'd had a few near misses himself in the Market Foods lot.

Lila led them to the pale yellow Jag. Damn, Lucas thought, he'd just paid four hundred bucks to get that thing tuned up. He sure didn't need body work on top of it. If someone dented the car, it was going to stay dented for a while.

He noticed the flat tire. "Oh, man, that's too bad Lila, but I can change it for you, you don't need Bob, here, he's a busy guy. It's a one-man job." Lucas stared at the extremely flat tire. It must have gotten a hell of a puncture. He felt some thoughts creep in like maybe someone slashed it on purpose. But why?

She didn't say anything, just opened the trunk with the key.

Bob looked in, scratched his head, and stood there for a while. Lucas came up behind him.

"Shit!" Lucas sucked in a breath and uttered a curse.

They both took a long look. Lucas started to reach in. Bob caught his arm. "Don't touch anything."

Then he did the oddest thing, he pulled a set of cuffs off his belt and slapped them on Lucas's wrists.

"Lucas Griffin, you are under arrest in connection with the murder of Emily Ruth Griffin."

Thirteen

Bob rattled off the Miranda rights. "You have the right to remain silent and refuse to answer questions. Anything you do say may be used against you in a court of law. You have the right to consult an attorney before speaking to the police and to have an attorney present during questioning now or in the future.

"If you cannot afford an attorney, one will be appointed for you before any questioning if you wish. If you decide to answer questions without an attorney present you will still have the right to stop answering at any time until you talk to an attorney. Do you understand all of these rights as I have presented them?" Bob said all that extremely fast.

"Bob, get real," Lucas said. "Why would I leave this stuff in her car?" Lucas had that déjà vu feeling of being arrested from when he was a kid. It wasn't a good feeling.

Lila was clearly not expecting this result. She screamed at Bob. "Bob, you *ass hole*. Lucas didn't kill her; I brought you over here so you could find out who *did*. Check this stuff for prints!"

Lucas looked at Bob. "Wow, I've never heard her curse," he said.

"Me neither," Bob said gruffly. "Look, Lucas, I have to detain you. There's no other way this can go down. The county guys would be calling me names worse than they already are."

"I'm seeing that," Lucas said calmly.

Lila was yanking on Bob's arm, yelling loudly. "Let him *go*, let him go you moron!"

"Lila, shut up and get in the back of the squad car. Don't make me cuff you. I promised your dad I wouldn't do that in public." Bob shoved her gently away.

"Watch it, Chief, I'll have to punch you if you hurt her in any way," Lucas said

"Duly noted. Now Lila, just calm down and come with me. I'm not arresting you, but you'll be safer in a jail cell than not." Bob got on his walkie-talkie and told his deputy to meet him by the Jaguar. They waited there for him, but Lila was yammering at Bob the entire time about what an incompetent ninny he was and how she was going to get Bernice Jensen to sue him for false arrest. Lucas felt a smile creep over his lips.

"Lila, it's okay, we'll get out of this. You know I didn't kill her, and maybe this stuff will help. Someone must have planted this in the trunk. After all, the car was in the garage parking lot for days. Very open to access. Bob, you should check to see if the trunk has been jimmied."

"I'll keep that in mind."

"Why don't you call Bernice and Stanley on my cell phone and they can come down to the station." Lucas gestured with his head to his jacket pocket. She reached in and pulled out his phone.

"I'm so sorry, Lucas, I had no idea Bob would do this." She sounded a notch less hysterical, but not much. Her voice was terse and angry: Irish redhead angry.

"Lila, I've got Stanley programmed into my phone under L-A-W, okay?" He was really just keeping her busy. He knew he'd be allowed a phone call at the station. She must not have had much of a cell signal from her motions. She stepped a few steps away.

"Lila, don't move or I'll have to shoot you," Bob said drolly.

"Shut up, you ass," Lila snapped and turned her back on them. She must have reached Stanley because she started in talking, gesturing with her arm in the air in a very animated way.

She was a live wire, that was for sure. And here she'd gone and gotten him arrested. God help the chief.

Two deputies showed up, one out of the store and one came screaming through the parking lot in his car, speeding up behind the Jag. Bob had to move Lucas out of the way. Lila jumped clear, too.

The officer got out of the squad car.

"Norm, if you do that again I'll fire you," Bob said.

"Sorry, Chief. I thought since you apprehended Griffin here, it was an emergency."

"Yeah, and Lord knows we don't get enough of those around here. Take Miss Abbott to your car and put her in the back, no cuffs, and no unnecessarily rough handling. I'm going to take Lucas with me. Barnes, you get a forensic kit for the contents of the Jag trunk, and make sure it's all done well. I don't want to lose even the slightest hair out of there, do you hear me? Then dust the car for prints and look for anything out of the ordinary besides what's in the trunk. Then tow it to the impound and we'll finish there."

"Gotcha, Chief."

Barnes took Lila by the arm and jerked his head toward the car. "It'll be okay, Lila, I'll be there in a few minutes, and this gentleman will drive safely instead of like a teenage jock, won't you, Norm?" Lucas called to her.

Norm just gave him a look.

"I'm so sorry, Lucas," Lila's voice broke. "Stanley will meet you at the station."

God, he just wanted to hold her and make everything better. But at the same time he wanted to detangle himself from her life to protect her. All he'd brought her was heartache and craziness. Before he'd gotten involved with her she probably played bingo on Saturday nights and had a nice quiet life. She didn't need this kind of trouble—going to jail.

But honestly, the thought of her in jail at the

moment didn't upset him that much because at least she'd be safe. If someone got into the Jag that way, planting all that stuff, well she was just so vulnerable. Of course it was most likely done while the car was at Roy's garage.

The whole off-the-road shove had been in the back of his mind every minute they'd been together this weekend. Even though he'd thought about showing her some of the papers he'd been gathering, he'd decided they'd both needed a crime-free, ghost-free weekend, and it had been great.

It was getting more and more obvious that someone very alive was out there and they were getting more and more deranged. Whoever it was must think Lila was getting messages from the ghost of Emily Ruth, and that made him, or her, very nervous.

Lucas walked tall beside the chief as the few people in the parking lot of Market Foods stared and whispered. In his business they used to say all press is good press, but he'd not found that true in his personal life so far.

When this was all over he was going to get out of this town and let Lila Abbott get back to normal.

* * *

Lila speed-dialed Bernice on her own cell phone.

"Bernice Jensen's office," her assistant, Rolly, answered.

"Rolly, this is Lila Abbott. I'm being arrested, or something."

"Oh dear, Bernice is out back in the garden. I'll send her right over, Lila, don't you worry."

"Thanks, Rolly, and tell her that my friend Lucas Griffin has been taken in as well. It's all my fault and I should be horsewhipped, I am such an idiot."

"Say no more, I'll take care of it. Chin up there, Miss Abbott."

"Thanks." Lila clicked off the phone. Rolly was from England too, but had a much more refined accent than Jenny Gardiner. Lots of Brits ended up in Port Gamble via Canada. Boy, it was amazing where her mind went when she was stressed. Just rambled all around. But it was Canada and Bonnie she was really thinking about. At times like these a girl needs her best friend and her parents—and Lucas, but he was busy.

Bonnie was probably up there being chased by some Mountie. She'd call her, but what was the point? All Bonnie would do is drop everything and run to Lila's side to hold her hand. Then she'd screw up her buying trip and basically make a pitiful nuisance of herself, as usual.

Lila sat quietly in the back of the squad car. She'd never really been in trouble before this. Except for getting pregnant, and that wasn't illegal, although it should be, she smirked to herself.

Always someone had come to her rescue. Sure she'd been a single mom, but mostly she'd been a kid living with her parents or next to them, who had a kid and they all took care of her while she took care of Mallory.

Even Bonnie was her rescuer sometimes. Now it was Lucas, apparently, although all it ever got him was a ton of trouble.

It was time for her to stand up on her own two feet. First thing she'd need to do is get herself out of this mess. Then she was going to take a long look at her connection to Lucas. Why was she with him anyhow, besides just a summer fling? To comfort herself in the wake of losing her daughter to college? Maybe it was revenge of the townie girl.

She took a long look in the mirror—the rearview mirror of the police car to be exact—and didn't like what she saw. For one thing, she needed some lipstick.

She dug in her handbag for a compact and a lipstick tube and noticed her hand was shaking when she twisted her "Baby" pink lipstick. That was *it* all over. She was a baby. She was naive and stuck in her little townie life. Imagine showing that stuff to the chief and thinking it would help clear Lucas. How naive was that?

She better smarten up in a whole lot of ways. Bonnie had always said that she was living in her own little dream world. And her answer had always been . . . don't wake me up.

When they reached the police station she saw that Lucas was being taken in the door. She bolted away from the stupid deputy after he let her out the car door and ran over to Lucas.

"Lucas, I was such an idiot to think that showing Bob that stuff would help. I'm really not this stupid, usually."

"You're not stupid. I love you, Lila Abbott." He leaned over and kissed her.

She looked up to see the police photographer snapping a picture.

"Oh, real nice, are you going to sell that to the *National Enquirer* or something? This is small-town crap buddy, so don't count your scandal money yet."

Lucas laughed at her. She rolled her eyes and looked sheepish. "I have a tendency to lash out when I'm pissed off."

Bob gave him a yank toward the door.

"Later, Abbott."

"Later, Griffin." Lila was captured by Norm who must have been a little peeved at her for running off by the way he held her arm. She felt kind of giddy because—Lucas had just told her he loved her. And she hadn't even replied.

"Ah-ah, there, Norm, no police brutality." She shook her arm and he loosened up.

"Sally, I need you to process Mr. Griffin here as an arrest. I'm going to lunch," Bob said to the female deputy behind the desk. "And no photographs. Tell that idiot Jeff to knock off the paparazzi routine. His job is to take crime-scene photos. That should be enough."

Lila walked next to Deputy Norm, who she could tell was still pissed. "She's a runner, Sal, lock her up."

Bob gave him an exasperated look. "I'll take

Lucas into the holding room, you put Lila somewhere safe. She's not arrested, but consider her
detained. Take her prints, too. We need them.
And give them both some lunch after you take
prints. We don't want them starving. But keep
them apart, okay?" Bob said all this as he headed past Lila and took Lucas down the hall. Lila
saw he'd taken the cuffs off Lucas.

"Sure, sure, Chief. Hi, Lila, remember me?
Sally Jo Johanson. We went to high school together."

"Wow, Sally, you look great!"

"Yeah, dropped thirty pounds and found my
inner cop. Don't worry, I'll take good care of
you."

There was no escaping the fact that this town
would always take care of her, she sighed
quietly.

Sally gently led Lila through the humiliating
process of having her fingerprints taken, and all
the corresponding paperwork. They gossiped
about the McInnis boys and Sally confessed that
her divorce from Bart Witherspoon was final
and she was dating Dave, the cute one. And that
he was great with her two kids. Wow, good gossip, Lila thought.

After the bad part, Sally had salads and sodas from the Port Gamble Café delivered. Lila sat with Sally at her desk. No cell for her, she guessed. Sally took Lucas's lunch to him, her keys jangling. She wondered how he was doing.

"I'm here for Lucas Griffin." A guy that looked like someone's crusty old grandpa in a rumpled suit stood at the railing.

"Hey, Rooster, how's business?"

"Bernice called me. She's on her way, Lila," said Rooster. "She had to build a shade screen for her pumpkin. They say we're in for a rise in temperature and she's aiming to win this year's competition."

"Why do pumpkins need shade?" Sally asked, letting Rooster in the gate.

"They crack in the heat."

"Oh." Sally looked funny at Lila, then led the attorney down to Lucas's room.

When she returned, Lila was waiting. "Rooster? What happened to Stanley?"

"That is Stanley, also known as Rooster Millard, best criminal attorney in the area." Sally settled back down and popped her can of root beer open. "Damn, this case is a stumper. I heard the dead lady has really been making everyone nuts, mostly you. Did you know we have more ghosts in Port Gamble than any town in Kitsap County? Probably because of all the historic buildings."

"I'm thinking that must be it. I read a book about local haunts and half of them were here. Kind of spooky, isn't it?"

"Hey, its worse for you, you actually see them. Have you seen her?"

"Yup, she decided to make her first appearance over the bed where Lucas and I had been well . . . it was a surprise visit," Lila laughed.

"I woulda had a heart attack. I wonder if she's trying to tell you who murdered her. Or maybe who knocked her up. You'd be a person to turn to on that one, Lila." Sally took a stab at her salad.

Lila, for once in her life, didn't say a word. *Knocked her up?* Oh God, that was really sad. It made her sad. Her murderer probably didn't know she was pregnant. That was just *so* sad. Or maybe he *did* know. That was even worse.

And more than that, she knew without a doubt this was the missing piece of information they were holding back. Sally just assumed she knew. "I do think she's been trying to tell me that. She pulled a christening gown down from the closet one night," Lila baited Sally to tell her more.

"Wow, really? We've all been trying to figure out what happened to the baby. She must have put it up for adoption, but we can't find any records or anything. I mean it's been at least three or four months since she had it according to the autopsy."

Lila practically choked. "Um, wow, she really lost the weight, didn't she?"

"Emily was always thin as a rail. It must have really bugged the crap out of her being pregnant."

"You know, I didn't see her around all last spring. She must have holed up in the Griffin estate," Lila said.

"Well, someone must have seen her, she had to eat, unless she ordered in twenty million Lean Cuisines for the fat months. I sure as hell didn't trim down very fast after my second kid, but the first, I lost it pretty fast," Sally said.

"I gained like fifty pounds, but over the years I've gotten at least thirty of it off. That leaves a nice extra twenty." Lila patted her hip and made small talk like a champ. Oh *God*, Lucas needed to hear this. Where was Bernice anyhow? To hell with her pumpkin.

Bob walked by and headed for Lucas's room. He hadn't heard a thing. Wow, somebody up there must like her. Poor Emily Ruth, it was all just clear as a foggy mirror now. She was worried about her baby. Where the heck was that baby? And whose baby was it?

Sally was talking about her divorce, which gave Lila time to just nod and say "men are pigs" once in a while. She needed to think.

Well, unless Lucas hadn't told her something, it sure wasn't his baby. Lila thought over everything that had happened: the way Emily Ruth had kept the Griffins from protesting her life estate by saying she was pregnant with the brother's child; the christening gown given to her by Mrs. Griffin; the supposed miscarriage; the Cheez Whiz; the L's and the cans in the car trunk complete with the peanut butter syringes; the fact that Emily Ruth had been hiding a pregnancy and that she was going out on a date—it was all so confusing. If she had told Mrs. Griffin she was pregnant, why didn't she just have the baby and keep it? It would have assured her claim on the beach house. Lucas said she'd told the family she'd miscarried.

That Monday was probably the first day Emily Ruth had been out for months. Out to get the ingredients for a gourmet dinner for Prentice Cortland. Out to snag herself another rich summer guy. Lila's head spun with all the information.

"... And then he just blurted out that the panties belonged to Brenda Stark, you know, the chick reporter at the newspaper office? I took out my service revolver and pointed it straight at his dick and slowly pulled back the safety. You should have seen him. It was the funniest thing I've ever seen. He ran like a buck being chased by a mountain lion." Sally, laughing until she spurt root beer out her nose, slapped at the table and continued, "Of course I wouldn't have actually shot him."

Lila laughed with her. She'd heard that part, for sure. She had to admit the thought of Bart Witherspoon running for dear life from his crazed cop wife was a good image. He'd cheated on her, the dickhead.

Bernice came in the door, overalls and all. Lila wanted to bounce up and down in her chair and go *"Oh-oh-oh! Me-me-me!* I know, I know!" But she didn't do that. She just stood up and took her root beer with her.

"Hey, Bernice."

Sally opened the gate and let her through.

"Sorry, Lila, I was knee-deep in pumpkin vines."

Lila smiled at her. "Oh, hey, there's a green thing with legs on your bandanna. Hold still." She reached over and plucked it off. It was one of those strange leafy bugs.

"Thanks, Lila. You haven't been chatting too much with Sally here, have you? Remember, she's still a cop."

"Oh, no, we were just swapping girl stories," Lila said calmly. She was feeling very calm for the first time in days. She gave Sally a little elbow in the ribs and Sally laughed. "Sally, do you have a room where Bernice and I can talk? She's got to tell me all her pumpkin secrets."

"Sure, this way." Sally led them to another room down the same hall as Lucas.

"Oh, and Sal, can you call my mom and tell her I'm in jail again, and could she go pick up the dog from Lucas's house and keep it till I'm out?"

"Sure, and be sure and holler if you want

out or you need to pee or something. I've got to lock you in otherwise Bob will yell at me." Sally clucked and closed the door behind Lila and Bernice.

"What's up?" Bernice could sense Lila's excitement.

"You know that saying 'loose lips sink ships'? Well, Sally just sank a big fat ocean liner. Sit down, I'll tell you all about it."

Lucas had seen plenty of lawyers but, he had to say, that Rooster Millard was one of the sharpest tacks he'd ever met. Apparently this down-home rumpled façade was a great cover and led to people underestimating him. They'd made quite a bit of progress in their short conversation.

"Mr. Millard, I don't like what's been happening. Her slashed tire on top of the road incident is a warning. I thought I could protect her but I'm not so sure. I think this thing is going to get worse."

"We can count on that. With everything you've told me, I think we've got a lunatic out there and he, or she, is about to blow. But we need to draw this person out. If you both walk, then the whole setup hasn't worked and they'll have to try something else. That's my theory anyhow."

"So what, that makes Lila a sitting duck? I don't like that. We need to get the chief moving on what we've talked about. Then maybe we won't have to do any of this."

"I think it's our best course of action. We've got to have you out on bail quick so we can go shake the bushes. Judge Hunt is hearing arraignments at the county courthouse this week. We're golfing buddies. I'll check with his bailiff and see if she can get us a hearing this afternoon. All we need is the prosecutor and a judge and we're set. We'll wave the reading, like I said, plead not guilty, and get you back on the street fast."

"And what about Lila?"

"She'll be fine. Bob hasn't actually pressed charges on her anyway. He just wants you both where he can find you. She is officially a person of interest and he can detain her for about twenty-four hours. That should be enough."

"I want her safe in jail."

"If things go beyond today we'll set up a body guard for Lila. And we'll set up a real live mousetrap for our rat. Having Emily Ruth come back from the grave is really working in our favor."

"Speak for yourself, Mr. Millard." Lucas ran his hand over his forehead.

"Call me Rooster, son, everyone else does. I knew your grandfather, did you know that? He and I used to go fishing together. Your dad too, and your uncle."

"Really? I miss them all. I'm going back to California when this is over and put things right. The whole family has a strong connection with the house here and it was partially my fault it ended up in Emily Ruth's hands, as I told you. I'm sorry she died, but I'm not sorry that the house is back in the family. I've done my job."

"I hear you, Lucas. Now let's call over to the bailiff and see if we can get you on the docket. As I recall bailiff Margo has a weakness for chocolate-covered cherries and she knows I always bring her a box. But if you're stuck, we'll get you a cell in the county lockup with a view of Port Orchard and try again in the morning," Rooster said.

"At least Emily Ruth's ghost won't be haunting the jail." Lucas had the superstitious foresight to knock on wood after he said that.

Fourteen

The Indian summer heat wave started early with a sunset that made the old jail soar up into the nineties, and for Lila that was just too damn hot to sleep. Not that she could sleep anyhow, even with Sally's great contributions: a goose down pillow and a very clean set of sheets on the small cot.

If her daughter could see her now—her mother in jail. What kind of mom ends up in jail? Maybe she could keep her daughter from ever hearing about this. No, that would be wrong. She'd have to know. Family secrets sucked.

Lila's mother had dropped by with a tooth-

some women's prison. She'd take one more rescue before she got on with being independent—
please?

A strange light flickered across the way. Probably the mercury vapor lights of the high school football field half a mile away. Wait, school hadn't started. There weren't any football games yet. Lila watched with curiosity as the flickering came closer and closer.

It came up right to the edge of the lot, then like some kind of creature, it sped right to her window. She covered her eyes it was so bright, and the glare beamed in the cell as if someone had a floodlight pointed in the room. Lila instinctively moved to the side.

She looked out the window again and what she saw made her blood run cold. A shiver moved over her entire body. The face of Emily Ruth floated there in the light. And Emily Ruth was crying. She cried hard, and loud, and her sobs filled the room with echoes. Lila could see tears shimmering on the clear, misty image of Emily Ruth. If she didn't know better, she'd have thought it was a movie effect.

Lila knew, in a flash of a second, that Emily Ruth was filled with remorse. She had done something she regretted and it pained her to her very soul. The sobs turned into screams and Lila had to cover her ears.

Then everything went black again.

"Lila? Are you okay?" It was Sally at her cell door. "What the hell was that?"

Lila pulled the velour blanket off the cot and wrapped it around herself. A chill had replaced her overheated condition. "*That* was Emily Ruth. Apparently she makes house calls. Or jail calls. Sally, where is Lucas?"

"He's been arraigned and released into Rooster's custody. Oh, I'm probably not supposed to tell you that, but I'm terrified beyond the ability to think." Sally opened the cell door. "Want a cup of cocoa?"

"Sure. Are you on night duty tonight?"

"Only when there's a prisoner. That'd be you. Can't you sleep? Of course, who could think with that sort of thing going on. How do you handle these spirits, Lila, I'm a hard-ass girl and I just can't even wrap my head around it."

"Weirdly, I'm more curious than afraid. So I just barge in there to see what's going on and there you go, I'm in the middle of it." She shivered. "So, Sally, why can't I be in someone's custody? There aren't any charges against me, are there?"

"Hmm, I've probably already said too much, Lila. Everyone just wants you where you are safe and sound."

"How about my mother's house?" Lila asked. "Her cooking is better."

Sally had filled a hot pot and punched down the button to make it heat up. "Too dangerous. There are theories flying around. They were all buzzing about some theory. Someone tried to run you down, you know."

"Lucas didn't, oh, say I murdered his ex, did he? Because I didn't."

"I can't tell you anymore, Lila. I've already gotten in trouble for a few things I spilled." Sally gave her a look. "But Lucas Griffin sure is cute, isn't he? For a summer boy, I mean. Although they *were* always cuter than the townie boys."

"Yes, he's cute, just like the cute boy who got me pregnant at sixteen. They're *all* cute in the dark, then they leave."

"Don't we all know it? And I heard him tell Rooster he was going back to California when this was all over," Sally said casually.

Lila was getting as steamed as that hot pot. Oh he was, was he? That was just swell. Apparently he had it on good authority he wasn't going to be arrested for the murder of his ex-wife. If that rat ratted her out to save his own ass, *she'd* die and come back and haunt him forever. Then he'd have both her and Emily Ruth on him. A regular dead-chicks convention. He'd just hate that. She almost laughed out loud, but a part of her inside was just . . . dying. She felt sick.

She *would* haunt him, she knew that. Dead *or* alive, he wouldn't forget their time together quickly. She wiped away a tear.

They had theories. *Theories*, those bastards. A bunch of men keeping her in here just so she didn't screw up whatever game they were playing.

Oh, did she really need a guy in her life who thought it would be better if she were kept in jail? Except, if Lucas had done that horrible thing and implicated her, then wouldn't they have already charged her with murder? No doubt she wouldn't be sitting here having hot chocolate with Sally. Besides, that would mean *he* killed Emily Ruth, and Lila knew that just wasn't the case. So they must be on a wild goose chase. Well, he could just have his California goose.

Sally handed her a hot cup of cocoa made from a packet. There were tiny little marshmallows floating in it. She slurped some of them. She felt miserable. Her thoughts were so confused.

"Thanks, Sally," Lila said. She sat quietly while Sally went on about ghosts and Port Gamble and how the girl that ran the theater said the second story was haunted for sure, but that probably she didn't care because she was so eccentric anyhow, and that the Walker-Ames house where the mill manager used to live has been haunted by his youngest daughter since she died in 1908.

Lila lost the rest of it as she thought about maybe . . . escaping. It's not like she was charged with anything; they were just being good-ol' boys and keeping her safe. And she sure as hell didn't owe Lucas Griffin any loyalty. She could take care of herself. She'd been doing it for thirty-three years, with a little help from friends and family.

Of course, she was in a SpongeBob sleep shirt and had no shoes. But her house was really only about four blocks from here, and she knew all the back porches and trails and trees to hide behind. She was a *townie*! Townie girls were tough.

At home she could take a nice shower, maybe call Lucas and tell him what a giant prick he was; that kind of thing.

Her mother would say to just follow the rules and everything will come out well in the end. But that hadn't always worked for her. Her life had been ass-backwards for quite a while now, and she might as well embrace it.

"Um, Sal, I'm getting kind of tired. How about I hit the sack. And I know it's against the rules, but can you leave the cell door open? I don't want to be trapped in there if the dead ex-Mrs. Griffin comes back to play." Lila got up out of her chair, cocoa and all.

"Wow, I guess. Sure, Lila. I'll flake out in the big chair back in Bob's office and you yell to me if that woman's ghost comes back. I've never seen anything like that in my entire life." Sally stood up and took her own cocoa with her. "I'm damn tired anyhow. Ol' Dave's been wearing me out."

They both snort-laughed and patted each other on the back, but Lila was faking it. She felt guilty, but she'd have to apologize to Sally later.

There was a chance Sally would actually let her go based on her distain for stupid men, but then again, Sally was a cop and she did have her limits. No use testing them. Officer Sally Jo Johanson was armed, even if she'd have to put down the cocoa to get to her revolver.

Lila faked herself into the cot, fussing with the blankets and groaning. If she hadn't been all jazzed up with ghost adrenaline, cocoa, and escape thoughts, she probably could have gone to sleep. It was about 1:30 according to the historic old clock on the historic old police department office wall.

She laid low and thought about whether her actions would result in something bad down the road. Something her mother had trained her to do over the years.

She'd been playing it safe and careful for the last seventeen years, making up for her one mistake. Stifling every impulse, following every rule. Wow, that was getting old. Lila smiled to herself. No one would ever suspect her of sneaking out of jail. It just wasn't in her nature.

When she heard Sally snoring, she threw back the sheets and grabbed the blanket off the cot to be her coat. It was gray velour and no one would see her in the dark night. SpongeBob had that glow-in-the-dark tendency. Her stuff was locked up in some police locker, so she'd have to forgo the cell phone and purse. No time to dress, she'd get clean clothes at home anyhow.

Without as much as a rustled paper, she walked out of the cell, hopped over the low railing, waltzed on out the door, and closed it quietly behind her.

The sliver of a moon added a nightlight along with a million pinpoints of stars to lead her home. Her bare feet squished into the soft grass of the Port Gamble lawns patchworking the town from one end to the other. Most folks were sleeping and she knew who wasn't. She also knew who had dogs and who didn't. She really did love this town.

All her sneaking-out-at-night skills came back to her. She remembered her mother saying, "*Now Lila, nothing good ever happens after midnight when you're a teenager.*" Oops, too late, but the exhilaration was the best. It was just like she'd gone back to being sixteen and running wild in the secret parts of town. Parts only teenagers knew about—like the big maple tree on the edge of the graveyard. It was so huge and wide you could climb up inside and practically lie down.

That's where Mallory was conceived, in a tree. Lila giggled. Teenagers can have sex anywhere. They used to hang an apple by a string from a particular branch to let other horny teenagers know the tree was in use.

Either that or in the back of William Shaul the Third's father's sleek black Jag. And here she'd been driving one. That was really strange.

Sweet William, whose kisses had made her completely, insanely wild. Wild enough to let him go all the way. Wild enough to believe a condom did its job.

No one had made her feel like that again. Until recently, that is. It was just possible that Lucas Griffin was the best kisser ever. Of course, this must be his cue to exit, stage right. Dump the girls and make them cry.

Must be the cool night air and the hint of danger making her remember these things. She reached her own house and fumbled for the hidden key under the ceramic cat on the front porch.

As quietly as possible she slipped in her own front door and closed it behind her. She heaved a big sigh of relief. She wanted to dance a little happy dance having given the lot of them the slip.

Maybe she'd take a shower, have a nap, then stroll back over there in the morning after a stop-off at The Port Bakery. Bring Sally some bear claws or something, stick her tongue out at them all. Damn, she was hungry. Salad never really did it for her, and by the time they'd had dinner she'd lost her appetite.

Maybe she'd just whip up some scrambled eggs and toast right now. A little comfort food. She slipped off the jail blanket and grabbed her slippers out of the tiny downstairs closet—the fuzzy blue ones, and they felt great on her bare feet.

Something rustled. Something made a footstep. A rush of fear shot through Lila. She quietly edged toward the sound. It was coming from the kitchen. Probably a rat or something. Or like one other night, a rat named Lucas Griffin.

She hadn't turned any lights on and her eyes had adapted to the dark. Pressing herself against the wall she peered around the doorframe into the unlit kitchen. A figure stood very close to her, just to her right. She stopped breathing, almost ready to scream. But then she realized who it was.

"Oh my God, you scared me to death." She took a deep breath in and pressed her hand to her chest. "Hey, what the hell are you doing in my . . . ?"

A frying pan?

A frying pan came swinging at her like some kind of horrible cartoon, so fast she didn't even *think* to duck. In a split second she fought to keep herself together, then sank deep, deep into a painfully dark hole.

Duct tape—aisle nine. Household Goods. Lila's eyes flew open and she found herself staring into the bottom of a metal rack—after the fog cleared a bit from her vision. Her mouth was taped shut, her hands were taped in front of her, all the way from her wrists to her fingertips, and from what she could feel above the splitting headache, her legs were taped together, too. She was lying on her back on the cold black and white tiles of Market Foods. How extremely strange.

It was amazing to her how fast she figured out exactly what was going on. It must be about 2:30

A.M., when the store was closed for about three hours, from 1:30 to 4:30. Then the bakery crew would come in and start baking for the day, and the doors opened at five.

Larry was tidying up the wrappers from the duct tape, tucking them in his blue vest pockets.

Larry. Larry? Larry. L L L. For heaven sakes, why would Larry kill Emily Ruth?

Wow, she might have instincts when it came to ghosts, but her instincts about live people just sucked. Larry put on a pair of store work gloves and grabbed her feet and dragged her down the aisle, which made her nightgown ride up. Her mother was right, nothing good happens after midnight. Except maybe with Lucas. She also always said wear clean underwear in case you are hit by a car. Or hit over the head with a frying pan and kidnapped by some lunatic produce manager.

Lila felt calm for some reason, even as Larry muttered and dragged her down the main back aisle. But then again, that was what she did when things were really bad, get very calm.

Gosh, she could almost figure out what he was going to do with her. It either involved lemons or Cheese Whiz. He was going to try and make it look like Emily Ruth killed her. Or Lucas maybe.

She didn't know how long she had, but she better do some thinking while she could. He obviously knew she wasn't dead.

Larry wasn't that strong and it was a whole lot of work to drag her. He had to stop a couple of times to catch his breath. She lost one fuzzy blue slipper at the end cap with the Progresso soup. Wow, two-for-one sale. She liked Progresso, especially the chicken dumpling.

Lila made herself as heavy as possible. That was sort of interesting you could do that. Deadweight. You know, Larry was getting really sloppy. Here's this guy who went from the extremely subtle injecting of peanut butter into Cheez Whiz cans on the random chance Emily Ruth would pop a demo cracker in her mouth, banking on her weakness for cheese, to taping a woman's hands together. Like the tape wouldn't show. Like a ghost was going to tape someone up.

She still couldn't figure out why Larry Pierson would target a woman like Emily Ruth. Maybe he had a thing for her. They'd always connected on a neat-freak level. And produce. Emily Ruth always gushed about Larry's produce.

Wait, wait. Sally was saying that Emily Ruth must have holed up in the house while she was pregnant, and where the heck did she get her food? Could Larry have been her delivery boy? Did Emily Ruth share her secrets with Larry? Wow, she probably used him like she used everyone, then off she went to Prentice Cortland.

As if Emily Ruth would go for a guy like Larry. And hello, he was *married*.

Poor Larry. Smitten with the beautiful Emily Ruth. Of course she was only guessing. They passed the frozen-food aisles in the center of the store. Brrr.

Wow, she regretted sneaking out of jail. Sally was probably still asleep.

Where was that bitch of a ghost when she needed her? Oh, and where was that rat of a summer fling of hers, Lucas? Probably on a plane back to Los Angeles. Yep, long gone, slam, bam, see ya ma'am.

At least the dead chick could make a nice appearance about now and scare Larry to death. It would be only fitting. She'd been trying to tell them all that Larry was the guy for weeks now. How about making a spectacle of herself now? Or a specter as the case may be.

Lila thought back to her dream of the lemons and the bracelet, which they never found, and all that Cheez Whiz and, for heaven sakes, did a whole rack of condiments have to fall on her before she figured it out?

That's probably what Larry had in mind, as he parked her next to the olives, Cheez Whiz, and pickles. Probably didn't want to sully up his own aisles. That murdering weasel. Well, she wasn't going to go down easy.

Lila sat straight up and screamed at him through her duct tape. He fell backward he was so startled. She wriggled like a fish and tried to kick him.

"Stop that, Lila. I didn't *want* to hurt you. You've always been so nice to me. But she made me. She wouldn't leave it alone. Pretty soon you'd figure it out."

Lila arched an eyebrow at him and cocked her head.

Larry crouched next to her.

"You see, that woman, she was the devil. She was evil, and she's a demon now. She's haunting me night and day and you, too. We need some peace. I can't have you telling people I killed her. I didn't mean to kill her; I left it to God anyway.

I just put the peanut butter in every other can. That gave her a fair chance, see? If she deserved to live she'd take one that didn't have peanut butter in it. Can you believe she actually called me and told me she'd be coming in that day? She didn't want a scene. Well, I didn't make a scene, she did."

Lila nodded and looked like she agreed. She'd try the sympathy card.

"I did everything for that woman. I waited on her, I brought her things, I took care of her when she needed help. She . . . did things to me. She made me think she loved me. That's when I figured out she was the devil.

"She didn't even want her own child. She was going to give it to strangers. After I found her that nurse to deliver it and kept everything hidden for her. I knew it was a special child and made sure it was given to someone special. My own mother. My mother is a wonderful person. But she's getting old, and that baby isn't easy, so I'm going to help her take care of it myself. It's the best part of Emily Ruth, before she went bad. She trusted me to put that baby in a good home, and I did. My own mother."

Lila felt sick, but she gave him a really, really

sympathetic look. Oh, she just *bet* his mom was swell. Good grief. And how would his wife feel about him bringing home the stray baby of his former lover? Probably not too keen.

"Mmm, mmm." Lila made like she wanted to talk, since he was apparently in the mood.

"Promise not to scream?"

What was she going to say, no? She nodded yes. He ripped off the six-inch piece of tape covering her mouth.

"Ouch." She wiggled her mouth to make it work again. "Larry, that woman was evil and she deserved to die. But I'm nice. I won't tell anyone, I promise."

He looked at her, staring down from his crouched position. For a moment he looked like he might believe her. Then his face went all twisted and dark. "That's what Pauline said. But she lied. No, I'm sorry Lila. I've got to be here and keep this store in shape. Can you imagine letting someone new take over my department? This store would never survive without me. And I have a son to look after, now."

"Is he yours?"

Larry slapped her face. God, he was fast, just like a horrible mean parent, she imagined. He stuck the duct tape back over her mouth. Her cheek stung, and that *really* made her head hurt. Her calm was starting to wear off. She inch-wormed away from him as slowly as possible.

"How stupid of you, Lila, it's a Griffin baby. But I helped it be born and took care of it. I loved Emily Ruth, and it's like having the good part of her all to myself. It's more mine than anyone's."

Larry got busy again, mumbling to himself. He left her in the aisle and went in the produce department. He must have gotten distracted with some lettuce leaf that wasn't lying perfectly in line because he really took a long time. She kept inch-worming toward the door, but that was a really, really long way away. If she could get on her feet she could hop to the window and break it maybe, and that would make the alarms go off.

She didn't even want to know what his idea of her demise might be, but again, if he managed it, she'd haunt his ass forever. Her and Emily Ruth. They'd make a great team.

Back came Larry, and dragged her right back to where she'd started, smack in the middle of the condiment aisle with the Cheese Whiz cans to one side. He ceased making eye contact or talking to her at all, probably to keep himself from straying off task, she guessed. No sympathy to creep in there.

Well, if she was going to go, she was going to go down fighting. She kicked him a good one in the leg right before he let her go. She was starting to get the hang of what she could do in her present state. He hollered and clutched his shin. The remaining blue slipper was too soft, but her bare heel wasn't bad. She scooted toward him and kicked him again.

"Stop that, Lila, you're only making this harder."

Lila squirmed like a worm and worked a couple of fingernails loose. She ripped off her mouth tape.

"Oh what, I should make it easy for you?" Lila screamed. Then she just kept screaming. She screamed at Larry, Emily Ruth, and Lucas, and that boy that left her seventeen years ago. "Listen up, Emily Ruth, no one will ever find your kid if you don't help me now!" she screamed. As soon as she said that, she smelled the familiar, overpowering scent of "Passion."

Larry was looking around frantically, probably trying to decide whether a jar of pickles would knock her out. He grabbed a can of olives, fittingly, and started toward her. He stopped once, sniffed the air, then went even nuttier.

Lila really freaked out then, and not at Larry, but what she saw above Larry. Pretty as you please, Emily Ruth floated above the entire aisle, just behind Larry. Way up there where they stocked the cocktail onions and odd things. "Oh God, watch out Larry!"

Now why she said that, she had no idea, but it did distract Larry for a split second as he was just about to bean her with a can of large black olives. He turned, caught sight of Emily Ruth, and screamed like a girl. They always did that.

Lila put her elbows on the second rack and managed to get herself up on her feet. She started hopping away to get to where the division of the racks occurred—pasta was softer. But too late, she saw Emily Ruth effortlessly shove the thousand-pound rack in Larry's direction—and hers.

"LILA!" Lucas yelled. He didn't think, he just ran for her, hoisted her over his shoulder like forty pounds of dog kibble, twisted, and ran in the other direction. He felt his leg give him a nasty knife-pierce of pain, but he kept going.

The sound of Larry being pinned under a giant supermarket rack of condiments wasn't a good sound. The rack hit the next rack, and knocked over the opposite rack, right into the produce department.

Lucas smelled squished cantaloupe.

"Oh, *finally*, Dudley Do-Right to the rescue," Lila cried out.

"Shut up, Nell, or I'll put you back on the railroad tracks and let Snidely have you." He shifted her to the floor.

"Snidely is busy right now. Boy, you've got some nerve, Griffin."

Chief Bob was next to them. "Wow, nice save there, Lucas. You take care of her; I'll see if our friend is still alive."

Lucas picked her up again and carried her in his arms. He found the lawn chairs and sat down on a cushy chaise with Lila in his lap. He held her close, taped up as she was.

"Do you think he's dead?" he asked her.

"Nope, I'd have seen his stinkin' little ghost. But we should help him because I want him alive so I can make sure he's in a really horrible messy cell somewhere. Larry Pierson, can you believe it?"

"I figured it out. Bob and Rooster and I went to find him at his house, but he wasn't there. He gave us the slip."

"Wow, Sherlock, he was at my house. And what, you didn't think maybe to share this information with me?"

"You were supposed to be safely in jail. We tracked down his car to this parking lot. It had a huge dent in the front end. Black Ford Escort. My, my, aren't we snippy."

"I've had a bad night," Lila pouted.

"You've been a bad girl. If you weren't already bruised up, I'd spank you."

"Ha." Lila thought about that and nuzzled up to his neck. "Okay, that sounded interesting, for a minute. But I'm more of the tender, hot, crazy type."

"That you are." He kissed her.

"I'm going to be really mad when I get out of this tape. You putzes just threw me in jail and left me there. The big, strong, smart men." She said that in a very sarcastic tone, but still snuggled next to him. "And I know something you don't, but I'm not going to tell you."

"Yes you will, because you're a better person than I am."

"Well, *that's* true. Get me out of this tape, will you?"

Lucas pulled a stray strip of tape from her hair.

"Ouch. Goddamn it, Griffin, I'm attached to that hair."

"I can't believe the swearing you've done lately. Your mother would be appalled." Lucas put the tape back over her mouth.

"Hmmmmmmrrrrrggggghhh!"

He took it back off, laughing. "Sorry, I couldn't help myself." He started unpeeling the tape from her hands.

"What's this I hear about you leaving for California?" was the first thing that came out of her untaped mouth.

"Lila, this isn't the time to discuss this. We'll have a calm, quiet talk later. Did you know that Larry murdered his wife? I saw her obituary come through the stacks in the paper and that's what tipped me off about the possibility it was him. But I'm still not sure why."

She burst out crying. Probably more from what just happened to her than anything. He just held her while he unpeeled the tape, letting her head rest on his shoulder. When he shifted her around to get her feet he looked at his shirt and saw blood.

"Did he hurt you?" He came back up and felt her head. A sticky patch of dried blood was on one side. She was still sobbing. "Frying pan," she sobbed out.

"Lie down here," he commanded her. "Stay."

The medics had arrived and were trying to unbury Larry from the tons of pickled cauliflower and capers and of course, busted jars of cheese spread that created the strangest smell. They were trying to heave the rack off.

"Hey, guys, I need someone to take a look at Lila. I think she's hurt."

Lila felt really strange. Like she was alone in a sea of people. The blur of paramedics and police just felt like that—a blur. No one came over to her, and Lucas had left her there alone.

When she had Mallory at home she always had company.

A sea of self-pity swallowed her and made her cry without even meaning to. Just think, Larry had already killed two women that they knew about. She was going to be the third.

They had to get that baby away from Larry's

mother right now. It must only be about four months old. The bakery crew would be in soon. The sun didn't really come up till seven. She tried to get up off the chaise, but her head started pounding something fierce. Her thoughts were turning random on her, she could tell.

Lucas and good old Dave McInnis came up beside her. Dave had his little medic kit with him. Lucas handed her a brand-new box of the best Kleenex in the store, opened and ready to pull. She grabbed a few and blew her nose.

"Ow, Dave, I need an aspirin. Stupid Larry hit me with a frying pan. It didn't hurt too bad, but now it does."

"That's because you've been running on adrenaline, and now you're crashing. Lucas, grab a blanket off the equipment pile over there."

"Did you lose consciousness when he hit you?"

"Ya, like long enough for him to get me from my house to here, I guess."

Dave ran a penlight back and forth in front of her eyes. "She's got a concussion."

"You're so cute, Dave, and Sally told me everything, you know, like about the back of the ambulance, woohoo, Dave."

"She sounds drunk." Lucas bent over her and wrapped her up in the blanket like a sausage.

"She's going into shock."

"I love you, too, Lucas Griffin," she said.

Fifteen

 Lila looked up into the fuzzy faces of Dave, Lucas, and Emily Ruth staring down at her. Wait a minute, Emily Ruth was dead. Thank goodness for Emily Ruth, or she'd be pickled and squished like Larry.

Well, actually the woman practically squished her as well, if it hadn't been for Lucas. She made a face at Emily Ruth. The ghostly Emily Ruth actually looked apologetic. Wow.

"Listen to me so your ex-wife will stop haunting me." Lila took Lucas's arm and shook it. "Emily Ruth had a baby."

"We know, sweetie, Bob finally came clean about the autopsy. We can't find any records of the birth, though, or any adoption. I don't know how she did it, but she hid the whole thing."

"He left it with his mother. And, Lucas, he said it was a Griffin baby."

Lucas looked pale. Paler than Emily Ruth, who smiled at her. "He told you this? We thought it was Larry's baby. It's my brother's child?"

"Yup, must be. Larry got some nurse to deliver it at home, then he took it to be adopted but gave it to his mother instead. Emily Ruth didn't want to be a mother. She wanted to date Prentice Cortland." Lila made a face at Emily Ruth's ghost to show her how much she disapproved. Emily Ruth vanished.

"God, I wish I could go with you, Lucas, but I have a really, really nasty headache. Be careful. I think Larry's mom is the source of a whole lot of his problems," Lila said.

Lucas pulled Dave over to the side. Oh, those men and their secrets. Well, hopefully they'd get that baby safely away from good old Granny Pierson. She just wanted to take a long nap. She pulled the blanket over herself. A chill ran all over her body.

Lucas came back and gave Lila a kiss on the cheek. "Thanks, Abbott, I've got to go see a woman about a baby. Dave will take good care of you."

"Good night," she whispered. Dave came over and put another blanket on her. She closed her eyes and heard all sorts of commotion, but it didn't bother her anymore.

A soft touch on her forehead woke her. She looked up to see Pilar, and half the checker chicks gathered around her. The bakery gals in their hairnets were all in white and angelic looking. Lila smiled at them. Her little family for the last fifteen years. All that was missing was Mallory, Bonnie, and well . . . Lucas. But he was going AWOL on her after he rescued the baby anyway.

She thought about that baby. Oh, the poor little thing. She wondered about whether Lucas would want to keep it and raise it. And how would she feel about starting all over again on the child-raising adventure? Not that Lucas asked her. What a joke. She'd known the guy a couple of weeks.

Pretty soon some guys came and lifted her onto a gurney, then rolled her out the door. Her friends followed her till they were about to lift her into the medic van.

"Becky," she called out.

"Yes, Lila?" Becky came closer.

"Wet cleanup on aisle two."

Becky laughed and patted her hand, then waved goodbye.

Lucas went in first, despite the protests of his police backup. He insisted that a calm approach would be the best.

Oddly, the lights were all on. The small house looked fairly orderly on the outside, no peeling paint, no broken fence, just a little cottage-type house about fifteen minutes away in the Lofall area. It was deep in the woods, surrounded by tall evergreens.

He went straight up to the front door and knocked. After a long time he heard the sound of a walker coming across the floor, or he imagined that's what he heard. The door opened and a very elderly woman stood looking at him, leaning on her walker.

"Well? I thought you were the milkman it's so early."

"Mrs. Pierson?"

"Who wants to know?"

"I'm from Port Gamble. Your son Larry had a little accident at work and he asked me to come and tell you."

"Did you bring back my car?"

Lucas took note that her first response was not about the well-being of her son. "No. It's in the shop, with the dent and all," he took a guess.

"Kids. Always getting into trouble."

"Where's the baby, Mrs. Pierson?"

She looked at him, her face becoming more suspicious. "Larry told you about the baby?"

"He was worried since he wouldn't be able to come home after work that you'd need things. Diapers, that sort of thing."

"Well, look for yourself. He's fine. Larry left enough this weekend." Mrs. Pierson moved out of the way and Lucas stepped into the house. This was Larry Pierson's mother? The house was not spotless. The house was a disaster.

Magazines, clothes, boxes of stuff were stacked on every surface. Books filled the bookshelves until they fell to the floor. She read, he'd have to give her that. The kitchen was a nightmare. Lucas saw baby bottles on the counter. No wonder Larry was a neat-freak.

Lucas moved down the hallway, looking in each room and found more of the same. At the end of the hall to the right he stopped and turned to see a completely immaculate room. A single bed and dresser, with the bed made tight. On the bedside table stood a lamp and a clock.

In the corner stood a crib, and he quietly moved toward it. Inside a small infant slept on his back, clean blankets around him, a clean long-sleeved T-shirt covering him. The kind that tied on the side. He'd seen those before on one of his cousin's babies. He looked very carefully at the baby. It was a Griffin, all right.

"See, he's fed and bathed. He woke up at four A.M. just screamin' his little head off like he'd seen a ghost. But he was just hungry. Larry said you're supposed to put them on their backs to sleep now. In our day it was the opposite. This is Larry's old room," she said with pride.

"Mrs. Pierson, this is my brother Jason's baby. Larry stole it from Emily Ruth Griffin, the mother."

"That horrible woman? Larry didn't steal it, she gave it away to him to get rid of. He helped deliver that baby himself, did you know?"

Well, Lucas knew he had the right baby, that

was for sure. Looked like Mrs. Pierson knew the whole picture pretty well.

"The baby is my nephew. I'm Lucas Griffin." Lucas turned to look at her. "I'm going to take him with me. Your son murdered Emily Ruth."

"You're not taking Larry's baby, I won't let you!" The mild-looking old woman picked up her walker and hit Lucas with it, repeatedly. "Emily Ruth deserved to die. She was the devil. She broke my son's heart," she screamed.

Lucas shielded himself, and the child. He grabbed hold of the walker and gently took it away from her. Before she could come at him, claws flailing, Sally Jo Johanson stepped into the doorway and caught Mrs. Pierson by the arm. In a couple of smooth moves, she subdued the woman.

Lucas picked up the now-awake baby and wrapped it snugly in the blankets. He scooped it close to him and dodged past Sally and Mrs. Pierson, who was yelling very loudly.

He walked to Sally's squad car and climbed in the back where she'd left the door open for him. Two other uniformed police officers from the county went into the house.

The department kept an infant car seat and he

nestled the tiny baby into the curve of the carrier. His eyes were large and very blue, just like Jason's. He didn't cry at all.

Lucas strapped him in and stared at each little baby feature. He put his finger in his perfect miniature hand and the baby closed his fist around it.

Thank God the woman had actually taken care of him. He didn't even want to think about anything else but being grateful this baby was healthy and fed and clean.

Boy, he was going to need some baby stuff.

Sally came back and slid into the backseat with them. "Wow, Griffin, I really saved your bacon," she joked.

"She was pretty good with that thing, but I could have taken her."

"I figured, but you had your hands full. Isn't he just a doll?" She cooed over him and the baby made some funny sounds. "Is he yours?"

"Nope, but I'm pretty sure he's my brother Jason's baby."

"Ohh, you've got a nephew, that's cool. You and Lila can get married and start a family and little Griffy here can have some siblings."

Sally had it all figured out, Lucas guessed.

"I'm not sure Lila is up for round two, Sally, and we'll have to talk to my family about what's to be done. I'm just glad we found him."

"Damn, I guess otherwise you'd have a little Larry Junior running around town with his lunatic un-father." Sally patted the baby again then slid out and went to the driver's seat.

"Take us to the hospital, Sally, we'll get this little guy checked out and see what's become of our Lila." Lucas sat back and rested against the seat. The baby kept hold of his finger, and he let him. It had been one long night. His mind was reeling. He was grateful for the quiet while Sally drove toward the Silverburg medical center.

Not only had Emily Ruth left him a slightly neurotic but cute Pomeranian to take care of, but a baby as well. He knew it was Jason's, but they'd have to do the paternity tests to be sure. They still had all Jason's information from his death—blood type and all that, and maybe being his uncle would even help.

Maybe this was his chance to do something for his brother. He'd waited to tell his parents about the baby, not knowing how things were going to go. And he'd probably wait to get positive confirmation from the test, but he knew it was Jason's in his heart.

Ever since yesterday he'd thought of his sister, who had been through hell trying to conceive a baby with her husband, Nate. This might be the answer to her prayers. A very strange way to have her prayers answered, but still, it was her own nephew. Most likely.

He had no hesitation himself about taking the boy to raise. But his status with Lila wasn't at the point to spring something like this on her. He hadn't even decided whether he'd stay in Port Gamble. With a baby, he'd want to be near his folks.

He just needed some time with them anyway. Time to sort things out and get things straight. He didn't want another week to go by without that happening.

Lila would understand that. Heck, look what happened with Emily Ruth and her unfinished business. He didn't want to have to look up Lila from the afterlife to get straight with his parents.

"Hey, little guy, I don't know what your name is, but you're going to be okay now. We've got a great family, and before you know it you'll be playing on the beach building forts and hunting for sand fleas and hermit crabs."

"Lucas, he looks just like a Griffin." Lila sat in her hospital room bed and held the new arrival. "And you're sure you've got the right formula and everything you need, right?"

"Yes, I swear, they brought me everything he'd been using from Mrs. Pierson's house. Larry actually did a fairly decent job of picking out the right stuff." Lucas sat on the bed beside them.

"Poor baby, taken away from your mother like that, all lonely and only strange people to care for you."

"I don't think even Emily Ruth expected Larry to hide the little thing away. Before he died he told Dave everything. He'd convinced Emily Ruth he had adoptive parents all picked out." Lucas shook his head.

"I'd say she was such a selfish bitch she just wanted to believe him and be free of the shackles of motherhood, but I'm trying to give old Emily Ruth a break. I'm sure she thought someone else could raise the baby better than she could. She was a woman who didn't have a lot of self-esteem," Lila said. "And poor Larry."

"Poor Larry? Larry who murdered two women?"

"Well, hey, we're being charitable. I've known the guy for years. I feel very bad for him. He fell under her spell so hard it drove him crazy."

"It was a short trip, darlin." Lucas looked in her eyes. "And speaking of a short trip, I want you to know I've booked a flight tomorrow to L.A. It's really important I go see my family and we talk about what to do regarding the future of the littlest Griffin here. It's something I need to do. We've got lots to talk about. I don't want to end up like Emily Ruth with many sins to correct before I can get to heaven."

"And will you be coming back?"

"You mean after I die?"

"No, after you correct your sins."

Lucas looked at the ground. "I don't know, Lila, I'm not sure."

Lila knew she had two choices here. She could get all bent out of shape and yell, or she could be gracious. Her mother always said being gracious was the higher path. And it was looking like mother knew best in this case. Who was she to stand in the way of a family reuniting?

"Take little Griffy here, and go to your family, Lucas, I've got no ties on you. We were just a summer fling, you and I. Brought together by adverse circumstances."

"Actually it was your pink bikini underwear under your white work pants. That and the red hair and the kindness to animals."

"Gee, such a sweet-talker. For me it was your amazing pecks. Where'd a soft rich guy get pecks like that?

"The gym, of course."

"Time to go, Lucas, my head is still pounding."

"I thought the MRI turned out okay."

"Yea, they just want me to stay the night for observation in case my brain swells or something." Lila figured it already had, way back at the beginning of August when she laid eyes on Lucas Griffin.

She needed to get this over with. She gave the sweet-faced little spawn of Emily Ruth a kiss on his soft little forehead. Surely the woman had some good in her to have given birth to such an angel.

"Here, take your nephew. I'm supposed to rest." Lila handed Lucas the baby. Lucas gathered him up and stood.

"Hard to believe he's hers, isn't it? I see a whole lot of Griffin in him. We'll have that confirmed by tonight, the lab guy was so interested he's working late."

"Well, Emily Ruth sure fought the good fight to get him rescued. We've got to give her that."

"Lila." Lucas was rocking back and forth like a good uncle with his little bundle of nephew. "This was more than a summer fling. You are a very special woman. You're probably the most unique woman I've ever met."

Not unique enough to actually make a commitment to, of course. "Thanks, Lucas. And what about your dog?"

"Can you keep her? She loves you."

"Sure. My mother's taken quite a shine to her, too. I'm sure Mallory will adore her." Lila slid down so she was under the hospital sheets, her head, which hadn't even needed a stitch, was actually doing much better. Larry didn't pack too much of a wallop.

"Thank you, Lila, for everything. I'll . . . I'll write to you."

"That would be great, Lucas. Good luck with your family."

Lucas looked like he was thinking about kissing her but didn't know how to position his little nephew. Finally he just managed himself down to her lips and gave her the softest most loving kiss she'd ever received. She better treasure it because that was the last one she'd ever get from Lucas Griffin.

"Later, Griffin."

"Later, Abbott." He looked at her for a moment, then walked quietly out of the room.

Lila closed her eyes and waited. She counted to one hundred. He'd be far enough down the hall by one hundred. When she got to ninety-nine she let out a deep, wailing sob that shook her body like a very unfriendly vibration. But a very familiar one. She turned her face into the pillow and cried herself to sleep.

Sixteen

Lila opened her eyes when the nurse came in on morning rounds. Beside her in a chair sat Bonnie. Or more correctly, slumped in a chair, sleeping.

The nurse proceeded to take Lila's blood pressure and temperature. "She came in last night and we didn't have the heart to throw her out."

"Or the nerve, probably," Lila said with a thermometer in her mouth.

"Yes, that either," the nurse said and winked. "Dr. Keyes said if you had a good night and normal readings you could be released." She took Lila's thermometer when it beeped. "Your head feeling okay?"

"Great."

"Okay, you're good to go. Call in right away if you have dizziness or nausea, or a headache that lasts longer than an hour. And you get three more days off work according to your chart. Oh, and your parents were here last night while you were sleeping, but they didn't want to wake you. Your mom brought you some clothes."

Lila threw back the covers. "Thanks, but I'd rather get back to work."

"Well, you might as well stay home because Market Foods is closed for the rest of the week. The police closed it and the place is getting cleaned up. I live near Port Gamble myself. We're all going to the Kingston Albertson's and from what I hear, they've discontinued Cheez Whiz, too." The nurse gave a nervous laugh.

"Wow, thanks for the update." Lila smiled, just to let her know it was okay to talk about.

Bonnie groaned and stood up as Lila tied the flimsy robe over her flimsy gown. The nurse gathered her charts and departed. Bonnie came over to Lila and gave her a huge hug. "You could have called me," she said and thudded her in the arm.

"I was busy being an idiot."

"Lucas?"

"Gone."

"*Damn* it."

"Life goes on. He's got to get his little nephew squared away. And himself, I guess. He left me the dog."

"Come on, get dressed. I'll take you home and tell you stories. I had a summer fling with a Canadian."

"Was he a Mountie?"

"I can't go there because I'll make really bad jokes and laugh too hard and we're supposed to be quiet in the hospital." Bonnie smirked. "Let's get out of here. You've got a whole lot of free-flow stream of consciousness ghost stories to tell me."

"Speed exit." Lila went into action and in ten minutes she was dressed and ready to escape—again. In the bathroom she decided not to even look at herself in the mirror. Her face probably had the blotches of her crying jag all over it.

Well, no more crying for this gal.

"The nurse brought an envelope while you were dressing." Bonnie handed her the lumpy packet.

Car keys. She read the note out loud. "Lila, the

Jag is yours. Your car is being repaired at Roy's. Car parked in north lot, row B. Lucas."

"Oh, man." Bonnie let out a low whistle. And Lila knew it wasn't about her getting a Jag, it was about the short, curt note. No *Love, Lucas*, not even a *Best Wishes* or *Warmest Regards*.

Lila crumpled up the note and threw it in the trash. "Hey, this time I got a car."

"And a dog."

The two women made their way to the parking lot and found the Jag. It had a huge bouquet of flowers in the front seat. It was a wild mixture of dahlias and Gerber daisies, tiger lilies and hops. Pipper's Flowers, the card read. That's all. Good old Pipper, the local florist, ready to spread the floral joy at any occasion.

"Are you okay to drive? Not dizzy or anything?"

"I'm fine. Just follow me and we'll be home in a heartbeat."

"I'm around the corner. Wait for me here."

Lila unlocked the car and slid onto the white leather seat. The car smelled like a garden. She got the thing purring and pretty soon Bonnie was behind her, waiting.

She was going to be okay. She'd just get herself

back to work and back in the groove and she'd survive. Women all over the world survived. If she knew one thing, it was that heartache fades after two or three years. Maybe she'd shorten that up this time.

They both pulled out of the parking lot and took the back roads home to Port Gamble. The leaves were starting to turn and the trees looked like someone had dipped their edges in gold and red paint. It seemed more vivid than she remembered from past years. It was a beautiful town full of people who loved her.

Back at her house her parents rushed out as soon as she closed the car door. They pulled her into a big embrace and held her tight. Schatzie barked like crazy and danced on her hind legs like a circus dog till Lila picked her up and gave her a nuzzle. Her dad broke the news that Mallory was flying home, and that Lucas Griffin had paid for the ticket. Lila was actually so glad to hear that her daughter would be here she didn't think about the other part.

Her mother tried to insist she go straight to bed but settled for making her breakfast when Lila resisted strongly. But . . . shower first. Mom sent Bonnie to keep an eye on her.

Bonnie knew just what to do and made like she was going to be a mother hen, then when they were in the house she went in the kitchen and got the coffee going. She knew that's what they both needed most.

Lila took the hottest shower she could stand. Her head hurt where she'd gotten beaned, and there was a cut there, but nothing too bad. She shampooed out the blood and watched it drain down the shower drain.

In her room she looked around and decided she must clean house. She'd like things spruced up for Mallory.

Her room had the strangest feel to it. She'd been sleeping at Lucas's house so much and not living her old life. She had a flash of the night he came to her bedroom and scared the daylights out of her. And how they'd made love. That flash hurt.

"Coffee." Bonnie came up the stairs and hollered. She stood in the doorframe holding Lila's favorite cup.

"Saved by the best friend." Lila took the coffee and let it soak into her like a secret cure. Maybe it was. "Will you help me clean my place up? Mallory is coming home some time today."

"Consider me your indentured servant. Besides, we still have much to talk about, and what better way than over the scrubbing of floors. An ancient female ritual," Bonnie laughed. "Now get dressed, I want your mother's breakfast."

Lila set her coffee down and picked out a dress she hadn't worn for a long time. It was a periwinkle blue floral number with flirty little sleeves and a longish skirt. The whole thing buttoned up the front. She even found some clean undies.

She actually felt better.

Over at her mother and dad's, Bonnie went in the kitchen to help and pretty soon she was pouring coffee for everyone at the dining room table. Lila still clung to her favorite mug from her house.

The familiar raspberry pink dining room, where they'd all gathered during crisis times since she could remember, felt comforting.

Her mom handed her a plate of scrambled eggs with bacon and cheese and bits of green onion mixed in, her favorite.

"You've got to tell us what happened." Her father sat on one side of her as her mother handed out plates all around.

"It's almost unbelievable, but I'll do my best."

Lila sipped her coffee and started in with the twisted tale of Larry and Emily Ruth's ghost and her final revenge on the man who killed her, and how Lucas ended up with a baby in his arms, the baby of his dead brother.

The part she left out was how she'd fallen in love with Lucas Griffin and he'd done the unspeakably heartbreakingly predictable thing and left her. For good reasons, but that was that. Perhaps her life wasn't meant to have that kind of love. She had other kinds. She looked around the table and cherished each person there. She missed her daughter terribly, and could hardly wait to hold her in her arms again.

Speak of the devil, the door flew open and her daughter came running straight to her. She pushed her chair back and held her Mallory, who was taller, she swore.

"Mom, mom, for heaven sakes, are you in one piece? I leave for a few weeks and you've gotten into all sorts of trouble."

Lila ruffled Mallory's short red hair. "I'm fine now that you're here. Come on, have breakfast; I'll start the story all over again." More hugs, more coffee, more breakfast, and Lila felt like she just might be okay, Lucas or not.

* * *

Mallory and Bonnie and Lila spent the day airing out the entire cottage. They washed and hung the sheets on the old clothesline and let the sun brighten everything. They even gave the dog a bath and tied a new blue bow around her neck.

Mallory said that Stanford was fabulous. She loved the dog, and swore to steal it and take it back with her.

Lila spent much time making sure that Mallory felt like she was fine and dandy and able to be left in the hands of Bonnie and her folks.

They put Lucas's flowers in a huge vase and set them on Lila's little white painted dining table. They were like a neon sign that read—*Thanks for the summer and goodbye*.

Lila made them all promise not to talk about any of it anymore, and they moved onto Bonnie's adventures, which had to be censured for Mallory, Lila could tell. After lunch they decided to take one of the many cars they now had in tow over to see the container of goodies Bonnie had sent back from Canada via a large truck.

They passed by Market Foods and saw police cars and cleaning company trucks outside. Lila got a horrible flashback of the sound of Larry being crushed under the rack. She shuddered. It would be harder than she thought to go back. Mallory gave her a car-squeeze. "Don't worry mom, you can come to college with me if you want. You never have to go back there again."

"Thanks, honey, but the checker chicks would miss me. It's my life, I guess." Lila felt a strange independence in that. She'd get back on her old schedule and all her after-work activities and groups. Why, she hadn't been bowling in a month.

Lila was going to treasure every minute of her daughter's visit and not think about anything else. Not Larry, not Emily Ruth, not ghosts, and not Lucas Griffin.

It was Monday. A quiet Monday. A September Monday. Her first Monday back at work. Lila put her purse in her locker and slipped on the clean blue vest she'd brought in with her, complete with all her collected pins reattached: Disney characters and sunflowers and pins customers had given her.

It hadn't been easy coming in today; she'd felt a horrible apprehension walking through the familiar glass doors, but so far nothing had occurred.

Let's hope that Emily Ruth had been set free and Larry had been escorted to a proper after-death rehabilitation center, and that 10:36 would go by without as much as a cleanup on aisle anything.

She slipped her cell phone in her vest pocket and padded down the stairs in her thick blue sneakers. She'd gotten new shoes, new pants, new everything just to cheer herself up. She was new and blue.

Pilar was waiting for her at her check stand and handed her a paper cup of Starbucks coffee.

"What's up with that?"

"Many days closed, we put in the new coffee area. Now we drink the good stuff."

"Wow, thanks."

Lila walked in a circle around the store to see what was new. They'd moved all the school supplies out front and ditched the summer lawn furniture. Everything was polished and clean and you couldn't even tell that two people had died there over the summer. She liked how clean everything was. Maybe she was the new Larry. *Not*.

The floral department had gone nuts with sunflowers and fake fall leaves, and, well, Phil was nervously fluttering around the produce department.

"Hey, Phil."

"Hey, Lila."

"It looks good, Phil, just make it your own." She tipped her coffee cup to him. Phil nodded and looked relieved, like she'd taken some pressure off of him.

When she started aisle walking she couldn't make herself go through aisle two. She'd tackle that later. Her heart ached with bad memories. It filled her with a strange, anxious dread and she dodged right down the chip-and-pop aisle instead. The lunchbox packs of chips were on sale.

Tom Boscov was at the check stand end of the aisle.

"Hey, Tom, nice coffee."

"Hey, Lila, just you take it easy today. If you need to leave or anything, we'll understand."

"Tom, just keep me busy. Give me work. But keep me out of aisle two," Lila said.

"Gotcha. How about you stock in the baking aisle today. We've got brownie mix coming out our ears."

"Great. Call me if you need me to check."

Lila walked to the front and grabbed a box cutter. She passed each of her friends and although they all had the same look on their faces, they just said two or three words like, "Glad you're alive, Lila," and went about their work. Lila appreciated that.

Okay, brownies on aisle twelve. She liked that. She got to ripping open boxes and shelving mixes till she was in the zone. The restocking zone. She even hummed. Mallory had gone back to Stanford this morning, and she was back to her regular life. She lost track of time moving in the rhythm she'd come to know so well.

There was some sort of rippling gasp rolling over the store patrons like a wave rolls over the fans at a football game. Oh, no, not again. She'd kick that ghost's scrawny butt back to the moon if she made another appearance in this store.

Lila sealed her box cutter and stomped her way toward the other end of the store, ready to do battle.

But instead of spray cheese or flying lemons, she saw a walking floral monster. It came right up to her. She parted some ferns and saw Lucas Griffin staring back at her.

* * *

"What, more flowers?" she snapped.

Well, he knew it wasn't going to be easy. "You are so cute when you're angry," Lucas said. "I've got something else, too."

"What, another dog?"

Lucas put down the two vases of flowers and got down on his knee. He winced from the pain. He probably should have picked the other knee. He took out the little black velvet box and opened it so the pretty diamond sparkled under the lights of the store.

"Will you marry me?"

Lila crossed her arms and tapped her foot, saying nothing. She stared at the ring.

"No," she said firmly.

By now a crowd of her co-workers and customers had formed nearby. A collective "awwwww" went around the group.

Lucas stood up. "Why not?"

"Because, I like it here. And I'm not even sure we're right for each other. We haven't known each other that long."

He scratched his chin, then put the ring back in his pocket. "Would you like to go to the movies tonight?"

"No, it's bowling night for the Checker Chicks. I've got some practices to catch up on. You and your, your, complications"—she waved her hands in the air—"*distracted* me. First Monday of the month, bowling. Also every Sunday is league night. Third Monday is Mystery Book group. That's my life. I'm not sure I've got room for you in it. Later, Griffin."

She turned, actually *turned* around and walked away from him. Wow.

"Well, I think you're going to have to make room, Lila Abbott, because I'm not going anywhere, and I'd love to come bowling with you tonight, and I'll take Fridays if you're open, there's a double feature playing at the Strand Theater this weekend, but right now we've got some catching up to do, so if you don't mind . . ." Lucas strode past her, turned, and stood right in front of her, making her stop in her tracks. "I'm going to alter your schedule a bit," he said, then picked her up and hoisted her over his shoulder, holding her very firmly in place.

"Put me down this instant!" Lila screamed, but everyone clapped, and as Lucas carried her out to his Jeep, he noticed she stopped screaming and started laughing.

When he reached the passenger side of his jeep he put her down next to it and pinned her against the door. He started kissing her neck and worked his way up to her lips, holding her head gently, his fingers weaving into her hair at the temples. Most tenderly, then more intensely, he kissed her.

She must have been trying to say something as he kissed her but finally, instead, her arms slowly moved around him and she melted like a marshmallow under his smooth, loving, repeated kisses, which got deeper and deeper the more she melted.

"Oh, Lucas," she groaned. "Don't make anything of this, I just have a serious weakness for hot summer boys," she mumbled.

"I'm not a summer boy anymore, I'm a local guy. I'm going to live in the beach house and maybe write the history of Port Gamble, with all its ghosts and . . . historic stuff, and that's going to take me years, you know." He said all that through more kisses that ran down her neck. He unzipped her blue vest.

"And I'm going to need an assistant. Someone who knows this town backward." He slid his hands to her soft, lovely rear and pressed her into him, making his jeans get even tighter. "And forward." He ran his mouth down the front of her crisp white blouse and as far down into her clean white cotton bra as he could push to her ample breasts. Her top button popped open, making it a little easier. She groaned and arched against him.

"Get a room, will you?" Mrs. Mills laughed as she wheeled one of the new plastic carts by them.

"Let's do," he whispered in her ear. "My room."

"I have to be at the bowling alley by seven," she said between breathing heavily.

"Bowling it is." He could hardly stop himself, but he refastened her button, zipped her vest back up, and moved her without letting her go till he could open the Jeep door. He deposited her in the seat and buckled her in. "No escaping, now." He kissed her again, then ran to the other side, jumped in, turned the key, and drove them out of there at an L.A. pace.

She had lipstick smears and she looked very messed up from his messing with her, but she leaned against him and didn't say a word.

Down in L.A. he'd seen the most wonderful

thing, he'd seen his sister and brother-in-law so happy they wept, and he'd seen his parents cry, and he'd seen himself freed from some very old pains. When the emotions had settled and they'd figured everything out, he'd still felt like something was missing. That something was Lila. He was in love with Lila Abbott.

And he wasn't going to lose her ever again. This time was forever.

Seventeen

St. Paul's Church had never been so decked out, as far as she knew, as it was today.

They'd had Thomas Griffin christened a week ago Sunday morning in the late June sunshine. He was a little big for the Griffin family christening gown, so they made him a new blue sailor suit. He was an absolute doll and Lila couldn't believe how much happiness Lucas's sister, Victoria, and her husband, Nate, had been given by the magical gift of that child.

Lila had realized somewhere around Christmas that she'd never actually been married in her entire life, and the whole bridal mystique had taken over. She'd accepted Lucas's ring at last. Mallory was due for summer break in June, and it just seemed the perfect time for Lila to finally give in and marry Lucas.

She even went to stay at the cottage with Mallory for two days before the wedding so he could *miss her* again.

So *this* Sunday afternoon she stood in St. Paul's with her favorite minister, Reverend Dee, and married Lucas Griffin, surrounded by their families. His sister joined Mallory and Bonnie beside her in decidedly unghastly blue bridesmaid dresses with bundles of white roses and blue statice, and her mother had actually wept under her white picture hat.

Pipper had outdone herself with late lilacs and all kinds of dogwood and cherry tree blooms, plus yellow daylilies in pots all the way up the stairs and tons and tons of white roses and blue hyacinth.

Schatzie had a big white bow on and yapped a couple of times, from the safety of Deputy Sally's lap. Sally was sitting next to Dave McInnis with her two boys all in a row, wearing a girl dress, as she'd promised Lila when she'd gotten the invitation.

The Griffins added that special touch of . . . cash, and a wedding feast right out of the movies was waiting for them under the tents at the end of town, looking out to the sea, where all the brides had their outdoor receptions. They were blessed with unusually good weather.

Lucas just blew her away with his very English-looking morning suit attire, and when they walked out into the light through the big double doors, she saw a horse and carriage at the bottom of the stairs waiting to take them to the reception.

She turned to Bonnie and gave her the *look*. That little smile—the look they both knew was every townie girl's dream come true. Lucas whispered, "I love you, Mrs. Griffin," and took her arm.

"I love you too, Mr. Griffin," she replied.

Then she walked down the stone stairs of St. Paul's Church with her antique veil billowing in the breeze, her organza sleeves rustling, and her soft pale blue petticoats rippling. Her heart was as light as a bird soaring above the tall steeple.

She handed the white-rose bouquet to the driver and Lucas helped her climb in, gown and all. The driver took his place and got the horses going. They'd take two turns around the town square then stop at the reception tents, like all the brides did.

She'd seen many, many summers in Port Gamble but none more beautiful than this one. *This* summer was the forever summer.